SHADOW SOLDIERS

LAYNE PARRISH BOOK 1

JIM HESKETT

OFFER

Want to get the Layne Parrish novella **Museum Attack** for FREE? It's not available for sale **anywhere**. Check out www.jimheskett.com/free for this free, exclusive thriller.

PART I

A WILD RUMPUS

1

LAYNE PARRISH ALWAYS LOVED A GOOD RUMPUS. Nestled in a cramped bed next to a little girl named Cameron, he flipped to the last page of *Where the Wild Things Are*.

"Daddy," she said.

"Yes, little one."

"Why did Max go home? Why can't he stay with the wild things?"

"Because he missed his family."

Cameron stared at the page, an illustration of the protagonist sailing across the water toward home. Pale brow creased, her face riddled with confusion. Thinking. Her eyes were kaleidoscopic puddles of blue crystal, glistening under the meager light of the bedside lamp. The young child readjusted herself on the twin bed, and Layne had to pivot his weight to keep from slipping over the side.

"He missed his mommy and daddy?"

Layne nodded. "He did."

In his pocket, a phone buzzed. He slipped it out to find a

call from an unknown number lighting up the screen. Unknown to the phone companies, but Layne had a strong suspicion who was on the line.

The same person who had been calling and texting him relentlessly for the last two days.

"Daddy, put it away. You said no more screens."

"You're right," he said as he jabbed it back into his pocket. "Watching screens after dark makes our eyes cross, right?" He crossed his eyes and let his tongue loll out.

She giggled and poked his chest with a finger not much bigger than a toothpick. "Daddy, stop."

Cameron traced one of her fingers along his arm, gliding across one particular section of the tattoos that covered it from wrist to shoulder. A cherub in the middle of his forearm, obscuring a gunshot wound from long ago. The cherub now appeared faded and blurry on his forty-year-old arms.

The phone squirmed inside his pocket again, demanding attention. A repeat call. This time, though, he ignored the eager person on the other end of the line.

"It's time for bed," he said.

She pondered this for a moment and then frowned. "Are the wild things going to get me?"

"You're a wild thing," he said, and his fingers leaped to her belly for a tickle. She cackled, writhing, and he instantly regretted it. Bedtime was supposed to be calm time. But he couldn't resist torturing such an easy target.

"Okay, okay, little one. Time for bed, for real."

She pushed out a breath, the remnants of tickle energy fading. Her lids were heavy, her motions thick, like a person wading through swampy water. She was an inch away from sleep. Layne anticipated no bedtime false starts tonight.

"I love you much, Daddy."

He kissed her forehead as he drew the covers up to her shoulders. "And I love you much, little one."

He sneaked across the room and rested a hand on the light switch. "I'll be right downstairs, okay?"

"Okay, Daddy."

Layne flicked out the light and stole one last look at her, a miniature head nestled on a Thomas the Tank Engine pillow. He closed the door behind him as his phone buzzed yet again. Didn't bother to take it out.

Next, a knock came at the front door, downstairs. He paused for a moment in front of his daughter's room to make sure she wouldn't call out. No way she was asleep already, but maybe she hadn't heard it. The excitement of someone coming to the door would turn bedtime into a circus requiring a whole new set of little kid cooldown routines.

She made no sound. No vibration through the door.

Layne held perfectly still until another knock came. He wasn't unreachable in this small town, but he almost never had visitors. And never unannounced or after dark. The neighbors knew about bedtime policy and wouldn't betray Layne's evening ritual.

He hustled down the stairs, past the fireplace, and through the living room to the front door. Keeping his large body close to the wall, he eased toward the framed art print of a stretch of highway cutting across a Nevada desert. Three motorcycle riders blurred with speed, the stark highway underneath them rippling with heat.

After lifting that off the wall, he accessed the hidden vault behind it. He pressed his thumb against a small pad in the lower left corner. A moment later, it clicked and then opened. Inside were two Glock 19 MOS with Trijicon RMR sights and four extra magazines. He loaded a magazine into each pistol but left them inside the safe.

He inched toward the door and slid open a small cover on the other side, revealing a six-inch LCD panel connected to a video camera concealed above the front door. With squinted eyes, he tapped the screen to wake it. A hefty sigh then escaped his lips. A tall brunette with curly hair posed on his front porch, wrapped in a heavy winter coat. Shivering against the flakes of snow cascading down around her.

He gritted his teeth and shut the wall vault. Rehung the framed poster.

Layne opened the front door. "Hello, Daphne."

"Let me in?" she said, grimacing. "It's cold as hell out here."

"It's December at eight thousand feet. Obviously it's cold."

She strutted inside and hooked a heel to kick the door shut behind her. Spent a couple of seconds unspooling the scarf around her neck like a mummy unwrapping herself. "I don't know why you insisted on Colorado. And not even somewhere sensible like Denver, but way the hell up here in the backwoods."

"What can I do for you?"

She let her coat slip off her shoulders and crash to the floor. Layne did not miss the fact that she was wearing a formfitting business suit, one that amplified every one of her curves.

Daphne strutted around the living room, rubbing her hands together and casting narrow eyes at the decor in his house. It wasn't much, but Layne didn't care about decorating. He cared more about childproofing the electrical outlets and making sure Cameron had plenty of space for her toys, which littered the floor like grenade shrapnel.

As she glanced into the kitchen, she grinned at his refrigerator. "Still adding to your magnet collection, I see."

Layne said nothing.

Daphne paused before a framed print of the Denver skyline hanging above the modest television in the living room. "What do you have to drink?"

He shook his head. "We're not doing that. Why don't you just tell me why you're here, so I can politely refuse and send you on your way?"

"Aww, Boy Scout," she said, mock-pouting, "you really need to work on your conversational skills. I haven't seen you in so long, and all you have to offer me is hostility and bitterness?"

"You know when you drop a lobster into a cold pot and then slowly turn up the heat so he doesn't know he's boiling? That's how this feels right now."

Wearing a wry grin, Daphne sashayed across the room and slipped her hands around Layne's waist. "This is a far cry from how you used to greet me after a long absence. Remember the Radisson in Houston? I thought we were going to break the bed."

"I just put my daughter down for the night. She sometimes doesn't sleep well at this altitude, so I would like to sit in my recliner and drink a Fat Tire while I read my book. After that, I'm going to bed, so I can be ready when she wakes up to go potty two or three hours from now. How can I hurry this conversation along so I can get to my alone time faster?"

She removed her arms and stepped away from him. "Fine, dear. I'll get to the point. You're needed for something, and it's important. Give me two minutes, and I can lay it all out for you."

He shook his head, feeling the familiar burn of a headache ignite behind his eyes.

"You're not even curious?" she said. "Not even a little?"

"Nope."

"You have to trust me, Layne. I can tell you most of it now and the rest when we're at our destination. This operation is something that affects you personally."

"I'm not interested. I appreciate you coming all this way, but it was a wasted trip." He pointed up at the ceiling, toward the room where Cameron slept. "That's the only thing that affects me personally anymore."

"We don't have time for this cat-and-mouse foreplay."

"No cat and mouse. There's nothing you can say to make me jump back into that life, and whatever is at stake here, you can get your own people to handle it. I'm done."

Daphne chewed on her lower lip for a second, then sighed. "You're making a mistake."

"I can live with that."

"Hundred percent, this is your final answer?"

He stared, stone-faced. Figured he'd said all he needed to say.

"So be it." She dropped into a crouch to pick up her coat, slipped it on, and carried the scarf in her hand as she marched toward the door. Layne opened it for her, saying nothing as she exited.

When the door had closed, he stood there watching the LCD screen as she shuffled through the snow toward the street. A brief pang of guilt thumped his chest. That he should have agreed to hear her out, at least. She'd come a long way, and it couldn't have been for no reason.

But then again, Layne didn't do this kind of work anymore. He'd left that life behind years ago for something simpler. Something less dangerous.

He continued to study her tiny avatar on the screen as she reached the edge of his yard. Couldn't see what car she'd arrived in.

As she shucked snow from her shoes, Daphne lifted a phone to her ear. Her head peeked back toward his front door as she mouthed some words into the phone.

He could see it in her eyes.

His finger jabbed the button next to the LCD screen to change the view. First it cycled to the camera at the side of the house, then to the rear porch. At two black-clad shadows, breaking into his back door.

Their footsteps padded across the threshold, into his house.

He spun around as he felt the first pinch. A jab in the side of his stomach, like a heavy-duty mosquito bite. His eyes flicked down to see a stick no longer than a match jutting from his shirt. An instant of wooziness struck him, and his vision filled with stars.

Through his living room, Layne could see two figures slinking into his kitchen from the back laundry room. Both were dressed head-to-toe in black, one man and one woman. The female had an arm extended, a device like a pistol in her hands. Stun dart gun. Layne turned back toward the wall safe next to his front door when the second pinch happened, this one in his back. Like a needle jabbed into his spine.

He wrenched a hand back to pluck the dart from his skin. Wobbling on his feet, not sure if he could keep himself upright for much longer. His eyelids fluttered.

The two figures in the kitchen continued to advance.

Layne spun and raced toward them. He swerved along the way, bumping against his recliner. Could barely keep his eyes open. His hands felt like meat dumbbells hanging from his arms.

From around the corner by the fireplace emerged a third assailant, same attire. Layne pivoted and drove his shoulder into the man's chest, knocking him back against the wall.

He noted one odd thing: aside from the stun dart pistol, they'd brought no other weapons.

Not here to kill him.

He ducked down and swept the nearest attacker's leg, knocking the man off-balance and sending him to the floor. The third pinch hit him, this time in the shoulder blade. The world spun. His chest tightened while his limbs flopped, feeling out of control. Couldn't raise his arms.

His eyelids wanted to slam shut. His body weighed a thousand pounds. He sank to one knee, a few inches away from the man on the floor, now incapacitated. Layne struggled to draw in a breath as the weight of his own frame succeeded in pulling him to the floor.

Layne rotated onto his back as he fell to the carpet. The ceiling swam, and his mouth lolled open. Two figures loomed over him, both of them wearing dark fabric over their faces. Layne made one last attempt to swipe at a nearby ankle before his eyes closed completely.

Then darkness.

2

GROGGY.

AT FIRST, Layne couldn't see. He experienced the revival of his senses in quick succession, but at first, each one was a shadow of what it should have been. He could hear something akin to a repetitive drone fading into his ears, and then he felt his skin. Something touching it, like a fan, or maybe a breeze. He was on his back, judging by the pressure on his hips and shoulders.

The oddest thing was the warmth he felt. The humidity. Pores accustomed to dry, open air now felt slick and clogged.

This wasn't South Fork, Colorado.

With some effort, he fluttered his eyes a few times to find himself staring at a ceiling with a revolving blade fan. The fan made him nauseous, so he closed his eyes again. Drew in a deep breath, heavy and thick. His arms engaged, and he lifted them to wipe his face a few times. He could smell salt in the sweat he'd dabbed from his brow.

After a few breaths, the queasy feeling in his stomach abated.

Last thing he remembered, he'd been at the South Fork house, had just put his daughter to bed—

Cameron.

He pistoned up into a sit, panicked. Heart racing. Flashed open his eyes to find himself inside what looked like a bedroom. No windows, only a dim lamp cutting through the room's darkness.

No, that wasn't right. There was a single window in the room, covered with a heavy brown curtain.

The room contained a bed, a nightstand, and a dresser. On top of that dresser sat a folded piece of paper, with the single letter "L" written on top. The piece of paper was pointed in his direction, beckoning him.

That could wait a minute. First priority was self-defense and a threat assessment.

He swung his legs over the edge of the bed and planted them on the floor. The carpet was warm, his feet achy and sore. He eased over to the curtain and discovered it was stapled to the window frame.

He was wearing only boxers. His eyes searched around the room for a weapon. Nothing immediately came into view. He considered breaking off a leg of the nightstand to use as a spike, but the splitting of the wood would make too much noise. Sequestered in this room, he couldn't predict the scope of what he'd find outside the only visible door.

Layne picked up the lamp to check the weight, but it was made of plastic or some other material too flimsy to use as a weapon.

There had to be a better option. He sneaked across the

room and opened the sliding closet door, hoping to find a tool set with a hefty screwdriver.

No such luck. The closet was bare except for a few clothes hangers. Layne grabbed a wire hanger and bent it around his palm, sharp end sticking out between his index and middle fingers. A crappy weapon, but better than nothing. It might slice a throat if he hit the target in exactly the right spot.

Layne wobbled across the room toward the dresser. He snatched the piece of paper from the top and opened it.

I imagine you're furious. That's to be expected. The room you're in right now is not secure. Please leave and go down to the beach hut marked #58. It's right outside the apartment.

He gripped the paper. *Beach* hut? Where the hell was he?

More details of his last lucid moments flooded back into awareness. Daphne coming to visit him. Her making a phone call on her way out, and then seconds later, those three thugs filling him with a toxin heavy enough to knock him out. They'd been lying in wait at his back door.

Daphne had anticipated Layne would refuse her and then would require force to comply with her wishes. She knew him too well.

But what about Cameron? They'd knocked him out and kidnapped him with his daughter asleep upstairs. That was too much, even for Daphne. A line that couldn't be uncrossed.

He opened the top drawer of the dresser and found a pair of correctly sized cargo shorts and a short-sleeved polo shirt. No wallet or keys. The possessions he'd had on him before those people had invaded his house were nowhere to be seen.

He slipped on the clothes as he opened the other drawers to find them completely empty. Even with the clothes on, he felt naked. Layne slinked across the room and held his hand on the knob. He half expected it to be locked or to find more of those black-clad figures in the hallway outside. The hope that he might locate his daughter was slipping fast.

But the door wasn't locked. He creaked it open to a hallway on the other side, with pastel walls and thick carpet underfoot. Natural light spilling across his vision from unseen windows.

Daytime. How long had he been out?

He peered into the hallway and listened for any sounds. Nothing but that repetitive droning sound.

"Cameron?" he said. "Little one, are you here?"

Only the echo of his voice came back.

With a deep breath, he raised his wire hanger weapon and readied himself for a fight.

He leaped into the living room of this small apartment to see a place devoid of any decorations or furniture. Nice, but empty. And now he understood exactly what the droning sound was: the ocean. Through the window of this spartan living room, he stared out at the curve of an orange beach with foamy white suds pelting the shoreline. Hundreds of people sunbathing. Umbrellas casting shadows. Girls in bikinis smacking volleyballs over nets rippling in a slight breeze.

His head grew woozy again, but only for a second. A pulse of tension throbbed behind his eyes. Was that feeling jet lag?

Layne eased across the carpeted room and stumbled on a

pair of size-thirteen sandals sitting on a square of tile in front of the door to the outside. He slipped them on and then stepped out into the bright sunlight. Had to raise a hand to shield himself from its power. Blinked a few times.

Not only humid here, but breathtakingly hot. The kind of hot that sucks the air right from your lungs and makes your skin sizzle, even in the shade.

He stumbled a few steps forward, off the tile porch and into the beige sand of the beach. Gulped air as seagulls cawed overhead.

What the hell was happening here?

And then his eyes followed a collection of people on the beach, many of them pointing and hoisting phones to snap pictures of something occurring in the distance.

Layne raised his other hand to block out the sun so he could follow their gaze. Took his eyes a few seconds to adjust to the brightness of the sand and waves.

A little ways down the beach, he saw what they were all watching: a kangaroo hopping through the sand.

3

THE KANGAROO HOPPED, BIG FLOPPY FEET KICKING UP sand with each leap into the air. Little T. rex arms wiggled near its chest as the roo traversed the beach. Head like a deer, pointy ears.

Okay, so this was Australia. The people snapping pictures and pointing were tourists. A beach, so somewhere along one of the coasts. He'd never been to the red continent before. Sydney? There was no opera house in sight, and he knew of no other landmarks.

Behind him were houses and apartments and a few taller buildings. In front was the ocean. Between sat an orange beach littered with people. Layne Parrish was unaccustomed to feeling so lost and out of sorts. Out of control.

He had no choice but to take the next action available to him. The note had said something about beach huts.

He stumbled forward across the beach as his sandals whipped grainy particles up onto the backs of his legs. Warm and grating on his calves. Had been a long time since he'd been to a beach, and never in this level of heat.

He now understood the grogginess running through his brain to be jet lag and possibly leftover chemicals from those darts they'd used to take him down. But how he'd gotten here and how long he'd been here were still mysteries.

Daphne knew the answers, and he had a feeling he would find her at this *beach hut*, whatever that was.

Ahead and to the right, Layne spotted a series of tiny, colorful buildings with flat roofs, like storage sheds. They butted up to the beach. The note had said to find hut #58. He approached the back of them and rounded the nearest one, marked #49. The next was #50. He stumbled along the beach huts, kicking up sand, searching for #58.

He had to work harder to breathe in the thickness of this air. The heat was already punishing him, sending beads of sweat from his short hair down into his eyebrows. Droplets plunged to their deaths in the oddly colored sand.

He found #58, a bright pink hut with a few pieces of spray-paint graffiti and a single roll-up door, as a garage would have. Padlock sitting on the door. Instinctively, his hand went to the pockets on his new shorts, and he felt a small indentation in his left pocket he hadn't noticed before.

Paper clip.

He fished it out and broke the paper clip into two pieces to make it suitable for lock picking. He jabbed both ends into the lock and fished them around. In about five seconds, it clicked and opened.

After a pause, he whipped off his shirt and wiped down the area, then he wrapped the shirt around his hand to open the door.

A whistling sound behind him cut the air. He turned to find two young girls in bikinis, blonde and tanned, grinning at him.

"Won't you be late for your firefighter calendar shoot?" said the one on the left, and they both devolved into hysterical laughter.

"Flex for us," said the other one.

Layne gave them a wave and opted not to reply so the conversation could end. They both blew him kisses and skipped away after lingering for a few more seconds.

Once he was alone, Layne took a last look around before opening the door. No one was paying attention to him. Aside from his two teenage fans, everyone was too busy enjoying this sunny day.

Took Layne a moment to realize that since the seasons were reversed, December in Australia would be summer. That explained the brutal heat.

He lifted the roll-up door about three feet and then ducked underneath it, then let the door roll closed behind him. Found himself in a ten-by-ten shed, lit by an LED light on a chain up above. The only other objects in the room were a wooden chair, a desk opposite that chair, and a laptop sitting on top of the table. Finally, next to the laptop was a stack of what looked like money. Non-American currency, with small, transparent windows, made from a thick material. Almost like plastic. The bills were yellow and had a large number *50* printed on each. At least thirty or forty of them.

Layne slid into the chair. He used the hand wearing his shirt-glove to lift the lid of the laptop. The screen faded in from black to display a Notepad text file, with this message typed in the middle of the page:

Please wait for call.

A cursor blinked next to the text. In another few seconds,

the program Skype jumped into focus with a familiar jingle and an incoming call message. With his shirt-glove, he tapped on the space bar to accept the call.

Daphne Kurek's face appeared, framed by her curly hair. Layne fumed, but silently. So many phrases popped into his head at once, he didn't know which one to choose. Better to let her make the first move and then calculate his response.

Daphne lifted a hand to offer a little wave, which jerked across the screen due to the poor internet connection. Like it was skipping frames.

Her face filled most of the Skype window, but Layne could see she was sitting against a simple white background, most likely a wall. Probably didn't want him to know where she was.

"You're angry," she said.

He unclenched his jaw. "I don't even know where to begin."

"Before you start yelling—"

"Where is my daughter?"

Daphne held up her hands in surrender. "Cameron is totally fine. One hundred percent fine. She's with her mother, and she will stay with her mother for the next four days. She was asleep when we collected her in South Fork, and she woke up at your ex's in Denver the next morning. Had no idea about any of it."

"I need proof."

She frowned. "You're serious?"

"Yes, I'm serious. I want to see what she's doing, right now."

Daphne blew out a frustrated sigh, then she leaned out of frame. She whispered to someone, then nodded. "Okay. It'll take us a couple of minutes to get a drone into range."

"Why four days?" he asked.

"Because someone is going to assassinate the governor of Victoria."

He racked his brain to remember what he could of Australian geography. Wasn't much. Then it clicked into place. "So that's where I am. Melbourne."

She nodded. "You're in Frankston, to be exact. Just south of Melbourne. And if you want to fit in, you better learn how to pronounce it like *Mel-bun,* not *Mel-born.*"

Layne sat back and grunted as he tugged on his lower lip. A nicotine craving blossomed in his chest. "I can't believe you, Daphne. After everything I had to do to get away from you people. After the absolutely catastrophic way we left things, and you pull this shit? Is the end going to justify the means this time?"

"I get it. But I'd like you to hear me out. There's a lot more to this story than you might think." She turned her head to the side, listening to someone. "Stand by, Layne. One second." Then she scrolled through her phone and held it up to the camera. There, from above, he watched his ex-wife standing in a park playground in her neighborhood in Broomfield, north of Denver. A moment later, his daughter came rushing down a nearby slide, her arms in the air. Wearing her bright red parka, the one he'd bought her last month.

His heart ached at the sight of her. Even from this height, he could read the smile on her face.

"This is live?" he said.

Daphne nodded. "In a way. It's live to you, but it's yesterday afternoon to them."

"Prove it to me. I want you to pan over to the warehouse

across the street from the park. Pan over to it and focus on the big tree in the parking lot."

"Fine." She tapped on her phone and then held it up. She raised her eyes off camera at whoever was controlling the drone, and it did as Layne had asked. Made a sweep into the air, showing the glass manufacturing building across the street. Big tree, doused with snow.

"Believe me now?" she said.

"Am I killing the governor or stopping the person who's going to kill him?"

"Stopping," she said with a smirk, lowering her phone. "The governor is getting on a flight five days from now, to arrive in Pakistan. There is an immense amount of secrecy surrounding this flight, and it has a lot of people worried."

"Why is the governor of Victoria going to Pakistan?"

"We're not sure why, but we're working on finding that out. Whatever the reason, someone is trying to make sure it doesn't happen. Your job is to stop that person."

"Why can't you talk to the governor?"

She shook her head.

"Okay, then why don't you kidnap him? Keep him under wraps for a few days? That seems to be your specialty lately."

"Surprisingly, the governor's office has been antagonistic to us. Not willing to take our meetings or even acknowledge the existence of his travel plans."

"Maybe you're not as charming as you used to be."

"We have theories about what's going on in Pakistan, and it's all quite chaotic right now. We're trying to muddle through the data, but we're running out of time."

Layne flexed his hands. "So try harder."

"We've done all we can through official channels, even tried going above his head. He's not interested. This speech is too important to him, and he won't accept help from outside. We've tried to get local police involved, but they refuse to believe their security can be compromised."

"Maybe you should trust them to do their jobs. Either way, I don't care. I'm not interested in taking on a new assignment. So why don't you tell me where my passport is, and I'll be on my way?"

Daphne sighed and rolled her head around her neck a couple of times. "Please, listen to me all the way through. This job is more than just a job. I tried to explain it to you in Colorado, but you were stubborn, as usual."

"I don't care, Daphne. If you won't give me my passport, then I'll handle it on my own. I'm going to end this call now and find out where the US embassy is. Please let this be the last conversation we ever have."

He reached to close the laptop, but she threw her hands up. "Wait! One more minute. Let me tell you the rest. I promise you will want to hear this."

Layne withdrew his hand and let it drop into his lap. "You have sixty seconds."

"There's a reason you were given this assignment. There's a reason we couldn't let you say no. There's a reason why we kidnapped you from Colorado and threw your unconscious body on a cargo plane and escorted you to a country halfway around the world."

"And what is that?"

"The person trying to kill the governor of Victoria is your brother, Randall."

4

LAYNE EVENTUALLY FOUND HIS WAY THROUGH Frankston to the nearest drugstore to buy nicotine lozenges. They didn't sell them, so he had to settle for nicotine gum, which was a distant second in his order of preference.

Afterward he found the Frankston railway station by wandering through the little beach town. There he picked up a train map and a myki card, which was good for trains, buses, and trams. *Trams* was apparently the local name for trolley cars. They ran along tracks in the middle of the street, bells clanging.

The sights and sounds here rattled him. Had been way too long since he'd been in another country, so he'd need to acclimate to new things like local transportation.

When Layne had stepped up to the booth and asked for a train ticket, he could barely understand the words coming out of the man's mouth. They were English, no doubt, but the musical way the man spoke made all the words run together. The Australian accent was one Layne had never familiarized himself with.

"Top up, tap on, and tap off," the man said, revealing a mouth full of yellow teeth.

Layne received more strangely colored currency as change, including several coins. Shiny gold two-dollar pieces.

He walked away with the card, destined for platform 8, on a trip to Flinders Street Station. Layne wasn't sure what would happen when he got there, but the trip would take over an hour. Plenty of time to figure out what to do next. Plenty of time to digest the bowlful of shit Daphne had served him.

Across the platform, he noticed two suspicious men. Both of them tall, dark-skinned, deliberately not looking at him. Both in T-shirts with logos for some sports team named the Essendon Football Club.

Layne observed their hands, which stayed in their pockets as they casually loitered. They were trying to look like they were not loitering, which was a dead giveaway. They'd been observing him.

He squinted at their pockets to check for bulges in the shapes of guns but couldn't detect anything. One man made eye contact with Layne, but only briefly. A split second of connection, and then he looked away.

The two men then turned and descended a ramp, disappearing from sight. A tension in Layne's chest told him something was wrong.

Above his head, the speaker squawked. "Good morning, passengers. The next train to depart from platform 8 will be the 9:15 Flinders Street, stopping all stations to Flinders Street."

The train approached, grinding gears and clanking against the tracks. It hummed as it came to a stop and wobbled in place for a moment before finishing. The doors whooshed open, dirty and speckled with graffiti.

Layne slid into the train car. Smelled of spilled beers and the remnants of cigarette smoke. He chose the last car in the line, mostly because it was empty. There had only been a handful of other passengers waiting on platform 8 this early in the morning. Made sense, since it was the end of the line.

He navigated to a seat halfway down the train car. The chairs were yellow and covered in bright blue fabric, like something you'd see on American buses from twenty years ago. Many were stained and speckled with bits of food or empty cans of beer with the letters *VB* printed on the label.

His head swam. He'd been around the world more than once, and jet lag used to be no big deal. But he was forty years old and hadn't made an intercontinental flight in quite some time.

Not since he'd quit the team.

Daphne Kurek was one of the main reasons he'd done such a rash thing when the decision to stay had become untenable. She had a propensity for using the most extreme methods available to complete the job. Layne had objected so many times, he'd lost count. But in the end, she always succeeded, and that meant their superiors saw fit to allow her to stay in command for one more mission. She'd been doing it since the tender young age of twenty-five, and her efficiency had only grown more lethal in the last seventeen years.

A quick jingle blurped over the loudspeaker, which gave way to a garbled warning about staying clear of the doors. After that, they all swung shut. Gears chugged, and he could feel the inertia building even before the train started to move.

Layne blinked and saw an image of his brother Randall's face. It had been so long since they'd seen each other . . . ten years, maybe a little longer. Their last encounter had been in Washington, DC, just a quick lunch as they happened to pass each other. Layne en route to London, and Randall coming back from Cairo, on his way to Vancouver.

Layne didn't know then it would be the last time he would see his brother. Didn't know he would receive word a year later that Randall had gone missing in South Africa and was presumed dead.

Layne had known there would be no official investigation. He knew, because of their job roles, nothing could be done publicly or even privately. Randall would never have a tombstone in any government-sanctioned cemetery. Just an occupational hazard of the sort of work they did.

Above Layne's head, lining the curved portions of the train car walls that met the ceiling, were a series of pictures demonstrating workplace safety. Horrific things, pictures of people burned and missing limbs. Gruesome. In America, someone would have complained and had these taken down as offensive. Maybe Aussies didn't have that same politically correct sensibility.

The train departed the station, and the sensation of movement made Layne's stomach rumble. Couldn't remember the last time he'd eaten. Perhaps they'd given him an IV drip on the plane ride over here. Maybe not. Either way, he had an hour until the train would arrive at Flinders Street, and he could probably grab food there. Hot dog, hamburger, or something local. Did Australians have their own cuisine? He didn't even know.

Food was step number one of the plan. What to do next needed work, though. He knew how to contact Randall, but if all the things Daphne had said were true, contacting him might be a foolish move.

But what other option did he have? Daphne had said not to bother trying to approach the governor. To avoid using any official channels because there were too many unknowns about which players were involved. Not to trust anyone.

Why would Randall want to kill the governor of an Australian state?

Layne glanced down at his forearms, at the maze of tattoos covering from his wrists up to his shoulders. Two in particular always stood out to him. A pair of cherubs, one on his left forearm and one on his right. The one on the left had a tattoo on its own little arm that read *id*. This cherub functioned as a cover for a scar on his forearm from a bullet wound he'd earned fifteen years ago. The cherub on the right also sported its own little metatattoo, reading *superego*.

One scowling, one smiling.

Layne's eyes flicked up when the door at the front of the train car opened. As he'd expected, the two shady characters he'd seen across the platform entered his train car. Both of their smug faces grinning at him.

Layne checked his immediate surroundings, hoping to spot something to use as a weapon. No luck. Everything around him on the train was bolted down, and he had nothing in his pockets except for the myki card and a wad of Australian cash. He'd even left the makeshift coat hanger blade back on the beach.

The two men marched toward him. One, the taller of the two, slid into a seat behind Layne. The shorter one chose the row in front, but he immediately pivoted and looked Layne straight in the eye. Rested his arm on the back of the seat.

"How you going, mate?"

Layne said nothing.

The man nodded at Layne's arms. "Like your tats. Looks like you've got quite a lot invested there."

Layne cleared his throat and settled his hands in his lap, flexing his fingers into fists.

"You get those at St. Kilda Ink? I've got a mate that works there."

"Nope," Layne said.

"Ah," the man said. "It speaks. Canadian or Yank?"

Layne shook his head. He used the opportunity to catch a look at the man behind him. Saw his hand reaching down toward his shoe.

Instinct and muscle memory took over. Layne drove an elbow straight back, cracking the man in the nose. Big grunt. Head smacked against the headrest behind him. Then Layne used the other hand to drive his palm up into the nose, knocking the man back.

The man in front of him tried to grab hold of Layne's shirt. Grubby fingers clawing. Layne lowered his shoulder to skirt away, resulting in fingernails scraping across his cheek.

Layne jumped to his feet to position both men in his view. Standing in the row across from them, both still sitting. Eyes narrowed.

The tall one lunged forward into the aisle, and Layne used that momentum to his advantage. He grabbed on to the man's neck and carried his weight, accelerating as the advancing torso twisted. Drove the attacker across the aisle and rammed his head into the opposite window. A tiny hair-line crack appeared in the glass. Layne could hear the sound of the man's forehead splitting open. Blood streaked the window.

The shorter man stood in the aisle, fists clenched. Hesitating. Layne touched a fingertip to his cheek, feeling the blood the scrape had drawn.

"Who sent you?" Layne said. "Tell me now, and I'll let you live."

A moment of confusion passed across the assailant's face, quickly replaced by desperation. "Just give us the bloody money."

Realization filled Layne as he drew in a breath. These two men had seen Layne pull the fat wad of bills out of his pocket when he'd purchased the myki card. His teeth clenched as he cursed himself.

Such a careless error.

The short man roared and then lunged. Layne lowered himself an inch to flex his legs and prepare for a punch. Layne sensed the man's right shoulder twitching backward, so he leaned in the opposite direction to avoid the punch. But the attacker surprised him and jabbed out with four fingers of his front hand. The blow landed right on Layne's Adam's apple. Flashbacks to the boxing ring appeared.

He gagged but had no time to wallow in the pain. Before the man could draw his hand away, Layne snatched it and twisted the hand to fold the wrist back on itself. The man howled, and Layne leaped out of the seat and into the aisle. Dragged him a couple of rows back to create space between them and the other guy.

"Next station: Kananook," said the scratchy voice through the intercom.

With the tall man pinned, Layne turned his attention to the man he'd smacked into the window. He was sitting in the seat, dabbing a stream of blood cascading down his forehead.

"Both of you will get off at the next stop. Yes?"

The short one grimaced, but the tall one said nothing, so Layne applied increased pressure to his wrist, which sent him to his knees. Too much more and he'd break it, which Layne didn't want to do. These were simple thugs, looking for an impulsive and quick score. They hadn't even brought weapons with them.

Layne added a touch more pressure, and the man on the floor nodded his approval. Sweat beading on his forehead.

The train slowed at the Kananook station, and Layne let go of his wrist. Took a few steps back in case either of them decided to cause any more problems. They didn't. Each of them scooted into the aisle and wobbled toward the doors as the train came to a stop. Dots of blood from the tall one's forehead flung onto the seats as he shuffled off the train.

Neither of them looked back at Layne as they departed.

Pulling out that wad of cash had been a terrible blunder. Jet lag or no, Layne needed to be more careful. Mistakes like that could lead to a bullet in the head.

A couple of people shuffled onto the train car. As the doors shut, standing on the platform was a young girl, no more than three or four years old. About the same age as Cameron, maybe a touch older. Holding a stuffed animal in one hand, the feet of the furry thing scraped on the train platform. Her eyes locked on Layne's. Pale blue, unblinking eyes.

Layne tapped the window and smiled at her. Gave her a wave.

She looked up at her mother, cracked a grin from the left half of her mouth, and then lifted a hand to wave back.

5

SERENA ROJAS WATCHED Layne pull out a fat wad of bills at the Frankston railway station to pay for his myki card. Given how careless he'd been, she wasn't at all surprised when those two bogans followed him onto the train with lust in their eyes. Only a matter of time before they would make their way back there and try to shake him down.

She chose a train car three ahead of Layne and one ahead of the bogans, hoping to avoid any potential run-ins. But she definitely wanted to see how Layne would react.

Serena slid her purse higher on her shoulder and peeked inside it as she stepped over the threshold to enter the train car. Inside her bag, the Walther PPK rested comfortably between her wallet and the small neoprene case that housed her noise suppressor.

She eased into the seat on the train car well ahead of Layne. She could see him through the rear window but made sure she could move her head an inch or two to break his sight line. Above all, Layne could not know she was on the same train. This spot provided her with a perfect view, but it would break if the train curved on any part of the track.

Only a minute or two after the train departed from Frankston Station, the two men left their car and entered Layne's. One sat behind him and one in front. Serena resisted the urge to dip a hand into her purse to feel the cold comfort of her pistol's trigger.

It was not her job to intervene. Not her job to either aid or stop these men from killing Layne Parrish. Her job, as ordered, was simply to follow Layne, note his movements, and never expose her presence to him.

If Layne were to be taken out, she would receive that order when the time came. Serena, a twenty-eight-year-old, highly trained operative, had been converted into a glorified surveillance camera. So disappointing.

As expected, the two men tried to rob Layne, and he dealt with them in short order. He was lithe on his feet, fast and efficient, like a boxer. Didn't move more than necessary. He delivered rapid blows that completely overwhelmed these two street-fighting thugs. The whole encounter lasted maybe fifteen seconds total.

The move to pin the man by his wrist had been so sudden and unexpected, she let out a little sigh when it happened. A giggle wormed its way up her throat, but she shoved it back down.

Serena hadn't had a worthy opponent such as this in quite some time.

At the next station, Layne ushered the men off and then returned to his seat. He sat, slumped, head down, at first probing the injury to his neck from a single lucky blow one of them had landed. After that, he stilled. Eyes closed in concentration. She could only tell he was alive by the subtle rise and fall of his bulky shoulders.

Layne was an attractive man, well built and classically handsome, like a square-jawed Hollywood actor from the black-and-white movies her grandparents watched. But Serena had no problems being objective about his appearance.

She'd killed handsome men before.

Over the next dozen or so stops, he occasionally checked his station map, but otherwise, he kept his eyes on the floor.

The beaches and suburban houses on the outskirts of Melbourne slurred into the central business district's dirty train stations and densely packed rows of houses and apartment buildings. The graffiti in this city fascinated her. Locals viewed it as a pure art form, or so she'd heard. If she had the time, she would spend a month in the city, photographing all the nooks and crannies of the underground illicit art spray-painted all over the train stations and alleys and laneways. Maybe when this job was done, she'd take a few personal days. If she didn't have to hurry off to Austria or Mozambique or Mexico City.

She sighed and thought about her cat. Had been a month since she'd seen her fluffy little partner, currently staying with her neighbor. Would the cat forget her after such a long trip away from home? Or would the little beast punish her by meowing incessantly once Serena finally picked him up from his foster home? Hopefully she would find closure on that question soon.

After an hour, they pulled into the covered Flinders Street Station. When Layne stood, so did Serena. And as she stepped off the train, she did slip a hand into her purse to grip the Walther PPK, on the off chance Layne looked in her direction.

6

AT THE FRENETIC Flinders Street station, Layne found a cart selling meat pies. He'd never had meat in pie form before, but he enjoyed the little circle of steak and curry. Gobbled the hand-size thing in four bites.

The clacking of dress shoes and high heels on the surrounding floor mingled with the continuous loudspeaker announcements to form a wall of sound in Layne's muddled head. He hadn't felt this out of sorts since he was first on the job, sixteen years ago.

He hated this feeling. Hated not being in control of himself and his environment. Hated that his daughter's face appeared before his eyes every few seconds, like a filter on the world. And most of all, he hated that he couldn't put his arms around her right now.

He wandered outside onto the steps of the station and basked in the glow of the yellow behemoth building towering over him. Across the street was an even crazier collection of buildings, marked with a plaque reading *Federa-*

tion Square. Ultramodern, which was a stark contrast to the classical architectural style of everything else around.

He took a few breaths and formulated a plan. Had to focus.

Step one would be to get in touch with Randall. Find out the truth behind all this. He had no reason to think Daphne would directly lie to him, but he would expect her to bury important facts if she thought it would benefit either the mission or her own agenda.

Maybe Layne's brother had a good reason to kill the governor of Victoria. Maybe the man was involved with something bad. Or maybe he planned to do something in Pakistan that would hurt America. Randall Parrish was still a patriot, as far as Layne knew.

But Layne didn't know very far. He hadn't seen his brother in more than a decade. A lot could happen in ten years.

Before step one, step zero would be acquiring a phone. To his left, across from the Flinders Street station, he noted the familiar Virgin logo above a ground-level store. Layne waited at the crosswalk with several dozen other people, then hurried across the street toward the store.

His senses felt like they were on fire. Adverts everywhere for sports betting. Dozens of them, plastered on the side of every building. Between the tall skyscrapers, little shopping areas packed with restaurants and cramped patios cluttered the alleyways. People moved in thick clusters, like oozing lava between crevices.

Plus it seemed a ton of people here smoked. The cigarette smokers threw him off because he was so unaccustomed to it. In Colorado hardly anyone smoked cigarettes. And that sort of distraction was the last thing he wanted because he needed to be alert and aware. To make use of the comfortable so he could focus on abnormalities.

He already felt the sensation of eyes on him and had felt it since Frankston. But he couldn't be sure how much the jet lag was still affecting him.

With a breath to steady himself, he ventured into the cell phone store. Bright lights and workers in red polo shirts assaulted his eyes.

"Morning," said a young woman with jet-black hair as she skirted over toward him. "Need a top-up?"

"Prepaid phone," he said, keeping his eyes low to make it less likely she might recall his face later.

She gave him a brief, odd look, and then her expression changed. She set him up with a phone (called a "mobile" in Australia) with only voice and text. No data, which would make him easier to track. She went through a whole spiel about flagfall and top-ups and lots of other things that barely registered in Layne's foggy brain.

Once he had the phone in his hands, he absconded from the store and wandered off to find a library or internet café. Last time he'd been in Europe, you could still find internet cafés. Who knew, though, with the prevalence of smartphones, if public internet terminals even existed in this country?

Layne had to hunt for a couple of blocks toward the center of the city to locate one. It was a combination convenience store and internet café, with a full coffee bar.

He sidled up to the counter to buy a coffee, careful only to withdraw a single fifty-dollar bill this time.

"Coffee," he said.

"Which kind, mate?" said the pale man behind the counter.

"Say what, man?"

"Flat white, short black, latte, cappuccino, strong black?"

"Cappuccino."

The man nodded and then went to work at the espresso machine. Layne studied the desktop computers in the internet café portion of the store as the machine whirred and chugged behind him. Saw three banks of four computers, with only a single one occupied at the moment. A teenage girl, flicking a mouse cursor along Facebook.

He took out the phone and sent a text message to the one person he knew in Australia, a woman named Tilda:

The beach is lovely today. Care to join me for a swim?

He had no idea if she was still living in the country, if she'd been killed in the line of duty, or had maybe even retired. No telling. He had to hope she would understand the code because he couldn't risk being any less vague with his terms.

When his coffee was ready, Layne grabbed a few napkins and walked his drink over to the computer and inserted a couple of one-dollar coins into the machine. The aging PC whirred to life, and he checked to see if this computer profile allowed installs. Surprisingly it did, so he opened a browser window. Downloaded VPN software he trusted to hide his tracks.

Once he felt confident that his browsing was private, he navigated to a certain forum and clicked on a message thread that hadn't been updated in over ten years. *The difficulty of being a Christian in today's world.* He scrolled down past a few posts and added a new reply to the bottom of the thread. He typed:

Seems to me the world keeps descending into hell, and the only thing that will save us is a return to Christian values. I agree with the OP in this case.

He paused and then took out the box with his new phone. Opened it and studied the number Virgin had assigned to him. Ten digits. He stared at the keypad on the phone and played with the numbers in his head. Had to turn it into a word.

After a moment, he came up with the gibberish name *HYALPABLY* as a possible letter combination. Entered that for the username of the poster and clicked Submit. The post appeared at the bottom of the other entries in the forum thread.

He sat back and sighed. Head still swimming.

Then he used Google Maps to locate a clothing store nearby. He was tempted to log on to his email and send a message to his ex, to inform her he was okay and to give their daughter his love. But that would be a mistake.

Later. He would contact her later, once he had a better grasp on the situation.

Finding a clothing store had been easy, but the bigger challenge was finding a costume shop. An internet search located one in Preston, a few miles away. Would have to figure out the train line to get there.

Layne cleared his search history, uninstalled the VPN software, then edited the Windows registry to remove all traces it had ever been there. Once the computer was clean, he wiped off the keyboard and tower and then shut it down.

He left the internet café and sat out front for a moment, studying what the pedestrians were wearing as they strolled by. Lots of people in shorts, few wearing long pants. Cargo shorts and a button-down shirt seemed acceptable for men his age.

As long as he didn't open his mouth, no one would have any reason to think him not a local. Not a chance in hell would he attempt to simulate an Australian accent.

Layne wandered back to the Flinders Street station and bought clothes, a watch, a wallet, tennis shoes, a pocket mirror, and a backpack to carry the spare clothes.

Two hours slipped by, and he mostly sat next to a tram stop, sipping at his coffee and watching people shuffle along. Occasionally wiping sweat from his brow. Eventually Layne returned to the internet café. Paid for another coffee and another session and then loaded up the message board.

There was a reply to his post:

I think the OP is an idiot.

Had been posted by a user named *Nash Bridges*. Layne recognized the handle instantly. It was a detective TV show from the 1990s. When Layne had been younger, he'd thought it was a dumb name for a TV show. Said it constantly for months as a euphemism to describe people whom he didn't like. His big brother, Randall, had also latched on to the phrase but used it as a nickname for Layne.

Randall had seen the post.

But there was nothing in this reply to indicate a number to contact him. Layne went over each word and character, trying to find a pattern that matched any code he could recall. There seemed to be absolutely no meaning beyond the snarky words themselves.

But then, the phone in Layne's pocket jingled. The tone sounded so unfamiliar, it took him a second to realize it was his. He fished it out to find one new text message from an unknown number.

MBS gym - Cato St, Prahran - 8 pm tonight

7

LAYNE WANDERED FROM Malvern Road to Cato Street. Peered down a slim road that was more like an alley than a proper street. The pocket of his cargo shorts clinked with the key to an apartment in the nearby neighborhood of South Yarra, one train stop away from his current location of Prahran. He figured it would be smarter to maintain a bit of distance. Whatever significance this city or town or suburb of Prahran held for Randall, Layne didn't want to be too close. Nearby, sure, but not right on top of it.

Besides, his new apartment was adjacent to the train line to help orient him. With his head being so foggy, orientation was an important factor to consider.

He was two hours early for his appointment to meet his brother, assuming that's who the text message had been from.

As he made a nonchalant pass in front of the gym, he cast eyes up to the sky and wondered if Daphne and her agents had satellite surveillance on him right now. Possibly, but that would be an expensive bit of tradecraft. More likely there was someone on his tail, although Layne had seen nothing. He'd kept to the train tracks and scrutinized every face that even casually glanced in his direction.

But that sensation of eyes on him persisted. Maybe it was the jet lag and multiple cups of strong coffee screwing with his senses, but still. Something wasn't right, for sure.

Past the gym was a Woolworths grocery store. Layne popped inside and purchased food to eat in the morning. Plus paper towels, toilet paper, Leatherman Multi-Tool, toothbrush, and toothpaste. A six-pack of Victoria Bitter and some snacks, including a package of cookies branded "Tim Tam," which seemed promising. He stashed the bag for these items behind the Woolworths, sandwiched between two dumpsters. No one saw him leave his food, and no one would have cared anyway. But he didn't want to walk into this Randall meeting with a big grocery bag as an accessory.

He kept the Leatherman on him, though. He had, in the past, used one as a weapon. On more than one occasion.

He conducted a lap around the edge of the parking lot, noting the mothers pushing strollers, the cars with their drivers on the right side, driving in the opposite lane. Something he hadn't been forced to do in a long time. He remembered the utter panic he'd felt in his twenties, driving through the streets of London in the wrong lane. The learning curve might not have felt as steep if he weren't being chased by a couple of Russian operatives in a Ferrari. Not much time to second-guess yourself in that situation.

After a full pass through the parking lot with nothing out of the ordinary materializing, he decided to check out the gym itself. He popped inside to find two men and a woman behind the front desk. Clanging of barbells, grunting of sweaty men and women. Relentless club music pumping through hidden speakers in an attempt to mask the grunt orchestra. The walls were adorned with posters of oily bodybuilders posing on stage.

The gym had a second floor, and he heard the warble of televisions wafting down from a set of stairs beyond the desk. This place was yellowing and grim. Reminded him of Glazer's gym back in Denver. A lifetime ago.

"Hi there!" said the cheery woman behind the counter. "You a member?" Her accent made the last word hit Layne's ears as *mim-bah*.

He approached and leaned in so he wouldn't have to shout. "I'm just poking around, thanks. Do you have a patio?"

"Sorry?"

"A patio out back that's accessible from the outside."

She shook her head. "The patio's fenced in. You can get to it by the hallway next to the loo."

"What about the second floor?"

"There's a fire escape, but no patio on the second floor."

"Got it. Thank you."

The woman was reaching over to snag a brochure from a display stand when Layne pivoted and walked out the front. She called after him, but the door was already closing before she could get the second word out.

He rounded the building and did see the enclosed area. A chain-link fence curved around the frame of a patio. No way to access it externally. Good. To the side, a ladder for a fire escape jutted out from the far end of the building. He made another pass around, looking for alternate ways to reach the roof, aside from the fire escape. Seemed there was only one way up.

He climbed the rusted fire escape to the second floor, which was a small landing barely wide enough to stand on.

47

Locked door leading to the second floor of the gym. Above him, the base of a smaller ladder leading to the roof hung only a few feet out of reach.

Layne bore down and then leaped. Barely wrapped one hand around the bottom rung of the ladder. Threw the other hand higher. As soon as he'd started to wrench himself up, the door below him swung open.

He pulled his feet under him to avoid them being smacked by the door. He stretched as hard as he could to hoist his lower torso out of view. Placed his feet against the side of the building and craned his neck to see below him.

On the second-floor landing, a muscular blonde woman decked from head to toe in formfitting spandex stepped outside, then she spun on her heels. "There, that's better. Let's get some air in here. All right, spinners, let's move those rear ends! Only twenty minutes left until you can shove off for the day!"

She returned inside, and Layne climbed the rest of the way to the roof. From up here, he had a good view of the four sides of the building. Could see all alleyways pointing in this direction. Every entrance and exit. He spent time mentally measuring the distances to the rooftops of the nearby buildings and decided they were far enough away to present no threats.

He found an empty milk crate, flipped it over, and sat. Held the Leatherman in his hands, pliers facing out. The weariness in his head and muscles added extra gravity to his body, and he shook his head a few times to clear out the cobwebs.

A memory obscured his vision. His daughter, Cameron, from three days ago, sitting on her little plastic potty, telling him a story as he hovered in the doorway to the bathroom.

She rambled for five minutes, inventing a tale about Thomas the Tank Engine becoming stuck on the tracks and how the other trains James and Gordon came to his rescue. Layne watched her, marveling at how this tiny little person's brain could think on the fly.

He checked his watch. Another ninety minutes to wait and see if his brother, Randall, would meet him in person or send someone to kill him.

8

EIGHT P.M. CAME AND WENT. THE SUN SANK IN THE western sky, disappearing behind the buildings and then blending into the horizon.

Layne wished he hadn't left the six-pack in the bag behind the grocery store, but he wasn't willing to surrender his secure spot to retrieve it. As his watch ticked to eight thirty and then nine o'clock, he decided to give up. Nothing but a stream of grocery shoppers, people in and out of the gym. Random pedestrians traversing the skinny streets. No one suspicious or out of the ordinary triggered Layne's warnings.

But since everything here was out of the ordinary, he wasn't sure how much to trust his senses right now.

Either way, he'd arrived at the conclusion that Randall Parrish would not show. Maybe it had been foolish for Layne to expect him to appear and explain himself. But the message had been from him, hadn't it? Who else in the world would know about the forum thread and the name *Nash Bridges*?

Maybe he'd had cold feet. Maybe he wasn't able to get away, for whatever reason. If Randall was working undercover for some organization, he might not get a chance to leave for the evening.

That had to be a viable explanation, right? Randall had a good reason for his involvement in a mess halfway around the world. There had to be more to this story than whatever intel Daphne had access to.

Or maybe she was right, and Randall was actually here to assassinate the state governor, something to do with the man's upcoming trip to Pakistan. Either way, Layne would not find out tonight. He wondered what time it was in Denver and if he should risk calling Inessa to speak to his daughter. He longed to talk to her but wasn't sure if it was a smart idea. Best to keep personal calls off the phone, even if it was a disposable burner.

Back home, if he felt tense and disconnected, he could whip out his cell and flip through an endless photo stream of Cameron. Her playing in the park, scratching huge sticks of colorful chalk along the sidewalk, giggling like crazy while descending a plastic slide next to a ball pit.

Here Layne had nothing. Not even a physical photo to stare at by the burgeoning moonlight.

After turning the Leatherman over and over in his hands a few hundred times, he decided to walk home. He slipped down the escape ladder and rounded the building to collect his groceries. Pondered trying to take a streetcar—known locally as a tram—but he wasn't sure if he could find his way back to the serviced apartment if he strayed from the train tracks. Operating without an internet-capable phone was a challenge Layne hadn't had to deal with in many years. He hadn't even noticed until now how dependent he'd become on the little piece of tech he usually carried around with him.

Layne crept to the edge of the parking lot and performed one more perimeter sweep. He still had that creepy feeling of being surveilled, and he couldn't shake it. On this pass around the block, he paid attention to the shadowy areas, looking for the glint of reflection from a camera lens. The muted LED of night-vision goggles.

But he saw absolutely nothing. All the empirical evidence available said no one was watching.

He followed the train tracks along various neighborhoods and alleys to reach Davis Street, where the small building sat. Tired hands escorted the groceries inside to the minifridge and then checked the shutters on the windows. This apartment had no air-conditioning, so he was forced to raise the windows a little. Fortunately, it was a shotgun-style apartment, so the open windows on each end pushed a breeze from the bedroom through the kitchen.

He cracked open the package of Tim Tams and shoved a few cookies in his mouth. Washed them down with a beer and then collapsed on the couch, exhausted. He wasn't even sure what time his internal body clock thought it was supposed to be. Late as hell. Like an all-nighter back in college, except he was nowhere near the peak level of physical stamina he'd been at back then.

All this international travel and espionage crap was a young man's game. Layne hadn't felt like a young man for some time now.

He opened the bag from the costume shop and picked through the disguises he'd bought. Wigs, glasses, colored contacts, nose prosthetics. The tattoos blanketing both of his arms presented a problem since the weather was unsuitable for long sleeves. Might draw attention.

The weight of his body pulled at him, and he left the costumes on the table as he reclined on the couch. He dropped the bag, his eyes fluttered a couple of times, and then he was out.

A knock came at the door.

Layne shot up, and his hand instinctively reached down under the couch. Maybe his muscle memory told him that's where the pistol would be.

But he had no gun. Daphne hadn't seen fit to leave him with one. She'd said he was better off foraging for what he needed as he went along, and Layne hadn't had the energy to argue with her at the time.

He considered the Leatherman but instead sneaked into the nearby kitchen and grabbed a knife from the magnetic strip on the wall. Slipped it behind his back as he padded over to the entrance. The door had no peephole, so he placed a hand on the knob and prepared himself for all possibilities. He took a few deep breaths and then whisked the door open.

Randall Parrish was standing on the front step of the apartment.

INTERLUDE 1

LAYNE PARRISH PLACES TWO FINGERS AGAINST THE underside of his wrist to check his pulse. He's slick with sweat, staring at the ceiling from a bed in the Radisson. Next to him, naked and half-covered by a bedsheet, Daphne Kurek breathes deeply to calm herself.

It's more than a decade and a half before Layne will wake up in Australia, transported there against his will. His light hair is not yet threaded with gray. There are no crow's-feet around his eyes nor wrinkles lining his face like bitter scalpel slashes.

He's twenty-four years old, and she is two years his senior. She's his boss, which Layne was unsure about at first, but he's warming to the idea. Not because his boss is a woman; that doesn't bother him at all. It's more that he expects a boss to be older, wiser, boasting a lifetime of experience. But their superiors see something in Daphne that experience can't provide: a ruthless efficiency. She's good with people. Bending them, persuading them, extracting the right results. She knows when to stick up for someone and when to jettison deadweight.

Layne saw it in her eyes on the day he met her. She will do anything it takes to come out on top. That both scares and excites him, and while he doesn't trust her, he respects her conviction.

Right now, Layne isn't so sure that having sex with his boss was a good idea, but Daphne was persuasive. His clothes seemingly shed themselves, and now they are in piles, scattered around the floor of her hotel room.

She always seems to get what she wants. Layne's body was no exception. That also worries him, but he respects how well she plays the game.

And in the afterglow of a fierce and cardio-intensive lovemaking session, he can't help but feel completely sated. He craves a cigarette, but the pack is in his pants, and he's not sure where his pants are.

Her body is a playground, and she knows how to use it. She did things to him Layne has never experienced in his twenty-four years on earth. Daphne is only two years older than him, but he feels like a teenager who's slept with the neighborhood divorcee and has been delivered to a whole new continent of wonder.

She turns in the bed and places a hand on his sweaty chest. Her fingers dance across his blond chest hair, nails tickling his skin.

"You were great," she says.

"So were you." He angles onto his side to meet her eyes. He loves the sound of her voice. It has a hint of rasp to it, like smoke seeping along rough wood.

"Tell me something about you," she says. "Something personal."

"I don't follow."

"What do you like to do for fun?"

"Oh," he says, "I like to read. Fantasy and sci-fi, mostly, but I dabble in everything."

"More."

"Okay. I like camping and national parks. I've been to twenty of them. Any new one I visit, I buy a magnet from the park gift shop and keep them all on my fridge." He chuckles a little to himself. "You could call it my life's work."

"Which one is your favorite?"

Layne thinks on this for a moment, cycling through a slide show of memories. "Bryce Canyon, in Utah. The biggest, bluest skies you've ever seen."

She's quiet. Staring at him. Layne feels the air conditioner pumping, the cold air seeping over his arms, drying the sweat. Feels good to be cold.

"Are you okay about this?" she asks.

He frowns but nods anyway. Not sure if it's better for him to speak his mind and be honest about how uncomfortable he is or to suck it up and act like it's no big deal. It's still many years until he will meet the mother of his future child, but Layne feels guilty due to someone else. Someone he can't forget.

His internal debate doesn't matter, though. He can see in her eyes that she knows everything hidden in his head.

"It's okay," she says. "Ethically, I mean. There's no conflict of interest with your training. I got permission."

His eyes open wide. "You asked them for permission to sleep with me?"

"Yes. Not exactly *asked*, more like I explained to them what I wanted to do and convinced them it wouldn't interfere with your progress."

His face draws heat, flush with embarrassment. It's odd how nonchalantly she's explained all this. "Okay, if you say so."

She giggles, a beautiful sound coming from her rosy red lips. "I know you're skeptical, but trust me. It's all going to be fine. No one will even mention it to you."

"Well, it is what it is."

"Everyone has been very impressed with you so far. You've exceeded expectations."

"Thank you. I'm just trying to keep my head above water."

Her eyes trace lines down his body for a few seconds, then she giggles again. "They gave you an official code name."

"Why is that funny?"

"You're not going to like it. I probably shouldn't even tell you yet."

He frowns. "Now you have to tell me."

"Your handle will be *Boy Scout*."

He turns again on his back and stares at the ceiling. She's right, he doesn't like it. "Anyone who thinks I'm a Boy Scout doesn't know me."

"Big, bad Layney Parrish. Compared to your brother, you're as pure as the driven snow."

"How is Randall? You seen him lately?"

She nods. "He's going to meet us in Seattle next week for a joint training assignment."

This makes Layne smile. He hasn't seen his brother in months, not since before this training program started. Hasn't even spoken with him in at least six weeks.

"I should call you Control," he says.

"Control? What does that mean?"

"It's from an old spy novel."

Daphne toys with a chunk of hair, flicking it between her fingers. "I like it. I'm gonna try that one on and see how it feels."

A knock comes at the door. He creases his brow at her, and she shrugs and pulls the covers up to her neck. "Go see."

Layne slips out of bed and grabs his boxer shorts from the top of the dresser. Daphne ogles him, licking her lips as he dresses.

Layne's first thought is that it's a neighbor here to complain about the noise. Another knock comes at the door, this time more urgent.

He crosses the room, his body slightly tilted, one shoulder back. Foot over foot toward the door. He leans against it, peering through the peephole. On the other side is a tall white man with dark hair, but with the dim light in the hallway, Layne can't make out his features. The man stands, stoic, no expression on his face.

Layne slips the chain onto the door and unlocks the dead bolt.

The chain shatters as the door bursts forward. It smacks Layne in the forehead, and he's so surprised, he can't help but take a step back. Has to blink a few times to see.

The man leaps into the room and kicks the door closed behind him. Fire in his eyes, teeth gritted, spittle dancing at the corners of his mouth. Layne glances down to see the man has a cylindrical object in his hand, like a miniature baseball bat or a baton.

He whips the baton upward, toward Layne's face. Layne swings an arm up, using his forearm to block the blow. Whatever that baton is made from, it's heavy. It cracks

Layne's forearm, and for a second, he worries the bone might be broken. But he doesn't have time to wail and cry.

He lowers his hips and spins, then delivers a backhand, pointed at the man's elbow. Priority number one is disarming the attacker.

But his opponent is too quick, and he draws his hand back. Layne's fist knocks against the man's bicep. The man responds with a hook from his free hand, cracking Layne across the jaw. It's a powerful punch. Jarring.

The attacker swings the baton, but this time, Layne is ready. He sidesteps and wraps his thumb and forefinger around the baton as it's whisking through the air. He uses the attacker's inertia and jerks it from his hand. Lets it fall to the floor, then he kicks it across the carpet.

Layne then drives his head forward, hoping to take the man by surprise. He does, and the crown of his head connects with the man's chest, driving him back. His shoulders slam against the front door.

Layne presses the advantage of surprise. He wraps one hand around the man's closest arm, locking his grip. Jerks it to force the man off-balance. Layne then wraps his other arm under and then around the man's far armpit. Now he has both of the man's arms pinned behind his back. All the leverage on Layne's side. Now all he has to watch out for is the man wriggling away from him.

Layne joins his hands together behind the man's neck, and he bears down for more leverage. Forcing the invader to lean over.

He jumps into the air, holding tight, bringing the man into the air with him. Layne slams the man's lower torso to the ground.

He loosens his grip to place one hand around the man's

throat. Squeezes. Not to kill him, but to knock him out. As quickly as possible because the man is now repeatedly driving his elbow into Layne's stomach. Vicious, rapid blows that make Layne want to retch the lasagna he and Daphne shared for dinner.

The man's face is starting to turn red. Eyes bugging out of his head. Only a few more seconds, and Layne will neutralize him.

"Layne, that's enough," Daphne says.

"What?" he says.

"Let him go. Let him go right this second before you do some serious damage."

Layne releases his grip and scoots back across the carpet until he butts up against the dresser. Above him, the TV wobbles. He snatches a comb from the dresser and grips it as a weapon. It's a shitty one but the only thing he has available.

The man rubs his neck, coughs, but makes no further attempt to retaliate.

And then it hits Layne: this is a training exercise.

"Damn it, Daphne," he says. "I could have killed him."

The former attacker grins. "You wouldn't have killed me." His accent has a slight tinge of Russian to it. He leans across the carpet, hand extended. "Oleg."

Layne pauses, then shakes his hand. "Layne."

"I know," Oleg says. "We will be teammates when you're done with training."

Layne flicks his eyes up at Daphne. He wants to growl, to complain, but he's mostly mad at himself. He should have seen this for what it was the instant Oleg burst through the door.

She clears her throat and whistles at Oleg. "Can you give us a minute?"

He nods, stands, and adjusts his clothes. "It was good to meet you, Layne Parrish. I look forward to working with you for many years to come." He nods at Daphne. "I'll see you in Montreal on Thursday if there's nothing else you need, ma'am."

"Call me Control," she says.

Oleg nods. "Of course, Control."

With a small salute to Layne, he exits the room.

Layne crawls to the edge of the bed, heart beating, ribs aching from Oleg's attack. But even more than injured, he's angry. "What the hell was that?"

"A test."

"You have to warn me next time when there's a test coming."

She shakes her head. "No can do, Boy Scout. Everything is a test."

PART II

EVERYTHING IS A TEST

9

LAYNE GRIPPED THE HILT OF THE STEAK KNIFE AND looked his brother in the eye. Whenever he studied Randall's face, he could see their father. The curve of his nose, the angle of his chin. Even more so now because it had been a decade since they'd laid eyes on each other. The formerly crease-free face of thirty-five-year-old Randall Parrish was now ten years older, with ten years of added wear and tear.

Randall flicked his gaze down at the knife. "You going to stab me or invite me in?"

"I haven't decided yet, man. I'm supposed to kill you, and now would be a perfect opportunity."

"While you're figuring it out, could I suggest you make your decision inside the apartment? I try to stay out of the public eye these days, if you know what I mean."

Randall lifted his shirt to expose his bare stomach, and he turned in a circle, showing he had no weapon. He then pulled the shirt higher to reveal his chest. He turned around and pulled the back of his pants down, exposing his butt crack. "Gun-and wire-free. We good now?"

Layne paused and then took a step back to let his older brother into the room. He entered, leaning a little in each direction as he strutted. Just like old times, with that classic Parrish swagger.

"You didn't show," Layne said.

"I had to be sure you weren't being followed."

Layne flinched. "I wasn't."

"I'm not so sure about that, but I don't think you're in any danger, at least." He pointed at the couch. "Can I sit, or is that where you're going to stab me?"

Layne nodded and pulled out a chair from the desk on the other side of the room. He slid into it, knife flat across his knee. Not taking his eyes off his big brother.

"Do you have a stereo in here," Randall said, "or something else loud like that?"

Layne shook his head, so Randall took out his phone, scrolled to a music app, and shuffled songs. Turned the volume all the way up. He set the phone on the coffee table between them."

"You still box?" Randall asked.

"A little."

Randall flicked his eyes at a pack of nicotine gum on the coffee table. "How long since you quit?"

"About eight years," Layne said.

"What? And you're still on the gum?"

Layne shrugged. "Not ready to let go of that habit just yet."

"Ah, I see." Randall inhaled as he cocked his head. "What did they tell you? About me?"

"That you're going to kill the governor of Victoria."

"Really?" he said, snickering. "And why am I going to do that?"

"They're not sure. Something about Pakistan and the governor's trip there."

Randall sighed and drummed his fingers across his knees. Layne recalled their father doing the same thing when he was thinking. "Daphne Kurek set this all up?"

"Control is still running things, yes."

"Did she give you supplies or drop you into the jungle with nothing?"

"With nothing."

Randall clucked his tongue a couple of times. "Not even a sidearm? And you're okay with that?"

"What I'm okay with is my business," Layne said, although Randall's words pierced him. Nothing Daphne had done so far had been aboveboard. Sent him here with no instructions, no gear, no backup. "You could say I'm figuring out where I stand with her."

Randall swished his lips back and forth a few times. "I saw on Facebook when you got married. What's her name? Ingrid? Anika?"

Layne gritted his teeth. Randall had been keeping tabs on him. "Inessa."

"Right. Inessa. How is she?"

"We split up."

"That sucks. I almost got married a few years ago."

"Is that so?"

Randall nodded. "I dated this woman for four whole years. Four years of my life I gave to her. Near the end, anytime we talked . . . if I asked her a question, she would ask me what I *meant* by what I said. 'What did you mean by that?' She'd say she wanted to go out for sushi, and I'd say I didn't want sushi, I wanted barbecue. She would ask me what I meant by that, like I was sending her a coded message."

"No more small talk."

"Okay, that's fine, we'll have plenty of time to catch up later. Here's what you need to know: There are two large crime syndicates in Melbourne. One is based out of St. Kilda, and they call themselves Reds. The other is a gang mainly located in Collingwood, and they call themselves Union. Magpies fans."

Layne detected a hint of the Australian accent in his big brother's speech. How long had he been in this country?

"Magpies?" Layne asked.

"Football. Footy. Anyway, Governor Phelps negotiated a cease-fire between them. Something of a peace treaty. There's been some back-and-forth about who ate the fat end of the hot dog. Most say the Unions got the better deal, and the Reds are not happy about it."

"Phelps is a pawn in a gang war?"

"Basically. The Reds are going to have someone at his speech at Fed Square in four days. A sniper to send a message that the Reds are too powerful to be told what to do by a politician and yadda, yadda, yadda."

"And why do you care?"

Randall leaned forward. "Because, mate. Your people were right about the Pakistan connection, but they've got me listed as hitting for the wrong team. I'm going to make sure Governor Phelps gets on that plane because he *has* to fly to Pakistan."

Layne noticed the knife drooping over his knee, and he reassured his grip. "What happens in Pakistan?"

"Abdul Abbad. You know that name?"

"Sounds familiar."

"He's assumed to be the leader of a small extremist group that calls themselves the Sons of the Imminent Dawn. And

Abbad also happens to have been Phelps's college roommate at Harvard twenty years ago."

"And?"

"Some concerned members of the European Union believe Abdul Abbad intends to acquire precursors for a nuclear weapon. And Phelps will try to talk him out of it. That's the purpose of the governor's Pakistan trip the day after his speech. This trip is important, and it needs to happen."

"You claim this gang war and the Pakistan trip aren't connected, they're just bad timing."

"Very bad timing."

Layne nodded. "So you're a mercenary these days."

"That's an ugly term for it. I'm doing contract work for our concerned friends from a certain European Union member country. Beyond that, I can't tell you which one. And you won't find any sanctioned mission that any of them will admit is on the books."

"Why does the US government think you're out to kill Phelps?"

Randall shrugged. "Could be the Reds spreading bad information. They do know about me, so I wouldn't be surprised. Could be the Union, because they're no fans of my work, either. Could be someone who is in Abdul Abbad's organization, not happy that he's willing to give an audience to his old college friend and potentially let himself be talked out of their future plans. Could be someone in Washington, just trying to cause havoc for some other reason. You know how they are in DC."

Layne had to concede that last point. Daphne had not so far behaved in a trustworthy manner, although he had no reason to think his handler wanted him dead. Why she had given him so little information did trouble him, though.

"Why would the Reds or Union care about you at all, man? What work of yours aren't they fans of?"

Randall sat back and grimaced. "About a year ago, the Union stole a collection of very expensive artwork from a gallery in a bush town named Dandenong. It's about an hour by train from here. A few days later, the Reds stole it from *them*. They were going to ship it out of the country, and I found out where and when. I showed up at the docks and hijacked their shipment. I returned it to the gallery and managed to make enemies of both of them at once."

"That sounds like something you would do."

Randall grinned. "Sometimes it's fun to play with matches."

"So how do you stop these Reds from killing Phelps?"

Randall breathed. Blinked a few times. "Tomorrow morning, take the train to Southern Cross Station. Walk up Bourke Street two blocks to the Macca's. I'll be inside at 9:00 a.m."

"Macca's?"

"McDonalds. Be prompt. I won't wait more than a couple of minutes. We'll be basically across the street from the lion's den, and we have to be extremely careful about who sees us moving around."

"How do I know you'll show this time?"

Randall leaned forward. "We have a chance to do something important here. Yes, I was hired to do this job, but I believe in it. The Sons of the Imminent Dawn are a nasty little cell. Friend of Phelps or not, Abdul Abbad is a wicked son of a bitch. If they get the power they're after, it's bad for everyone. Bad for Australia, bad for Europe, bad for the States."

"What will we be doing tomorrow?"

Randall opened his palms. "You're just going to have to meet me and see. I can't tell you anything else right now."

For a few moments, they both sat in silence. The song changed on Randall's phone. Finally he said, "I heard you retired."

"I did. Have been working as a security consultant in Colorado for the last few years."

"Is it good work?"

"I enjoy it. Companies hire me to find the weak spots in their physical and online security. It's a lot better than doing this kind of thing."

Randall spread his arms wide. "And yet, here you are, little brother, once again rushing headfirst as the whale opens its mouth to swallow you up." He stood and collected his phone, which made Layne instinctively clutch the knife in his hand tighter.

Randall pointed at it. "I'm going to walk out your door now. Please don't stab me in the back. If you kill me now, you'll seriously mess up my ability to explain myself."

Layne said nothing as his brother confidently strolled toward the door. Neither of them said goodbye when Randall slipped out into the night.

Sighing, Layne flicked a finger along the edge of the blade.

10

SERENA ROJAS ADJUSTED THE STEERING WHEEL TILT SO she could hike up her knee without feeling crowded. This street had voluminous trees with abundant leaf coverage. A nice feature. Even though it was late at night, having plenty of visual distractions helped. Layers of shadows upon layers of shadows.

Not that she was in too much danger of being spotted out here.

Nothing had happened since Layne had returned. She could see him through the angled blinds, on the couch, snoozing like he'd been hit with a tranq gun. His bulky shoulders rose and fell. He was shirtless, abs braced while he slept.

Shoulders rose and fell. Rose and fell. Rose and fell. From time to time, he jerked, like he was about to fall off the couch, then he would settle. Shoulders rose and fell.

Screw it.

She lifted her phone and dialed her neighbor's number. Any time she called across the world, she always felt like she was entering too many digits. The international dialing tone chirped, and a few seconds later, a voice picked up.

"Hello?" said a groggy man.

"Hi. I'm sorry to bother you. What time is it there?"

"Serena?"

"Yeah, it's me."

"I don't know what time it is. I had a late night."

"Sorry to wake you. I just wanted to see if he's okay."

The man grumbled. "The cat is fine. He's sleeping in a shoebox on the floor next to my bed."

"Did he eat all of his breakfast yesterday?"

"Yes."

Serena bit her lower lip. "And what about the cat condo? I wasn't sure if he would accept it being in your apartment."

"He was napping in the cat condo yesterday, no problem. You know, if something was wrong, I'd call you immediately, right?"

"Yeah, I know. I'm just bored."

"Want me to put him on the phone?"

Serena grinned. "No, I don't think we need to put him through all that. He's only chatty when he's hungry, anyway. I'm sorry I bothered you, so please, go back to bed."

"Thanks. Hope your business trip is going well."

The line clicked off, and Serena sighed at the phone. Thought of the cat in his massive, carpeted condo structure, sleeping on the top tier, six feet in the air. Raking his claws across the scratching posts mounted to the towers.

Serena pondered how long she would need to stay out here, watching a man sleeping on a couch through the slats in his window blinds. Studying endlessly, with nothing happening.

Like a flash, someone sneaked across the sidewalk, and

she sat bolt upright. Lifted her camera and adjusted the lens to bring the person into focus. She snapped a few pictures but couldn't grab any face shots. Whoever it was had a knack for keeping his or her face down and shrouded by the shadows. Someone deliberately trying not to be seen.

Although Serena had a good notion of the identity of the ninja.

The person entered the complex and knocked on the first door on the right. Disappeared inside after a brief conversation on the porch.

She retrieved the parabolic microphone dish from the passenger seat and pointed it at the living room window of the serviced apartment Layne had rented earlier that day. Listening through a small opening in the window was a long shot, but she had to try it.

With the headphones on, she angled the mic in a circle to find the best position. Static filled her ears. She adjusted the frequency as Randall Parrish briefly stepped into view.

Serena gasped. Definitely him. The Rattlesnake himself.

After a couple more knob tweaks, she could make out words. They were faint, faraway, and warbly, but definitely understandable, despite the music playing to mask their voices. When she closed her eyes and gave it her full attention, she could even make out individual words.

She flipped on her recorder and also retrieved a pen from her center console. Moved the notepad to her right thigh and wrote down anything discernible above the background noise in the room.

Governor Phelps
Abdul Abbad
Sons of the Imminent Dawn

Reds
Unions
McDonalds, 9 am tomorrow.

Layne said little, which was smart of him. In the cop shows on TV, they always portrayed the detectives as aggressive, battering the suspects with questions in an interrogation room. But in real life, Serena knew it was much better to sit back and let the interviewee tell his story. The more he talked, the more likely he would trip himself up and give something away.

When the conversation finished and Randall rose from his seat and left the apartment, Serena reclined in her chair and stowed all the equipment. Randall strolled along the road and then disappeared around the corner.

In the room, Layne held a kitchen knife clutched in his hand. Interesting. The younger Parrish brother didn't trust the older.

For a moment, she considered following Randall, but the odds were good he would spot the tail. She couldn't afford to blow her cover. At least, not yet.

She waited for two full minutes and then placed a phone call.

Two rings later, the call connected. "Yes?"

"This line secure?"

"It is, Serena. What'd you find out?"

"I had Rattlesnake and Boy Scout both in my sights. They had a meeting in Boy Scout's new apartment."

"You didn't kill them yet, did you?"

"No," Serena said. "I'm just gathering intel. And I have some actionable items, I believe. Sending data to you now."

She clicked the upload button on her recorder and then shifted the phone to her other ear.

"Got it."

"You need to look into Abdul Abbad in Pakistan. That should be priority one."

"I'll take it under advisement," said the voice on the phone. "Anything else?"

"Nope. They're meeting again tomorrow. What are my ROE?"

The voice on the phone hesitated. "Observe only, if possible. If you obtain concrete proof Layne is compromised, then you can do what needs to be done."

"I understand, Daphne. Serena out."

11

IN THE MORNING, LAYNE FELT BETTER. NOT A HUNDRED percent, but the jet lag had reduced to a low throb, like a constant state of dehydration.

He endured ten minutes of cardio exercises in the living room to shock his system and then a cold shower in the cramped bathroom. By the time he'd finished, he felt awake for the first time since arriving on the red continent.

He walked a couple of blocks from his apartment on Davis Street to the South Yarra station. Spent some time thinking how strange it was that, despite all his world travels, he'd never found a reason to land here before. No stops in New Zealand, either.

He bought a coffee and an egg sandwich from the little "take-away" place inside the station. As he stood on the train platform, admiring the graffiti that littered the station, he fished around in his pocket for the myki card. Had only a vague memory of buying it the day before. Many events from yesterday felt like shows he'd watched on a screen, instead of real life.

The train arrived and took him toward the tall buildings of downtown Melbourne. Richmond Station, then Flinders Street, then a loop around the downtown area. The train routes were starting to make sense to him. They were like a spiderweb that radiated out from this central loop, with long strands reaching out into the different suburbs.

As he passed Parliament Station, headed toward his final stop at Southern Cross, he noted Federation Square, the site of Governor Phelps's speech in three days. He'd seen it yesterday, walking out of the Flinders Street station.

Tall, angular buildings surrounded a narrow courtyard. Ultramodern and filled with dozens of nooks and crannies. Several excellent spots for snipers to gather. He assumed it would be snipers, but a bomb could be equally effective.

Layne exited at the Southern Cross station. The place was massive, with a giant wavy roof like a glass-and-steel version of a choppy sea. Impressive. Cameron would love this. She would stare, openmouthed, and then demand Layne hoist her onto his shoulders so she could move six feet closer for a better view. Thinking of her brought a pang of loneliness to the back of his head. Worse than the jet lag.

He needed to find a way to contact her soon. It was still a bad idea, but like a crack addict, the itch would have to be scratched, sooner rather than later. But definitely not right now.

Layne found his way to Bourke Street and hiked up toward the McDonalds. Even at this early hour, the city was abuzz with activity. Like New York or London, there were always crowds shifting and writhing like a communal organism. Never any place to be alone in a metropolis like this one.

He encountered his first aboriginal person, busking on

the street outside the train station. Skin as dark as he'd ever seen, chunky brown and gray dreadlocks hanging down over his face. The man was seated, with his mouth against a long wooden didgeridoo, far end resting on the pavement. In one hand he held a stick, thwacking it against the side of the didgeridoo to keep time.

The man looked up through his dreadlocks and eyed Layne as he passed on the street. Layne fished a two-dollar coin out of his pocket and tossed it in the open suitcase next to him. The man blinked once but didn't stop playing. Cheeks expanding and contracting, that earthy horn never stopping. Layne didn't *enjoy* the sound of the didgeridoo, but he appreciated the art of it.

He pressed on along Bourke until he saw the McDonalds. Spent a minute or two outside, watching people come and go. Nothing suspicious, mostly kids in matching school uniforms and backpacks. The backpacks wore intricate patches with names Layne didn't recognize. The children all like little carbon copies in their conformist attire.

When his watch ticked over to 9:00 a.m., he strutted inside the restaurant to the sight of a packed interior. Lots of college-age kids clustered around tables. Some had food, but most were leaning over laptops and tablets, fingers stabbing at keyboards.

And at a table in the back, dunking a chicken nugget into some purple sauce, sat Randall. His eyes flicked up, and he gave a subtle nod of the head.

Layne crossed the room and sat down with his older brother.

"McNugget?" Randall said.

"No, thank you. Why's it so crowded in here? Seems like it's after breakfast time."

"It's always like this. Macca's is one of the few places with free Wi-Fi. All the kids from uni hang out here before and after classes."

"I see."

Randall chewed, his eyes drifting down to the tattoos on Layne's arms. "Do you know the difference between faith and belief?"

Layne cleared his throat. "Why don't you tell me?"

"Belief is the hope something is true, without concrete evidence. Faith is the certainty something is true, despite evidence to the contrary."

Layne made a little grunt of an acknowledgment.

"Why did you and your wife split?"

Layne didn't want to get into the whole thing, so at first, he said nothing. Randall stared at him, insistent. Layne had to calibrate how antagonistic he would act toward his brother.

"We have a daughter together. She's three, going on thirteen."

Randall's eyes widened. "I'm an uncle? Holy shit."

"No, you're not."

"What do you mean?"

"To be an uncle, you have to be present. You have to take an interest."

Randall pursed his lips. "That's cold, little brother."

"I haven't seen you in ten years, man. I assumed you were dead after you went missing in South Africa and no one heard from you."

"Okay, that's fair. I'd rather not dredge up all the details. Let's just say Johannesburg was a real nightmare. I was lucky to get out of there alive, to be honest. After that, I decided to go off-grid and take some time to myself."

"A phone call would have been nice."

Randall dipped his head and dunked a nugget a few times until it was thoroughly coated with barbecue sauce. "You're totally right. I was mad, so I gave everyone back home the finger and made myself a brand-new identity. But it's a fair point: I shouldn't have cut you out, too. I'm sorry about that."

Layne breathed, considered an answer. He didn't like any of the options popping into his head, so he said nothing.

"So you were telling me why you and Inessa split."

"We have a daughter together, but I'm not sure she's mine."

Awareness passed over Randall's face. "I see. That's a heavy load to haul."

"It doesn't change how I feel about my daughter."

"It's a little hard to see you as a family man, to be honest. Changing diapers and having tea parties."

"My daughter and I have the best tea parties. They're legendary. But I don't want to talk about her right now. Tell me what we're doing here, man."

"I want to show you something." Randall pointed over Layne's shoulder. He turned to see an apartment building across the street, six stories tall, plain.

"What's that?"

"That's where a good chunk of the Reds live. You can call it their stronghold, if you will. But it's not all that secure, and they like it that way. Hiding in plain sight."

Layne shrugged. "And?"

"And we're going to break in. There's something in there I want to show you."

12

THE APARTMENT BUILDING ON BOURKE STREET SAT quiet at this hour. Pedestrians swarmed on the sidewalk in front of it. But no one peeking out of any windows above. No one coming in or out. Randall had said the building had residents, but Layne wasn't so sure.

He and Randall crossed the street and rounded the back of the building. Service entrance at the rear, with a roll-up bay door for deliveries. Layne kept watch across the tree-lined alley while Randall sifted through a small backpack over his shoulder.

"I'm not armed," Layne said.

"Not a problem. We're not here to blow the lid off a giant conspiracy. But there's a Word document I want you to see, and we might have to poke around a little to find which computer it's on."

Randall hovered near a smaller door to the side and removed an object the size of a flashlight from his back pocket. Held it up to the lock and jabbed it forward a few times. After a click, the door opened.

"That's a nice toy," Layne said.

Randall held it up for Layne to see. "Also functions as a stun gun. One shot only. Swiss-made."

"Have one for me?" Layne asked.

"Sorry, no. We're going to be ultraquiet with this one. Shouldn't encounter any resistance, though. This is where a few of them live but not where they do their work. I'd be surprised if we encountered a single person in this building today."

Randall pushed through the open door into an area like a garage, with tools hanging from the walls and a small bay with oil stains on the floor. He pointed over toward one corner. "There's a crowbar if it'll make you feel better to hold something."

Layne did retrieve the crowbar. Felt solid in his hands. A little cold, but satisfyingly heavy. The sort of object he hoped he wouldn't have to swing.

Randall paused and leaned against a workbench along one wall. "I heard you were in Beijing for that kerfuffle with the hacker six years ago."

Layne nodded. "I was."

"How did it turn out? I couldn't get any info."

"Not good. It was one of the last ops I was involved in before I finally pulled the plug and retired. We found where he was holed up, but he rigged the apartment with explosives."

Randall's eyes widened. "No."

"We lost four people that day."

"Sorry," Randall said, biting his lower lip. "That's awful."

"Yeah, man, we should have had better intel. Spent more time before engaging."

"Isn't that always the way?"

"Near the end," Layne said, "it was like that more often than it wasn't like that."

"You said it was 'one of' your last ops. Which one was the last? Which mission broke Layne Parrish?"

"I'm not going to talk about that." He pointed the crowbar toward the other side of the room. "Let's get to it."

They pressed on, through the room and to a door on the far side. Opened into a hallway. Randall paused, turning his ear toward a length of the corridor that seemed to stretch on forever. Layne also listened, and nothing but silence came back. Just the hum of an air conditioner.

Randall shifted into the hallway, foot over foot, grasping his door unlocker device in one hand. Several doors lined either side of the hallway. All dormant. At the end of the hall, the path split off to a door ahead and stairs to the left. Layne paused to study a message board with dozens of thumb-tacked and Post-it note messages. A quick glance told him many of the messages were in code. He didn't have the time or the energy to puzzle through them.

Randall headed up the stairs.

"What are we looking for?" Layne said.

"Proof. I'll know it when I see it."

Randall said no more as he ascended. He passed underneath a window, throwing sunlight on his face. The beams highlighted the wrinkles across his brow and around his eyes. Last time Layne had seen his older brother, those wrinkles had been faint. Now they were like deep grooves. Layne hadn't thought the difference between thirty-five and forty-five would be so stark.

For a brief moment, he contemplated his own declining features. But he quickly stowed those thoughts. There would be time for the mortality thought-spiral later.

At the second-floor landing, Randall turned to head up to the third floor, but Layne grabbed his wrist.

"Wait. What happens if we encounter anyone? Should we discuss a strategy?"

"The strategy is: don't hesitate. These people will kill intruders without a second's notice."

Layne wasn't sure if he wanted to leave a trail of bodies behind him. Plus, he had to keep one eye on Randall at all times. A couple of heart-to-heart meetings in an apartment and in a McDonalds weren't enough to make Layne blindly trust this man he'd been sent here to kill.

But he'd invested enough time to tag along this far, so he didn't have much choice. If it came to it, he would back up Randall as necessary.

They crested the third-floor landing, and Randall hesitated outside the entryway door.

"Are we looking for a specific person's apartment?"

Randall winced. "Not really. This isn't like a typical crime syndicate. They don't have a central leader or power structure. More like a council of people who make the decisions. One of the main guys lives on the third floor for sure, but I'm not positive about the others. One of them will have a laptop or desktop with the info we're looking for."

"Which is?"

Randall grinned. "Not yet, little brother. I want to keep you in suspense for a few more minutes."

Layne sighed. "Well, let's start with the one you know."

Randall nodded and opened the door into the third-floor hallway. Crept inside it. Layne followed him, feet light, keeping breaths even.

Then a door opened. Just behind Layne.

He whipped around to find a large man, shirtless,

wearing sweatpants. White guy, tattoos blanketing his arms, chest, and neck.

Plus, he was wearing a Ruger in a loose holster slung around his waist.

Layne reacted. Before the man could say or do anything, Layne jabbed the crowbar into his gut. Made him bend forward. With a flick of the wrist, Layne removed the pistol from the man's holster and dropped it to the floor. He kicked it down the hallway behind him. Layne then smacked him again in the arm but not hard enough to break bones.

The man let out a small yelp, and Layne drove a fist into his mouth to shut him up. The guy stumbled forward, leaving enough space in the doorway for Layne to maneuver. He dodged behind the man and pressed the crowbar under his chin, with the other arm over the top of his blocky head. He applied pressure as the man squirmed. If Layne could hold his grip and prevent the guy from wriggling out of it, the large man would be out in twenty seconds.

But he didn't get the chance to find out. Randall whipped a folding blade out of his pocket, flicked it open, and jabbed the blade into the man's heart. Held a hand over his mouth to keep his screams muted. Randall twisted the blade a few times, widening the hole. Blood gushed out onto Randall's wrist.

Layne, wide-eyed, released his grip. The man slumped to the floor. Randall stayed in place, blood dripping off the end of the knife.

On the floor, the man wriggled a few times, his mouth opening and closing. Layne watched the life race out of him, coating the floor on either side. Wasn't sure how to feel about it. For all he knew, this man was an insurance adjuster taking the day off to hang out at home and play video games.

"Help me get him inside," Randall said as he snatched the man's arms. Layne rounded him and picked up the man's legs, and they hauled the body a couple of feet to close the door.

After they'd dropped the body on the ground, Randall retrieved the gun and then knelt to study the man's face. "Son of a bitch. This is the guy. Name is Hallgren."

"What guy?"

Randall's eyes darted around the room. "Look for his desktop or a laptop, maybe a tablet. Might be a phone or something not easily found."

Layne had to step over the man's body as he surveyed the room. Couch, table, chairs, bookcases. A copy of *Mein Kampf* caught his eye on one of those shelves.

"Anything?" Layne said.

Randall sighed and lifted a stack of magazines from on top of a desk. "Nope."

Layne's neck craned toward a sound coming through the walls. A muffled cry. He gripped the crowbar and eased toward it. Eyes on a closed door.

Randall took notice and fell in step with him. Just like old times, they each stood on opposite sides of the door and made eye contact. Layne nodded his head three times and then opened the door.

Inside, Layne saw the definition of filth and squalor. A bedroom filled with food packages swarming with maggots and flies, dirty clothes piled several feet deep. The walls had been spray-painted with dozens of graffiti tags. Indiscernible symbols in every color of the rainbow. He had to breathe through his mouth to prevent retching.

The level of disarray was so bad that Layne didn't even notice the woman at first. She was on the bed, her hands duct taped to the bedpost. Wearing only panties, her olive skin glowing in the sliver of early morning light pouring in from the window.

"Holy shit," Randall said, an odd expression on his face.

She was Asian, tiny, hands and mouth covered in more tape. Her eyes bulged, and she wrestled against her restraints as Layne approached.

He held out his hands, palms out. "Hey, it's okay. I'm not here to hurt you. The man who did this to you is gone now. He's not coming back."

She tried to shrink away from him, but the duct tape held her upper body in place.

Layne pointed at his chest with one hand and hooked a thumb behind him with the other. "My name is Layne, and this is my brother. I'll untie you now, and then I'm going to step away. I will not hurt you."

She paused, beads of sweat dripping down her face and onto the duct tape over her mouth. Eventually, she nodded. Randall handed Layne the knife, and he flicked it along the duct tape over her hands. She grimaced as she lowered her shoulders, then used her hands to cover her exposed breasts. Shaky hands ripped off the duct tape from her mouth, and then she rolled over onto her side, sobbing. She formed a malnourished question mark. Vibrating, wheezing.

Layne pulled up the bedsheet and then folded it over her to give her some cover.

"Did Hallgren do this to you?" Randall said. "Did he tie you up here?"

The woman paused her crying long enough to turn toward them. She nodded.

"He's dead," Randall said. "In the next room."

Layne cleared his throat. "He won't hurt you anymore.

We can get you to a hospital if that's what you want. We can call an ambulance—"

Randall urgently cleared his throat as a protest, but Layne ignored him.

"I think you need medical attention," Layne said. "Let us help you."

The woman blinked a few times as the tears stopped. She slipped off the bed and crawled over to a pile of clothes on the floor. Without saying a word, she dressed. Layne and Randall stood in silence as the woman collected herself.

Layne considered reaching out to her but thought better of it.

When she was done, she limped to the doorway, then glanced back at both of them. She opened her mouth to say something, then caught herself. She heaved a few breaths before speaking.

"I want nothing from you people."

She disappeared into the next room and then out into the hallway. The door slammed behind her.

After a beat of silence, Layne said, "We should go after her."

"You heard her. She doesn't want help. You know the saying about how meth relationships are more like hostage situations?"

Layne nodded, still eyeing the closed door leading out of the apartment. His instinct said to go after the woman. But Randall was right: she wanted nothing to do with them. If he appeared in the hallway behind her, she was just as likely to run as let him aid her.

Randall crossed the room and swept a pile of junk off a desk. "Knife, please. This desk is locked, which is always a good sign."

Layne gave it back to him, and Randall broke open the lock on the bottom drawer. Spent a few seconds sifting through papers, then he chuckled. "I got something. Dumbass printed it out."

"What?" Layne said as he crossed the room to look in the drawer.

Randall lifted a printed page and showed it to Layne, who squinted to see a document with a list of items. Cargo manifest, to be delivered to some place named French Island, 11:00 p.m. tonight.

18x Sig Sauer P229
30x rounds x 50 9mm
6x AR15
4x Desert Tech SRS

There were several more items on the list, but Layne stopped when he saw the Desert Tech. A compact, easy-to-transport sniper rifle.

Randall met Layne's gaze. "Desert Tech is perfect for an easy-in, easy-out. Good for hauling up to a high location. Did you see what was underneath that page?"

Layne's eyes flicked back to the drawer. Inside it was a map of what looked like downtown Melbourne, folded so that Federation Square was visible. The same spot Governor Phelps would give a speech in three days.

Layne dropped the printed email on the desk. "I see the connection you're trying to make, but it's not proof. It's not enough for me, man."

"Come with me to French Island."

"Why?"

"It's not like America here. Much harder to get guns. All

the things on that list are coming to French Island via a boat tonight. If we can stop that shipment from coming in, we can seriously hurt their chances of killing the governor."

Layne stared at the folded map inside the drawer. Sighed.

"Come on, little brother. What do you say?"

13

***

ON TOORAK STREET, NOT FAR FROM LAYNE'S RENTED apartment, he ducked inside a Greek fast-food restaurant to buy a gyro. Watched as they shaved lamb from a rotating vertical spit. Heat from the kitchen nullified the air-conditioning, and he dabbed sweat from his brow as he waited for his food.

He sat and ate his lunch as he stared out the window at the trams chugging along the middle lane of the street. The bells clinging, the sounds of nearby horns blaring. Thousands of Melbournians marching along the sidewalks, smoking, chatting on phones, carrying shopping bags and briefcases.

His mind swirled with all the information of the last few hours. Particularly about the woman tied to the bed. The look on her face as she limped out of the room. Her patent refusal to accept his help.

Maybe he should have gone after her anyway. Escorted her out of the building and to a hospital. That moment of hesitation and letting her walk out throbbed in the back of Layne's brain like a headache.

But it wasn't the only puzzling moment he'd experienced since arriving in Melbourne.

He wanted to believe his brother. Wanted to stop the assassination of Governor Phelps using any means necessary. But there were already too many pieces in play. Reds, Union, Abdul Abbad, Pakistan. Too many variables to arrange into an easy solution.

As he ate, he studied the dueling cherub tattoos on his forearms. The sinister on the left and the angelic on the right. He held his arms together over the table, so they were next to each other.

The door to the restaurant opened, and in walked a brunette woman wearing giant sunglasses. Daphne. She smiled and edged up to the table, sitting in a chair across from him. He didn't even raise his eyebrows at her. That she'd taken pains to mask her whereabouts during their Skype call in the beach hut yesterday had suggested she was nearby. And also that she'd want to hide it from him, in case he was captured by someone.

The mission operator's location was always need-to-know information only. Often she was nothing but a voice on the end of a phone. And now, because she was here in person, that meant either she needed something from him or the situation was worse than she was letting on.

"How's the lamb here?" she said.

"Delicious."

"Tried the baklava?"

"I wasn't planning on it."

"I see. It looks promising, not all drenched in syrup the way they do it in America."

Layne chewed and swallowed. "So you're in Melbourne."

"Are you surprised?"

He shook his head. "But I am surprised you'd walk in here cold. It's a little too public for you."

She waved her hands around the restaurant. There were three tables, only this one occupied. The kitchen staff was standing at the spit, shaving meat, paying zero attention. Still, seemed sloppy.

"I wouldn't be here if I was concerned about security," she said. "But we should go somewhere else to talk. Outdoors, I mean."

He wadded up the remainder of his gyro and deposited it in the trash. After finishing his soda, he escorted Daphne out onto the sidewalk and back toward the train station. Across the street, a red metal arch led onto a path adjacent to the train line. The words *Lovers Walk* were emblazoned on the concrete.

"Who are the two brothers in your *Game of Thrones* books who are the big, dumb bodyguards? The ones with the funny names?"

"If you mean in the *A Song of Ice and Fire* novels," Layne said, "I assume you're referring to the Clegane brothers. The Hound and the Mountain."

"Right, right. That's you and Randall."

Layne scoffed but said nothing. He and Daphne padded a couple of hundred feet down the path, with a fence protecting the rails on one side and a row of trees protecting a neighborhood on the other.

"What's so special about this governor?" Layne said. "Why is he important?"

"That's above my pay grade. All you need to know is that he is the VIP in this operation."

A noisy train whooshed by. Clacking and banging. He raised his voice to speak above it. "What aren't you telling me?"

"Lots and lots of things. I know you met with your brother, and he's probably been filling your head with all sorts of info."

"So you have someone on me. I assumed you did, but I haven't been able to find him."

"Of course we have someone on you, dear. And you will never spot your tail unless your tail wants to be spotted. We can't afford to spook Randall."

"You've dangled me out in front of him as bait. Bringing me here was never about my skills or my training, was it? That's why you couldn't get someone else to conduct this op. It had to be me so you could trip him up. Make him work harder."

Daphne leaned against the railing. A sign behind her read *Keep off—Contact with overhead wires or fittings will cause death.*

"I had to be careful about what I told you," she said. "I didn't want Randall to sniff out too many things about this op before we'd had a chance to dig deeper into the situation."

Layne narrowed his eyes. "Are you being careful right now?"

"He's lying to you," she said. "We know that, for sure. But we haven't had the time or the resources yet to figure this all out on our end. The quick timeline of the speech has left us with few options regarding intelligence."

"I see."

"Did he mention Pakistan, or has he avoided the subject altogether?"

"We talked about it. The governor is flying there to meet with Abdul Abbad. Old college friend. Randall says he wants to make sure Phelps gets on that plane so this meeting can take place."

She nodded, with the slightest hesitation on her face. "We've learned about Pakistan, too. And did Randall tell you he has contacts with a mercenary group in India?"

Layne shook his head. "He did not."

"It's true. Your brother has had prior dealings with an anti-American group on the India-Pakistan border. This group wants Governor Phelps dead, to hurt Abbad. Maybe your brother plans on killing Phelps before he can leave. More likely, he wants to let Phelps get on that plane so he can have him killed in Pakistan. Easier to manage there."

Layne rubbed his chin and considered. "It doesn't make sense. I can't see why he would be so interested in this Pakistani squabble over the leader of some little cell."

"We have reason to believe that when Randall went missing in South Africa, it wasn't op-related. We think he got a better offer from a group in the Middle East, so he vanished himself for a couple of years as part of his new employment."

"I don't buy it. Randall was never in it for the money. He's never displayed any anti-American sentiment before, so I don't believe for a second he'd suddenly stop being a patriot."

She shrugged. "A lot can happen in ten years. What did *he* tell you about his motives?"

"This is all about a gang war between the Reds and the Union. Phelps is caught up in the middle of it because he tried to broker a treaty between them."

Daphne laughed. "Those two gangs are small time. Not even worth full investigation by the ASIO."

"Maybe. Maybe not. Whatever you're going to do,

Daphne, give me a chance to poke around first. I still have three days until the governor will give his speech at Fed Square. Please don't send in the cavalry until I've had a chance to ferret out the truth."

If Daphne had metabolized Layne's request, her face didn't show it. "Where is Randall now?"

Layne bit his lip, pondering the question.

14

LAYNE GRIPPED THE SIDES OF THE SMALL BOAT AS Randall piloted them across the rolling black of the water. A half-moon cut a line of white across the surrounding darkness. Bouncing up and down, the water's cool mist drifting up to his arms.

So many thoughts ran through Layne's head, but he didn't know how to categorize them all. The meeting with Daphne this afternoon had weighted Layne with a heavy backpack of doubt. He'd had trouble looking his brother in the eye, and the change couldn't have been lost on Randall.

But Layne had made no secret of his state of distrust. That he was only going along to find out the truth.

They were wearing simple low-grade body armor, no ceramics. Would stop pistol rounds, but not assault rifles. Each of them sported Maxim 9 pistols with built-in noise suppressors. Four extra magazines apiece stuffed into their cargo shorts to complement the fifteen-round mags.

First time Layne had held a gun in a few days. His arms were more used to holding a preschooler, lifting her up into the air. Swinging her around a room. Crawling across the carpet to complete an obstacle course made of repurposed cardboard boxes.

A pang of heartache hit Layne. A desire to contact Cameron. To see her face. But he knew it was a bad idea. Knew it was something he shouldn't (but probably would) do.

"How's your old Harley running these days?" Randall asked over the roar of the boat motor. "Or have you picked up a new one since I've seen you?"

"I sold it," Layne said as he popped in a piece of nicotine gum.

"You *what?*"

"Yep. I sold it two months ago, man."

"What in the world possessed you to do that?"

"I was sanding a rough edge on my new porch. Cameron was playing outside near me. I looked up, and she jabbed a garden hose into the exhaust. And just then, I had a flash of me crashing as a car cuts me off on the highway. Leaving my daughter without a father."

Randall was quiet for a moment. "I get it. I mean, I do get it, but that was a really nice bike."

"So it was. Where are we headed?"

"There's a small beach on the south end. We'll pull in there and hide the boat in the brush. Our approach should be far enough away, but keep your eyes open, just in case."

Layne squinted through the darkness. "What are we expecting to find beyond the beach?"

"There's a dock about a half mile up the coast, and that's where the boat will most likely come in."

"Do we round the coast?"

"Nah, most of it isn't beach. It's mostly mangroves and

jungle. We're better off going inland to find a different route. The Reds will send maybe a half dozen for security and to unload the shipment of weapons."

"Only a half dozen?"

Randall tilted his head from side to side. "Probably. Too many will attract attention. We'll set up shop nearby and pick them off after the boat arrives."

"What about this?" Layne said, pointing at Randall's backpack full of C-4.

"That's a fail-safe."

"I have a better idea than picking them off one by one."

"You do? Let's hear it, little brother."

Layne opened the backpack and counted the bricks of explosives. "We stack these on their boat and then wait until they've got all the gear. Sink them after they take off."

"Nice," Randall said. "It's dangerous and will attract a lot of attention, but I like it."

"I think it minimizes our exposure."

"True. You always were the more thoughtful one."

"So yeah?"

"Works for me," Randall said. "We'll have to find their boat and sneak on, then find a good hiding spot to monitor their departure. I'm not sure what kind of vantage point we're going to get."

They spent the rest of the trip across the water in silence. Mangrove trees shrouded their final approach. Pulled up onto the beach, lit only by the sliver of moon above. If there were buildings on this island, none of them had lights on at this hour.

Layne and Randall hauled the boat into some nearby trees, and there were plenty of bits of brush nearby to use as cover.

Layne checked his watch. Twenty minutes until the 11:00 p.m. arrival of the shipment. "We have to hurry."

He chambered a round into his pistol and ventured into the tall, spindly trees that made up the area beyond the beach. A shape in a tree caught his eye, and he gazed up to see a koala bear, clinging to a branch. Chest slowly rising and falling.

Randall stood next to him, eyes tracking the mangy little furball. "Any of the locals sell you the story about the drop bears?"

"Nope. I haven't really talked to anyone."

Randall shrugged and pushed ahead, then turned right in the next break of the trees. "We should stick close to the coast. The dock is about a kilometer ahead, so we're sure to find the boat somewhere nearby. On one side of it or the other."

Layne and Randall ventured through the thick, wooded area. Layne occasionally heard the calls of birds or howls of animals that sounded so foreign, each one caught him off guard. For a moment, Layne considered the possibility Randall was leading him into a trap. That they would pass some corner and happen upon a camp filled with soldiers from whatever Middle Eastern country was paying Randall to commit all this havoc.

If that happened, he'd be dead. One bullet to the head would leave his daughter without a father forever.

Layne checked the magazine of his pistol and eyed one of the bullets. No blanks. He had no solid reason to think Randall would betray him out here, but he let his older brother lead their hike, just in case.

They continued on like this for five minutes, ten minutes. And then they saw it. Through the trees, a boat tethered to a cluster of mangrove roots at the edge of the water. And more than half a dozen men exiting the boat. Ten or eleven of them. Each wearing semiautomatic rifles strapped across their chests.

Layne dropped to a knee and surveyed the surrounding jungle to evaluate their vulnerabilities. There were trees nearby to ascend, but elevation might work against Layne and Randall. Best bet was to stay low and use the brush as cover.

Once the men had cleared the area, Layne whispered in his brother's ear. "That's more than six."

"I noticed that. I said *probably* a half dozen."

Layne cinched the backpack full of C-4 over his shoulder and pressed forward. Kept an eye out for stragglers, but soon decided they were alone. He waded into the water to reach the vessel, swaying against the gentle waves.

"35 Sport Coupe," Randall said. "This is a nice boat."

Layne didn't care about how nice it was. He climbed up onto the aft and unzipped the backpack. Took two bricks of C-4 and two blasting caps and handed them to Randall, then clutched two more in his hands. Randall went down into the cabin, and Layne stayed up top. He placed one in a storage bin at the front of the boat, then another in the bin at the rear. Inserted the blasting caps.

He paused to consider if these men would search their boat before shoving off. Couldn't be sure, but he figured it wasn't likely. Layne didn't have time to find better hiding spots for the C-4 anyway.

When he and Randall met again in another minute, Layne opened the backpack and found a small cheap phone sitting at the bottom of the bag. He lifted it and showed it to Randall.

The elder Parrish brother nodded and held out his hand. "That's the one. I'll take it."

Layne hesitated, gripping the phone. Met his brother's eyes, and he could see Randall knew exactly what he was thinking.

After a moment, Randall withdrew his hand. "That's fine. Keep it. You'll just need to press *90 to detonate."

Layne slipped the phone into his pocket and exited the boat, back into the water. "Where to?"

"There's only one high point on the island," Randall said, pointing through the trees. "It might give us a good look at the dock, but it might not. What we don't know is if they will have a truck to move the gear or if they're carrying it on foot. Truck means road, so they'll have to come inland. Given all that gear, it's probably too heavy to carry."

Layne tilted his head in the direction Randall had pointed, and they set off. Past the outer rim of trees and brush, Layne could see the high point Randall had mentioned. Barely a hill, but it might be good enough.

And then there were voices.

Layne and Randall both dropped into a crouch, weapons raised. In front of them, maybe sixty feet away, were three men. They stood in a triangle at the intersection of two dirt roads. Armed, wearing camo fatigues and heavy boots.

"Sentries," Randall whispered. "We should go around."

Above their heads, a bird cawed. One of the men glanced in their direction, and his eyes met Layne's. A flash of white amid the darkness.

"Hey!" the man said.

The other two spun, lifting their assault rifles.

Layne aimed and squeezed off three quick shots. One whiffed the air, the second punched a hole in the head of one man, the last hitting a second man in the leg. Randall quickly finished him off with a blast to the chest.

But the third man turned and ran before Layne could aim again. He disappeared into the thick brush opposite the road. In a flash, the jungle was quiet again.

"Go," Randall said.

They leaped to their feet and sprinted through the trees. Layne paid attention to keep his knees high to avoid tripping on the brush underfoot. Each step landed in a tangle of foliage.

He raced out into the road, then paused. Listened.

Only the usual sounds of the island came back.

"What are you doing?" Randall said, panting. "He's got a head start on us already."

"No. He could lead us into an ambush. We have no visibility through all that. No night-vision and no backup. We go out there after him, and the odds are heavier in his favor."

"Then what do you suggest? We let him return to his people and tell them about us?"

Layne shrugged. "We don't have a choice. Let's get to the vantage point and finish what we started."

15

SERENA STOWED HER BOAT AND HURRIED THROUGH THE brush to find Layne and Randall. Each of them on their own wasn't so bad. But the two of them together created a formidable threat. Both trained by the US government for a specific purpose: to eliminate targets and escape unseen. They were cunning, smart, and ruthless.

If Serena were the kind of person to engage in self-doubt, she might have felt nervous. Unsure. Instead, she only had to remind herself how diligent she needed to be. If you want to tussle with the big boys, you have to think like one.

She caught up with them as they were making their way to a boat tethered to a mangrove tree. No markings on the boat indicating who it belonged to.

An odd series of events occurred next: they planted explosives on the boat and then had a slight disagreement about who should handle the detonator. She wished she'd brought her parabolic mic to the island, but doing so wasn't practical. She didn't need it, though, to see the tension on the men's faces as Randall reached for the phone and Layne wouldn't give it.

Did Layne believe the pile of shit Rattlesnake was trying to sell him? Obviously Layne was a partial convert, or he wouldn't be here on this island with a villain like Randall Parrish. This troubled Serena; Daphne had spent so much time heaping praise on Layne's judgment and abilities, yet here he was. Helping a man who had designs on murdering a politician for unclear reasons.

Layne had blinders on, didn't he? What other explanation could there be? Did he have some deep endgame to make Randall expose himself? If that was the case, Serena couldn't see it.

When they finished, she stashed her binoculars and set off to follow them. It became apparent they were headed for Mount Wellington. As Serena had been incoming, another boat headed toward the island from a dock on the west side. They were probably looking for this boat, to kill the inhabitants or stop them from doing something. The reason likely tied to the building they'd sneaked into this morning.

The uncertainty didn't bother her one bit.

Serena had to wonder if they knew anything about the traumatized Asian woman who had stumbled out of the front door of the building, holding up her hands to shield her eyes from the sun. Probably they did. But when Serena had caught up to the woman, she wouldn't say a thing. She had accepted Serena's offer of transport to a hospital but hadn't said a word about anything on the way there.

Since Serena could guess Layne's and Randall's destination, she cut an arc around them and headed to summit the hilly peak first. Better to scope it out beforehand and find a position to watch the watchers.

But as she neared within a few hundred feet of the mountain, she heard shouts and the thumps of silenced gunshots. Two from one gun and one from another.

There had been three men standing near the road, and Serena assumed Layne would have seen them. Maybe not. Perhaps he was still too jet-lagged to know what he was doing.

And then she heard frantic footsteps through the brush. Someone running in her direction. She focused her ears on listening for the angle of the oncoming rush. It was exactly behind her, on a direct path to her location. With one step to the right, she positioned herself behind a tree, blocking herself from view.

She placed her arms at her sides to become as small as possible. A frantic running man probably wouldn't see her in this dark, but she didn't want to take that chance.

The footsteps grew louder. She could hear the frantic breathing. Twigs crunched a few feet from her hiding spot. She readied herself, steeling her muscles.

At the last possible second, she whipped a hand out and smacked the person in the face. A body went flying, legs first, upper torso snapping back.

Serena jumped out in front of him and snatched the guy by the belt before he could land flat on his back. Yanked him toward her. His eyes were wide open, mouth agape.

She jabbed him in the throat with her free hand to keep him from yelling. He gagged, coughing. Then she let go of his belt, and he slumped to the ground. An assault rifle hung by a strap over his shoulder, and she first freed it and then tossed it up into the tree. The strap latched around a branch, and the rifle swung back and forth like a pendulum.

She jerked her hunting knife free and drove it down,

stabbing him in the chest. Pressed the blade to the hilt. Bloody spit bubbled at the man's mouth as his lips tried to form words.

Within ten seconds, he was dead.

Serena removed her blade and stood up. The dead man was clutching a phone in one hand, the screen off. A picture of what was going on here formed. This had been one of the three men by the roadside, and he'd escaped an attack by Layne and Randall.

Enough time to alert any others on the island?

The last thing Serena wanted was for Randall and Layne to engage in an all-out war on this tiny piece of land. To get themselves killed.

No, she wanted them all to herself.

16

ON THE OTHER side of the street, Layne pressed forward through the brush. Randall was close at his heels. But this time, they were slow and methodical. Careful to listen for every sound, every movement. Layne didn't need a repeat of the gunfight at the street. They'd been lucky the three hadn't gotten off any shots from their rifles or managed to sound any noticeable alarms. Might have woken the whole island.

Since arriving in Australia, this was the first quiet place Layne had found. No milling pedestrians. No omnipresent chatter.

In ten more paces, Layne came to a full stop. Held up a closed fist to make his brother notice.

"What?" Randall said.

Layne pointed at the body on the ground, fresh blood pouring from a knife wound in the man's chest. His eyes and mouth were open. Surprise on his face, the last expression he'd made before dying.

"Is that our runner?"

Layne nodded. His eyes tracked upward to see the man's assault rifle, strap hanging from a tree. Still swinging.

Randall put his hands on his hips. "Well, that's not good."

"I'm fairly sure Daphne has someone tracking me."

"I assumed so. It's just like her to send a shadow who oversteps his bounds. Is your shadow making sure you're a good boy, or is he trying to kill you?"

"I don't know yet."

"Well, one way or the other, the Reds will notice when these three dead people don't appear at the boat for the trip home."

"Maybe we should abort. We're not prepared for a war on a small island. We're outmanned and outgunned."

Randall looked around, scratched his neck a few times. "This is too important. Let's get on with it, and we'll figure out how to minimize the damage as we go."

Layne had to concede his brother's point. They had come too far to stop now.

They pressed on toward the hill in front of them. Whipping tree branches out of their way, fighting the incline.

Layne knew he wouldn't spot his shadow, not even catch a glimpse. Whoever Daphne had sent had to be one of the best. A little part of Layne hoped that was the case because the alternative wasn't pretty. It meant he was old and losing his edge, lost in the downward spiral of obsolescence. He used to detect a tail the instant he felt one on him. This new tail was like a ghost, deadly and invisible.

Someone he knew, maybe? Someone from the old team?

The hill provided no serious challenge to summit aside from the constant spiderweb of the brush underfoot. At the top, Randall pointed west, and Layne lifted the binoculars.

"Does your daughter look more like you or more like Inessa?"

Layne shook his head.

"Damn, little brother, can we not even make small talk? When did you turn to stone?"

Layne lowered the binoculars. "When I was plucked from my happy home in Colorado, kidnapped, and dragged halfway around the world to engage in some spy nonsense I want no part of."

Randall pushed out his lower lip. "Okay, yeah. I can see how that might make you grumpy. I know we haven't seen each other in a long time, but I'm trying here."

"I know," Layne said, feeling a pang of guilt as he resumed his watch. Now he saw a boat floating alongside a small wooden dock. A dozen men lifting boxes from the boat and hauling them onto the dock.

One man strolled along each box in the row and stopped at the last one. He pried it open with a crowbar. Setting the crowbar aside, he picked up items from inside the box and examined them. Guns, bulletproof vests, and then finally, the sniper rifles. Desert Tech SRS, compact and lethal. Moonlight glinted off the metal. Sent a chill down Layne's back.

"They got the cargo?" Randall said.

"Yep."

"Do you see a truck or a van?"

"Nope. There's only four boxes. They'll probably carry them and stick to the coast."

"Then we need to hustle back toward their escape boat. We're too far away to detonate."

Layne stowed the binoculars and began his descent down the hill. Kept his feet light to scramble through the brush. When they passed the spot where the runner's body had rested, they found it now empty, only a depression in the grass to mark his absence. The rifle still hung from the tree, swaying in the light island breeze.

"Shit," Randall said.

"It's okay, man. I don't think we've been made. If someone were going to stop us, they'd have done it already. My shadow came back to clean up his mess."

"Still, I don't like this."

"I know," Layne said, "but we have to move."

Took another five minutes of jungle-crossing to reach the mangroves near the boat. Assuming the Reds would transport the boxes in from the north, it made the most sense to hide out to the south of the boat. Layne picked a thick vein of mangrove roots and nestled into them. He had a view of the boat, but the spot felt totally sheltered.

And they waited.

Ten minutes passed. The sounds of the island jungle were off-putting to Layne. Animal calls he didn't recognize, the chirping of foreign bugs. Still felt like another planet.

Any minute now, they should hear those men grunting and sweating, lugging four crates toward the boat.

"What's your house like in Colorado?" Randall said.

Layne paused. Considered ignoring the question. Eventually he said, "I have a cabin in the little town of South Fork."

"That's up near Pagosa Springs, right? You get yourself a quaint log cabin in the woods?"

Layne nodded. "Sure, plus full exterior video surveillance, bulletproof windows, and a hermetically sealed panic room."

"I would expect nothing less. You ski much?"

Layne held out a hand and tilted it back and forth.

"Mostly I spend time with my daughter, when I can. She goes back and forth between there and Denver, with her mom."

"That must be rough."

Layne looked his brother in the eye. For a moment, he saw Randall Parrish at age twenty, coming home from college, having a late-night chat with his little brother on the front porch of their home. How much Layne worshipped him back then. How he begged the older Parrish to regale him with tales from college, and how Layne looked forward to escaping home to have adventures of his own, just like his big brother.

"It *can* be rough," Layne said. "I keep an apartment in Boulder, too."

"*What?* The Peoples' Republic of Boulder?"

Layne grinned. "Nobody calls it that anymore. It's a lot more corporate than liberal these days."

"Hmm. Times change. So your kid lives a double life."

"She does, for now. Not sure what will happen when she's old enough for school."

Randall nodded and said nothing. The sounds of the jungle faded back in. And they both stared into the darkness at the boat bobbing in the gentle waves that lapped against the trees.

Ten more minutes passed, and still no sign of their crate-wielding island crew.

"Something is wrong," Randall said.

Layne slipped out of the mangrove web and took a few hesitant steps through the water, toward the boat. With a clear line of sight into the woods in the area, he could see nothing. No movement. Just an empty boat, quiet in the night air.

JIM HESKETT

Realization bubbled up to the surface. He knew what had happened. They'd been fooled.

"Let's go," he said to Randall and then didn't wait to sprint. He raced into the trees, holding his gear close.

After fifteen minutes of shuffling through the trees, they emptied out of the jungle and into the spot where the delivery boat had been. Nothing but an empty dock and no people here now.

Randall, panting, caught up with him a few seconds later. "Son of a bitch," he said between breaths. "They fooled us."

They'd taken the delivery boat home instead.

INTERLUDE 2

LAYNE CLOSES HIS EYES FOR A MOMENT AND GRIPS THE binoculars before lifting them to his face. A quick adjustment to maintain his night vision. He opens his eyes and shifts the binocs around until he can see the second floor of the house across the street. It's a simple, two-level home, with shoddy shingles on the roof and a one-car garage out front.

A mist that's not quite rain leaves a haze between the house he's in and the one containing the target. Layne lowers the binoculars and tilts his head at Randall, seated in a chair across the room, eating his late dinner.

"See him?" Randall asks as he dabs a spot of mayo from his chin.

"I do. Second floor, guest bedroom. He's at a table, working on a train set."

"Train set?"

"That's what it looks like."

Randall wraps up his half-eaten tuna sub and puts his hands behind his head. With a grunt, he reclines in the chair.

"That's an odd development. The intel said nothing about him being a train set guy."

"Could be a cover. Explosives shaped like train cars?"

Randall shrugs. "Could be. Or maybe this asshole just likes trains, and we have shitty intel, as usual."

Layne leaves the window and takes a bite of the meatball sub on the nightstand. It's cold and he's not hungry, but he needs to eat. "Does it change anything?"

"Not a thing. Maybe wait until he leaves the room before you shoot him, just in case."

Layne shuffles across the room to the table next to Randall's chair. He steals one of Randall's barbecue potato chips.

Now, sixteen years before Australia, Randall is still on the light side of thirty, seems spry, and has a face full of life. Mischievous eyes and a permanent smirk on his lips. He's not yet the old and tired man he will later become when Layne finds him in Melbourne.

Layne sets down the binoculars and picks up the Beretta 92FS with SAK noise suppressor attached. When he hefts the gun, it jiggles in his hand a little. It's only two pounds but feels much heavier in his palm.

Randall eyes him. "You okay, little brother?"

"I'm fine, man."

"You don't look fine. You look nervous. It's okay to be nervous, you know."

Layne commands his hand to stop shaking, but it refuses. He lights a cigarette, the last one in his pack. "Okay, yeah. I'm nervous."

"Convert that fear into energy. Energy becomes adrenaline, and that gives you focus. You'll need it."

Layne's heart pounds. "Why are you saying that like you're not coming in with me?"

Randall shrugs. "Sorry. Control's orders. She said you need to pop your cherry all by yourself. Don't worry, though; I'll be here in case anything goes wrong."

"What can you do from across the street?"

Randall stands and puts his hands on Layne's shoulders. Light squeeze. "You were meant for this. Just remind yourself when you walk in the house and put a bullet in that man's head, you're saving lives. American lives."

"I know you're trying to make me feel better, but it hasn't worked yet."

Randall grins. "Ah, Boy Scout. It gets easier after the first time."

Layne holsters the Beretta and runs a hand over his stubbly scalp. He checks the window again and sees his target has now left the guest bedroom and moved back into the main bedroom. "Okay. In and out."

"In and out. You got this. Don't forget the backpack on the first floor."

Layne snuffs out his cigarette, exits the room, and slips out the front door. The mist has turned into wavy sheets of rain, warm in the summer night. His hair deflates in a couple of seconds. Feels like he's wearing a cap.

He makes sure there are no lights on in the windows, no eyes peering out through the curtains. Also, that no neighbors are watching. Not likely anyone is up at this hour.

He darts across the street and vaults the fence into the backyard. Feels his pulse with two fingers against his neck and holds them there until he's calmed a little. Five seconds, ten. He can barely think straight, his heart is pounding so fast.

Up to the porch, he opens the back sliding glass door leading into a kitchen. It wasn't even locked. Weapon out. Across the kitchen, through the living room, he ducks down below a couch to block the line of sight to the stairs next to the front door. No sounds, no lights.

He holds the Beretta low as he counts the doors in the room. There are two, plus the set of stairs leading up.

After a deep breath, he crosses the room toward a door next to the television, which he suspects is a closet. With an ear placed against the door, he can hear no vibrations coming through it.

He opens the door to find a raincoat and boots and an umbrella, and nothing else inside the small closet.

Now to the other door. He reminds himself of his training, to divide the room into quadrants and systematically check all four within one second of opening the door. If he had backup, he and Randall could split the work. But no, Daphne has commanded that Layne do this all on his own.

He's angry at her for doing it, but he also understands her reasoning. Rip off the bandage in one clean burst.

Layne pauses outside the door. Places his ear against it. There's something on the other side, but the sound isn't clear. It's not someone talking or a radio, but there's something other than normal house noise going on.

Layne steps back and raises his pistol with both hands. Arms locked out, eye looking down the Beretta's sight. Breathes.

Takes one hand off the pistol and opens the door. He checks all over the room in a flash, and this is what he finds: a bedroom with a made bed and a single dresser. A nightstand next to the bed.

And on the bed, a hulking German shepherd, head on

paws, sleeping. The backpack sits on the nightstand next to the bed.

Layne's not sure if his scent is enough to wake the dog. He's standing ten feet away, and the dog hasn't stirred. If Daphne were here, standing over his shoulder, she would tell him to shoot the beast. That his Beretta's noise suppressor will mask the shot well enough that the target upstairs won't notice. Randall would probably offer the same advice.

If the dog wakes and makes a fuss, the operation will turn sour.

But Layne can't do it.

Instead, he crosses the room, tiptoeing. Pistol out, just in case. He rounds the bed as the dog's frame rises and falls.

Layne slips his hand underneath the backpack's strap, lifts it, and slowly reverses out of the room. Slips the door shut behind him.

He lets out a breath. Feeling dizzy. Then he moves through the kitchen and deposits the backpack in front of the back door to grab on his way out.

Head cleared, he eases across the living room and starts up the stairs. The steps are carpeted, so not likely to creak, but he keeps his footfalls light, just in case. Pistol pointed up, ready for the target to appear at the top of the stairs.

Sometimes, he thinks, *the end justifies the means.*

He keeps telling himself that but hasn't yet believed it.

When he can see onto the second-floor landing, he leans around the bend in the stairs. Nothing there. He ascends to the second floor. The bedroom is the last one on the right. There are two other doors on this floor. One is a guest bedroom, the other a bathroom.

He pauses outside the bathroom and peers through the cracked door. Empty. A few feet down the hall is the guest bedroom, and Layne eases inside it. Six AK-47 assault rifles sit in a pile on top of the twin-size bed. Next to them, a dozen boxes of ammunition.

He continues on. Five steps to the next door. Now he can hear sounds. A faucet running from the bathroom inside the master bedroom.

Layne edges up to the doorframe. He knows the pistol's slide-mounted safety is disengaged, but he checks it again anyway.

He leans around the frame to find the bedroom empty. Light on in the bathroom. The sound of someone humming a tune, the melody thick and unclear. Probably brushing his teeth.

Layne stands in the doorway, Beretta at eye level. Squinting, trying to blink away the blurriness in his vision.

And waits.

A full minute goes by. Then another.

He's starting to feel woozy, a bit surreal. He keeps telling himself to live in the moment and that each second is *now*.

The water stops and then Layne blinks. Looks down the sight again. His arms shake. He bends his knees slightly, one foot in front, one foot a little behind, angling his shoulders to make himself a smaller target.

A shadow darkens the light spilling out of the bathroom. The humming resumes, but Layne doesn't recognize the tune.

His target emerges from the bathroom, toothbrush still in hand. A spot of toothpaste foam on his chin.

Their eyes meet.

Layne squeezes the trigger. The room lights up as the bullet leaves the gun.

The toothbrush falls to the floor.

17

WHEN LAYNE STIRRED IN THE BED IN HIS RENTED apartment, he woke from a dream about Cameron. They were playing in the hills behind the cabin in South Fork. Dandelions in her hands, both of them blowing the seeds out across the field. They fluttered in the air, dive-bombing to the grass below.

His eyes opened, and he first thought about Governor Phelps. Sunlight poured in through the window. Only two and a half days until the governor's speech. Two days until the Reds would make their assassination attempt.

Only setbacks and complications to this point.

With nothing promising so far, Layne decided to go straight to the target. To get an audience with the governor himself.

After a shower, he realized the jet lag was now only a dim vibration. He felt good. Lonely but good. No more tinny ache behind his eyes, no more feeling of extra weight on his limbs.

He popped by the train station to grab a coffee and an

egg sandwich. This one came with bacon, which turned out to be Canadian bacon. He debated asking the guy if he had a sandwich with *real* bacon but didn't want to seem like a tacky American. Layne tried to open his mouth in public as little as possible.

He consumed his breakfast while wandering down Toorak to locate an internet café. Found one a couple of blocks down, across the street from a large shopping mall. Like the one he'd used two days ago, this was a small place with a few rows of computers, but there were wooden cubicles around each one to provide a little privacy.

Before entering, he found an electronics shop in the nearby mall and picked out a cheap webcam with USB output. He hesitated before carrying it to the counter. Engaging in a video chat was risky, but he wasn't sure if he cared about the risks anymore. Not talking to his daughter for several days was like slowly bleeding out after an injury. He needed that connection.

So he bought the webcam and carried it over to the internet café. He didn't feel the eyes of his shadow on him. Wondered what that person would think about him strutting across the street with a webcam in his hands. How would that look in the daily surveillance report?

After purchasing some internet time, he first installed VPN software to ensure privacy, then connected the webcam and opened a video chat program. He wasn't sure about the time difference, but he had to try.

After he typed in her number, his ex-wife Inessa answered the call. Her high-cheekboned face appeared on the screen. The video came through pixelated and choppy, but there was no mistaking her. She sneered at him and asked in her Russian accent, "What do you want?"

"What time is it there?"

"Late afternoon. What do you want, Layne?"

He glanced around to check his privacy level. The internet café was empty, but his heart still thudded. This was a dangerous task, to contact his family. "Can I speak to her, please?"

Inessa rolled her eyes, but she handed the phone over to Cameron. Blonde hair, blue eyes, pale white skin. The sight of his little girl immediately made Layne wince as the corners of his eyes stung.

She was sitting on the couch, her face filling up the screen. "Daddy!"

"Hey, little one. I miss you."

"Me too, Daddy. I sleep at Mommy's house since you leave."

He cleared his throat to bite back the tears. "I know. I'm sorry I had to go. It's a work thing."

"You have to go to work?"

"Yes, little one. I have to go to work for a few more days, but I'm going to see you soon."

She pushed out her lower lip, pouting. "Okay."

"What's Mommy making for snack?"

Now her face lit up. "Mac and cheese with broccoli."

"Mmm, sounds amazing."

"I don't like the broccoli parts."

"I know, but if Mommy says you have to eat it all, then eat it all, please. It's good for you, and when you eat good food, that means you can play harder."

Cameron opened her mouth to say something, but the screen glitched and hiccuped. He could only catch bits and pieces of her response.

The front door of the café opened, and in walked a bald

white man with sunglasses. He waddled over to a soda machine and fished around in his pockets for change.

"I have to go," Layne said, eying the man. "I have to work. But I'm going to call you again soon, okay?"

She kissed the screen of Inessa's phone, which made Layne involuntarily chirp a laugh. Then Inessa appeared in the frame.

"I have to miss a *wery* important meeting in New York because of you. You said you were done with this sort of work."

"I thought I was. I'm sorry."

"You will not drop her on me again like this."

Before he could reply, the chat window turned to black. Call ended.

Layne wiped tears from the corners of his eyes and looked around again to make sure no one was paying attention. The soda-buying man retrieved his drink from the machine and then left the café. Seemed all clear, only one other person using the computers currently.

Back to work.

Layne spent a few minutes researching Randall's claim about the stolen artwork from the city of Dandenong last year. His explanation about why both Reds and Union considered him an enemy.

Layne found articles related to the original heist from the gallery, just as Randall had said. No mention of the Reds or the Union, but several articles referred to the mysterious fact that the artwork did magically reappear at the gallery four days after the original theft. No fingerprints were found, no useful evidence, but some witnesses claimed to have seen a solitary individual dressed in dark clothing fleeing through the streets the night the paintings had been returned. No arrests were made.

Layne stared at the screen, sighing. Randall's story seemed to check out. Layne kept looking for reasons to side with Daphne over Randall, but he continually came up short. Despite all the things Daphne had *said*, she had no evidence on her side. Randall could offer concrete points in his favor.

The outlook was still murky, at best.

Layne looked up the governor's website and schedule for the day. The governor would be at some place named Alexandra Gardens at 10:00 a.m. to escort a slew of visiting dignitaries to a festival taking place there.

Layne checked his watch. One hour until the festival.

He deleted his browser history, removed all traces of the VPN software, and logged off the computer. Jumped up, startling the young woman at the computer next to him. He tossed her an apologetic smile and raced out of the café, up the street toward the train station.

Trams clunked along the tracks as he darted across the road. Dodging pedestrians left and right. He skidded into the station and studied the board to find the next train to Flinders Street.

———

THE TRAIN ARRIVED at Flinders a few minutes before ten, and he raced out of the station, south along St. Kilda Road. Crossed the Yarra River, and then he saw the throngs of people. Some festival happening in the grassy area south of the river. Multiple stages set up with bands playing music, carnival rides, booths of sellers hawking wares. A few thousand people milling about, eating food, lounging on blankets in the grass.

Layne passed what looked like a boathouse as he entered the edge of the festival. The music carried and bounced off nearby surfaces. Little children played, running around in the dry midmorning heat.

He had no idea where the governor would be. Also, Layne wasn't sure what to do when he found the man. He had a vague notion of speaking with him, of asking him why he had so brazenly ignored warnings about an attempt on his life.

The smart thing to do would be to make a systematic sweep of the area. There were four stages opposite each other, so he counted each one as a quadrant of the festival. He would start with the northwest quadrant and work his way around.

Layne searched through booths and carny rides in one quadrant and then the next. Nothing to see but the usual assortment of carnival people and activities. But when he entered the southeast quadrant, he found exactly what he'd been looking for: an entourage of men in dark suits and dark sunglasses, forming a circle around a group of people.

Layne was next to a Ferris wheel, and he stepped up onto the ticket-taking platform to get a better look. Inside that protected circle was a fair-haired man whom he recognized as the governor, plus three other dark-skinned men wearing taqiyah caps and long, white robes. Middle Easterners.

"Oy," said a voice behind Layne.

He turned to find a teenager sitting at the Ferris wheel controls, giving him the stink eye.

"If you want to have a go, the line's down there."

Layne offered the kid a wave and then hopped off the

platform to carve a path toward the governor. He tried his best not to shove people out of the way, but the crowd was so thick, he had to fight the current.

Fifty feet from Governor Phelps, a security guard took an interest in Layne. He was a giant of a man, with slicked-back hair and mirrored sunglasses. A square jaw and biceps bullying the limits of his suit coat.

Layne wasn't deterred. He walked straight toward the giant.

"Can I help you, mate?" the man said, oozing breath that stank of curry.

Layne pointed at the governor, now within shouting distance. "I need to speak with Governor Phelps. It's important."

"I'm afraid that's not possible at this stage. The governor is entertaining guests. You can lodge a request with his secretary if you'd like."

Layne peered around the giant to see the governor escorting the three men to a booth with a ring toss. The carny handed Phelps a cluster of rings, and he aimed one at a row of bottles inside the booth.

Layne considered his options. Daphne had claimed the governor had already been warned of the threat against his life but brushed it off. If Layne declared he knew of the assassination attempt, these security guards would haul him in for questioning. Discover he lacked a passport. At best, that meant a call to his embassy, and he had no idea if this operation was sanctioned by anyone beyond Daphne and her superiors. At worst, confronting the governor meant spending at least a day or two in a holding cell.

But if he tried to play himself off as one of the governor's constituents, he could just as easily be discovered.

Apparently the giant didn't like Layne standing there pondering this choice. "Sir, I'll have to ask you to leave now."

"I'd rather not. I need to speak to Phelps, and it's important. He's gonna want to hear what I have to say."

The giant reached out and jabbed Layne in the chest with two fingers. It took everything within Layne's power to resist snatching and then breaking the man's wrist. Layne had taken down guys much bigger than this one.

"Piss off," the giant said. Layne had a feeling the giant didn't like the lack of fear on Layne's face.

He hesitated a moment longer, and two of the other security guards took notice. The giant swept his jacket back, revealing a holstered revolver at his hip.

Layne threw up his hands. No sense in making a scene. "Fine, man. No big deal. I'll write him a letter."

"Wise choice, mate."

Layne folded back into the crowd as the governor handed a ring to one of his guests. Laughing as the man's toss came nowhere close to the bottle he'd aimed for. As the governor took his own turn, he said something to the other three that made them explode with laughter.

Standing there, Layne observed someone he had a strong suspicion would be dead in a little over two days.

18

SINCE LAYNE WAS ONLY A FEW BLOCKS FROM FEDERATION Square, he decided to check it out in advance of the governor's speech.

Maybe contacting the governor directly wasn't the move to make. But then again, he'd only tried once so far.

He walked back along St. Kilda Road toward the Flinders Street railway station. Fed Square was across the street. A large, open bluestone-and-sandstone courtyard surrounded on three sides by various buildings of glass and metal, designed with odd geometric shapes. Very modern art-looking. Foot traffic flowed out of the buildings through the courtyard to the street.

A cop stood near a collection of tables on a restaurant patio. Layne wondered what would happen if he walked right up to the cop and told him all about the assassination attempt. Probably nothing.

His phone chirped, but he still wasn't used to the odd ringtone, so he hesitated a second before retrieving it from his pocket. Unknown number. "Hello?"

"Hey, little brother."

"Where've you been today?"

"I've been busy trying to find those crates we couldn't acquire last night. I have an idea of where they might have been taken, but I won't have confirmation for another hour or so. Now which do you want to hear first, the good news or the bad news?"

"Good news," Layne said.

"That woman tied to the bed yesterday morning? She went to a hospital, got checked out, and she's fine."

"How do you know this?"

"I've been doing this a lot longer than you have, little brother. I made a few calls and got the hospital records. She's going to be okay, though. That's what matters."

A pulse of relief swirled up from Layne's toes. "Okay, man, what's the bad news?"

"There is no bad news. It's all good. Anyway, you want to get lunch? There's a great place in Camberwell named *Wharf Rat* you should experience while you're here."

Layne eyed the buildings of Fed Square and thought about it. "Not right now. I'm in the middle of something."

"Okay, I'll check in with you in a bit."

The call ended, and Layne stared at the phone. He slipped it back into his pocket and strolled up the steps at the edge of the square.

His first concern was the contours of the building rooftops. The angular, sometimes jagged shapes of the roofs meant ample hiding spots for a sniper. Or multiple snipers.

Layne hiked up the steps to the main part of the square. A couple hundred people were here, browsing the shops and eating at tables sheltered from the late morning heat by fat umbrellas.

He wandered across the square, taking in the different buildings that lined the edges. Past the courtyard, an atrium connected two of the large buildings with a collection of bars and restaurants underneath.

He stared at it, letting his eyes trace the lines of the structure above his head.

This atrium was where they would set up their snipers. For sure. Near the back to make it easy to slip away into the small wooded area behind it. Close to the Yarra River if they intended to escape by boat.

That's where Layne would set up anyway.

At a table across the courtyard, a man was reading a newspaper as he sipped from a small espresso cup. After a moment, he folded the paper and dropped it on the table. He left it behind as he grabbed his briefcase and meandered toward the atrium.

Layne approached the table and picked up the newspaper. He flipped through a few pages to the classified section. Back in his active days, Daphne would leave messages for him. Usually if he spotted a newspaper classifieds post about a missed connection, that was something to read. A coded message with instructions.

But he saw nothing in today's paper.

A fragment of conversation between two people behind him caught his attention, though, and his head turned, but only for a second. And that's when he realized something wasn't right.

———

SERENA HELD her breath when Layne pivoted. She ducked back inside the Yarra building. The sign on the door said

Koorie Heritage Trust, flanked by a series of art prints. Some sort of museum.

Across the square, Layne turned his head back toward the atrium, his eyes aloft. Hands on his hips. Didn't take long for Serena to figure out what he was doing here. Scoping the square for shooters.

He wandered around for a few minutes, eyes up and down. Thorough. The more Serena watched him work, the more she could appreciate his style. After years of hearing about the great Layne Parrish, she could finally see him in action. And he wasn't half bad at his job. His first day, he'd obviously not been himself. He seemed to be growing back into those old habits. The plan with the C-4 on French Island had been a good one, even if it hadn't worked out.

His decision to tag along with Randall gave Serena pause, but she had to think Layne probably knew what he was doing. Or maybe he didn't. She kept changing her mind about his level of competency. Maybe he'd been at this spy game long enough to know how to make it *look* like he knew what he was doing.

He paused to pick up a newspaper, and he narrowed his eyes as he read through the classifieds. Looking for a message from Control, or maybe even someone else?

Layne was a shoebox full of mysteries.

Serena realized she hadn't checked in with Control yet today. She slipped out her phone and dialed the number. After two rings, Daphne picked up.

"Yes?"

"I've got him again. In Fed Square."

"Good. Stay on him as much as possible for as long as you can."

"He's more slippery than I'd expected. It's hard to stay with him."

"I know," Daphne said. "But do what you can."

Footsteps shuffled behind Serena, so she exited the building to find a more secluded spot. "He tried to speak to Governor Phelps at a festival across the river."

Daphne sighed. "That boy is going to get himself in trouble."

"How far should I let him go?"

"Meaning?"

"Do I let him speak to the governor?"

"Layne talking to him will only cause problems. If he winds up on the local news, we're all in for a real interesting time."

Serena felt perturbed at the way Daphne insisted on being so cryptic. Maybe a little angry at herself that she hadn't been able to get close enough in Alexandra Gardens to hear what Layne had said to the governor's security people. "Ma'am, I'll repeat my question: How far do I let him go?"

Daphne paused. "I'll leave that to your discretion. You have full authority on the ground."

And she hung up.

———

A LIGHT BREEZE ruffled Layne's hair as he paused amid a group of college kids fanning out around him. They treated him like a rock in midstream.

He didn't want to turn his head because he had a feeling his shadow was looking at him right at this second. The same shadow who had appeared on French Island, the mysterious person who stopped the fleeing gang member, most likely. Same one he'd felt near the apartment on Davis Street.

First time today he'd felt that presence, if that's who it was. Maybe.

Perhaps it was someone else.

Since no one was shooting at him, he didn't feel like he was in immediate danger.

Layne continued his tour of Fed Square, observing people and the angles of the buildings. So many places for a sniper to camp out, he wondered if placing his bets on the atrium was the right move. It did have a clean line of sight to where the stage would most likely be, plus the best access and exfiltration points. All signs indicated this would be the spot.

He passed under the atrium, glancing up at the sections of glass panels high above his head. Anyone crossing those could easily be spotted, but he doubted the people below would pay attention. Friday night, sun setting, everyone looking at where they're going and trying not to bump into other people. No one would crane their necks to gawk at something forty feet above their heads. Even if they did, they'd probably assume anyone up there had a right to be there, like a construction worker or building employee.

Past the atrium, Fed Square emptied onto the street. Train tracks from nearby Flinders Street Station knifed out the back of the buildings, rocks and metal streaming out into the city. The tracks might be another solid way to escape, although they seemed too exposed. But a trio of snipers in dark clothes might slip away unnoticed if they hit it at the magic hour after the sun disappeared but before the streetlights clicked on.

And then what would they do when it was done? Prepare a video to stream online, standing before a white background with ski masks obscuring their faces?

If the governor dies, Abdul Abbad goes underground most likely. His Sons of the Imminent Dawn carry on with their little cell's designs to become a big-time jihadist player.

Was Governor Phelps's continued existence an important link in the chain, or was he another politician destined to die for no good reason? Collateral damage with little butterfly ripples into the rest of the world?

Too much still didn't make sense. Layne wasn't even sure if he had found the corner pieces of the puzzle yet.

At the edge of his vision, Layne caught a burn of black clothing. Someone shifting, moving behind someone else, trying not to be seen. A woman.

The clothing vanished back into the crowd. Not in a clumsy way as a civilian would, awkward and slow. This had been a professional move.

So his shadow was not a man, as he'd assumed. He first thought it was Daphne, but that made no sense. Layne hadn't known Daphne to commit to fieldwork beyond managing her assets, so she wouldn't do it herself. But it was likely Daphne who had sent this tail.

Now the only question was: Someone sent to make sure Layne did his job or to make sure Layne didn't do his job?

As a glut of people exited a restaurant and traveled in front of Layne, his phone buzzed. He slipped it out to find a text message sitting on the phone's tiny screen, which brought a grin to his face:

Why yes, I would love to go for a swim. Give me a call.

19

LAYNE CHECKED HIS WATCH AS HE ENTERED THE JAM Factory on Chapel Street. Chapel was only a couple of blocks over from his apartment on Davis, but it was a world away. Posh. Lamborghinis and BMWs were the standard cars parked along the curb. Fancy people wearing fancy clothes having lunch at restaurant patios that intermingled with the sidewalks.

The Jam Factory was a shopping mall and movie theater a few blocks down from the intersection of Toorak and Chapel. On the inside, Layne welcomed the air-conditioning from what was shaping up to be a brutally hot December day.

He wiped sweat from his brow and navigated to the movie theater ticket stand. Stepped up to find a blasé young woman on the other side, heavy-lidded and bored.

"One for *Rocky Horror*," he said.

"It's already started."

"I know, that's fine. Just one ticket, please."

She rolled her eyes and gave him the ticket, and he

wondered if Cameron would turn into this sort of teenager —so fatigued and offended by the world. He hoped not, but he had little control over the future.

Layne entered theater #4, where the ancient movie played on a massive curved screen. Meatloaf was singing about something. Layne let his eyes adjust for a few seconds inside the spacious room until he could make out more than dim shapes. Much larger than the average American movie theater, complete with balcony seating up above.

Once his eyes had adapted, Layne scanned over the audience. Weren't many seats filled, and he easily located the shock of red hair, bent over, sipping a drink and shoveling popcorn into her face.

He grinned and climbed a couple of rows, then slid over to a seat next to her. She made no motion to acknowledge him. Tossed a handful of popcorn pieces into her mouth.

"Hi, Tilda. Thanks for getting back to me."

The heavyset woman to his left nodded but didn't take her eyes off the screen. "Sorry I took a couple of days. You go on holiday for two weeks, and everyone forgets how to do their bloody jobs." She cleared her throat. "Did you give change to any of those beggars outside?"

"No."

"Good. Don't." She then flicked her eyes to him, just for a moment. "You look like hell."

"I hear that a lot. How is life at the ASIO?"

"Pretty snowed under at the moment, but it's the same old same old. Catching bad guys sometimes, and sometimes they get away."

"Thanks for meeting with me."

Now she did pivot a little and grin at him. "It's good to see you, mate. Wife and kid good?"

"Me and the wife split."

Tilda frowned. "Sorry to hear that."

"No, it's okay. For the best actually. Our daughter is doing great, though. Getting into as much trouble as she can and making her mistakes a lot faster than I did. She's three, soaking up all life has to offer."

"Yeah," Tilda said, chuckling. "It's amazing how much they can learn. So many millions of words out there in the world, yet kids seem to pick up a thousand new ones every single day."

"Your family well?"

"Yes, all well. We just got back from a trip to Uluru. Our ankle biters love it up there, but it's *hot as* and a bit arid for my tastes. I miss air-con after a day or so." Her smile fell as she sipped from her soda. "What are you doing in Asia-Pacific?"

"Hunting someone, but I'm not sure if it's the right person."

"Do tell."

"You know about the proposed assassination attempt on Governor Phelps?"

Tilda nodded. "I do, and I have heaps of doubts about the credibility of the report."

"Why?"

"Someone's trying to sell you a little too hard, my friend. That rumor passed through our intelligence a few weeks ago, and we determined it has a low chance of legitimacy. Either way, we're keeping an eye on it. Phelps will be fine. We won't let anything bad befall one of the most beloved men in the country."

"I don't know if it's smart to be so cavalier about it. These people are pretty ruthless. I've seen them in action."

"Do you know how many death threats Phelps gets on a weekly basis?" When Layne didn't answer, she continued. "Every single one gets vetted. Usually it's some pensioner out in the bush with a grudge, and it goes nowhere."

"I've seen sniper rifles. I've seen crates of ammunition."

She flicked her wrist. "Probably toys. Some soldiers of fortune having a go at playing army. Seriously, you don't need to worry about it."

Layne watched the movie for a few moments, considering. Did Daphne have bad intel about all this? Was Randall manipulating the situation for some other goal?

"Who's running you? Who's your handler?"

"Daphne Kurek."

Tilda set her soda in the armrest holder and breathed a protracted sigh. "I know you've been out of the game for a while, Layne. Things have changed; they're different to what they used to be."

"They always are."

"Do you trust her?"

Layne shook his head. "She's all I've got over here."

"Well, now you have me, and you can be a lot of use to ASIO. What *we* have is a directive to find Randall Parrish. I assume that's what Daphne wants?"

He nodded.

"Your brother has been punching above his weight with all this mess he's in, and we think he might implode. There's a good chance all this bad intel comes directly from him."

"Why would he do that?"

"He's in league with some bad people."

Layne sucked his teeth. "Someone straddling the India and Pakistan border?"

"That's one possibility. Randall has business dealings up there, and some of his contacts could be very useful to us."

"How does that tie into the governor?"

Tilda shook her head. "It doesn't. Whatever Daphne has you doing here, it's a waste of your time. Your best plan is to tell Daphne where he is, then get back on a plane and get home." She studied his face for a moment, then smirked. "But you're not going to do that, are you?"

"I don't know. There are too many angles to process. So much of this makes no sense."

"Then let me give you a single piece of advice, mate: If you're not going to give him up and tell Daphne, then stay away from Randall. Being around him is poison and will only lead to trouble."

Layne chewed on this for a moment. "I'll think about it. In the meantime, I need you to get me some gear."

20

AS HE LEFT THE JAM FACTORY, LAYNE STOOD UNDER A grand awning for a minute as the organism of sidewalk pedestrians flowed around him. Nearby, a teenager wearing clothes much too thick for this sunny day was on his knees, sketching a chalk drawing of Kurt Cobain on the sidewalk. A close-up of his face, with a barbed wire fence obscuring from the lips down.

Layne stood next to him. "You look a little young to even know who Kurt Cobain is."

The kid grinned up at Layne, squinting against the sun. "You gotta appreciate the classics, mate." The teenager tilted his head at a coffee mug sitting next to the chalk drawing. Layne fished in his pocket for a two-dollar piece and dropped it into the cup. As he slipped his hand back into his pocket, the phone buzzed. Unknown number.

"Hello?"

Randall cleared his throat. "Hey, little brother."

"You need to give me your phone number, man. I can't wait around for you to call me."

"Sorry, I've got it set to hide my Caller ID. I always forget about that."

Randall then rattled off the number, and Layne committed it to memory. Layne, holding the phone to his ear, navigated along Chapel Street en route to Toorak. The afternoon lunch crowd was dispersing, headed back toward their fancy cars in their fancy clothes. The smells of curry and Italian food clogged Layne's nostrils. Expensive engines revved and jetted out into traffic.

"What have you been doing this morning?" Layne said.

"Well, for one, trying to make sure your shadow doesn't get stuck on me, too."

"Don't worry about that. I spotted her today. She's on me."

"Her, huh? Just like Daphne to send in a woman to blend in with the crowd."

"She doesn't blend in as well as she thinks she does, so I can handle that from now on. What else is going on?"

"Right," Randall said. "I went back to the building on Bourke Street. Spent a good hour or two staring at it, hoping to get an indication about our lost shipment from last night. Not a whole lotta action to see there for the most part. Anyway, the Reds are most definitely not keeping the shipment of weapons there. Not a damn thing in or out. But one of them got sloppy because I saw him exit out the back."

"You did?"

"Yep. I followed him and spotted those same crates from last night. I know where they're keeping the goods."

"And that is?"

"In St. Kilda, there's an amusement park named Luna Park. I saw them stop outside of a storage shed out back. That's where we need to go. Where are you now?"

"On Chapel, headed on foot toward Toorak."

"Good. Turn around and go to a mall named Jam Factory. You can't miss it; it's got a giant sign out front. There's an American-style diner inside. Go have a burger and a malt or whatever. I'll be there in half an hour."

The call ended, and Layne pulled the phone away from his ear. Stared at it. On the one hand, he had Daphne telling him to give up Randall because of the assassination attempt and Abdul Abbad. On the other hand, he had Tilda telling him there would be no assassination attempt and Randall was twisting the situation for his own gain. And finally, he had Randall telling him a completely different story.

He felt like a kid with a blindfold being spun around a dozen times and then told to find the piñata to take some whacks at it.

Someone was lying to him. But he didn't know enough yet to know which one or why. And in the meantime, he had doubts that trusting Randall was a smart move. But he didn't know if he had a better choice at the moment.

21

LAYNE WIPED BURGER GREASE FROM HIS CHIN AS HE paid the bill at the Soda Rock Diner. The standard burger had been topped with a fried egg and a slice of beetroot. He had to admit it was one of the best burgers he'd ever eaten.

Eating alone, just the jingly 1950s music from the diner, he'd felt at peace. Filled his thoughts with only good things: mainly visions of his daughter, playing, cuddling with him, sleeping.

One thing Layne knew for sure: his shadow hadn't been around since Fed Square. Now that he knew it was a woman, she would be much easier to spot. And she must have known he'd glimpsed her, too. She would be more careful, keep her distance. If she was smart.

Randall rolled up in front of the Jam Factory in a Toyota sedan, then lowered his sunglasses to wink at Layne. Revved the engine, a grin on his face.

Layne took one last look over his shoulder to make sure Tilda wasn't behind him since he didn't know when *Rocky Horror* let out. Didn't see her.

He slid into the passenger seat, and Randall gunned it onto Chapel Street. As the engine roared, Randall made his own car sounds to complement it.

"You're in a good mood," Layne said.

"Hell yeah, I am. We know where these assholes are, where the guns are, and now we just have to go get them."

"How far is St. Kilda?" Layne said.

"Not far. Was your burger good?"

"It was."

Randall nodded. "Tell me more about life back home. How is security consulting treating you?"

Layne paused. He knew Randall's intent with all this chitchat. Still, he *wanted* to catch up. Felt like he *should* catch up. "It's good money for easy work, man. Keeps me close to home in Colorado, which I like. Not how it was before."

After a quiet moment, Randall said, "I never wanted this life for you, little brother."

"Well, that's ironic, since they recruited me because of you."

Randall wagged a finger at him. "Not true. They recruited you because of that crazy stunt you pulled in college."

Layne cleared his throat and waited a few seconds to respond. "Yeah, but they never would have cared about that if you weren't already their star field agent."

"They never called me a *field agent*. The only job title I ever heard was *specialist*. Did they call you a field agent?"

"No. Daphne called me an assassin sometimes," Layne said, and left it at that.

"I understand why you wanted to retire. What we do is lonely, thankless work."

"Yet you're still doing it."

Randall shrugged. "There's still some good left to do. Plenty of adventures to have." He made weird eyes at Layne and said in an exaggerated, movie-announcer voice, "Wherever there is injustice in the world, the Parrish Brothers will foil those plans! Evildoers, beware!"

Layne smiled politely but kept his mouth shut. He had to remind himself of how susceptible he could be to Randall's charms.

They did have a forty-year history together.

He and his brother took the rest of the trip in silence. When they neared Luna Park, Layne knew they'd found it right away. Adjacent to the beach in St. Kilda, Luna Park was a walled amusement park with roller coasters and Ferris wheels, fronted by a giant entrance made to look like an openmouthed sun/clown face. Swallowing all those who ventured inside.

"Storage shed, right?" Layne asked. "We're not actually going into the park, are we?"

"Nope. Across the street, closer to the beach, there's a small building the park uses for storage. That's where I saw some guys unloading crates that looked like the ones taken from the boat. Given how secretive they were about it, this has to be our score."

"So we ditch the car nearby and find a back entrance?"

Randall nodded. "Sounds good to me. You always were the logistical one. I prefer to go in guns blazing and hope it all works out."

Randall piloted the Toyota past Luna Park and chose a spot near a tall apartment building on the next block. They left the car and rounded the back to the trunk. Randall opened it, removed a couple of heavy-duty Maglite flashlights, and handed one to Layne.

"No guns?" Layne said.

"This is much less suspicious. Too many people around. Even with noise suppressors, we'll cause a panic if anything happens."

Layne hefted the flashlight. Filled with D batteries, it was heavier and more sturdy than a baseball bat. "Fair point. But these won't do us much good in a firefight."

Randall beckoned him down the street. "We'll be in and out before that happens." Around the corner, he pointed at the building. Back door, no one guarding it. "This should be easy."

Layne studied the building, seemingly quiet. Despite the sleepy and bland appearance, going in unarmed was a gamble. "Think there's someone on the other side of that door?"

"Maybe. Let's hope not."

Layne sidled up next to the door to provide cover as Randall picked the lock.

"Your daughter," Randall said as he fiddled with the lock. "What's her favorite TV show?"

"It changes every week, but the longest-running favorite is Thomas the Train. We have a modular train set at the South Fork house, with hundreds of pieces. Stretches across most of the guest bedroom."

"Thomas the Train? You used to read those books when you were little."

Layne nodded, surprised Randall had remembered. He sometimes forgot that through all the teasing, Randall did take care of him. As far as brothers went, Layne could have done a lot worse.

"They're still making new ones," he said with a shrug.

Randall stepped away from the door, gesturing toward it. "We are *go* on the door."

Layne pulled back the handle an inch. Cool air rushed out, but no sign of a person on the inside.

Both of them entered the doorway to come face-to-face with a pallet taller than either of them. Layne leaned around it and noted rows and rows of these pallets inside a long, dark room like a warehouse. Not a person in sight, the front door closed. Light filtering into the building from windows near the ceiling, thirty feet up.

Layne motioned with his flashlight at his chest, then around the right side. Pointed at Randall and then to the left. Randall nodded and headed that way.

Layne hoisted the flashlight—beam off—and rested it on his shoulder as he crept through the warehouse. Careful with his footing in the dark. Up ahead, sitting on the floor at the far end were several crates and boxes identical to those that had been on the boat.

Layne made a slight clucking sound to get Randall's attention. Pointed the head of his flashlight toward the crates.

Randall nodded, but before they could take a step in that direction, a gunshot rang out. Somewhere outside the building. Front side.

"What the hell?" Layne said.

As the echo of the gunshot settled, more voices carried from outside. The front door burst open, and six men sprinted into the warehouse. One of them Layne recognized from the boat. A tall man with a rippling scar across his neck, like a burn mark.

These were Reds.

And hot on their heels were five more men, shooting at

them. These must be the opposing gang, the Union. Many of them were in black and white, with the words *Collingwood FC* or *Magpies* on their shirts.

The Reds scurried for cover behind pallets. One of the armed men looked up and saw Layne, standing near the back. He raised his pistol and fired, but the shot went nowhere close to Layne. Two others turned around and also shot at him. Within a second, everyone else was getting in on the action.

Layne ducked behind a stack of boxes nearby. Bullets pelted the other side but weren't passing through. He had no idea what could be inside those boxes, but it was something solid enough to stop bullets, at least. But no telling if whatever was in there would stop them for much longer.

"Out the back!" Randall shouted.

Layne spun and made a break for the door. He threw his shoulder against it and stumbled out on the street to find pandemonium. Civilians scrambling along the sidewalks, screaming, running. More gunshots cracking the sky from some unknown direction.

And a group of four men wielding cricket bats forming a barrier. Standing only a few feet away.

Before anyone could speak a word or make any moves, Randall swung his flashlight at the nearest man. Cracked him against the temple.

Layne spun and whipped his flashlight at the wrist of a dark-skinned man. The flashlight smashed into the man's forearms, sending his cricket bat clattering to the sidewalk.

A heavy *thud* connected with Layne's back, making him stumble forward a step. Pain shot up his spine, arching unnaturally as he stumbled from the sidewalk into the street. Layne continued his forward momentum and planted one foot to swing back around. Used the inertia to raise the flashlight again and cracked the base against the temple of the nearest man.

Now he had a chance to take stock of the situation. Two men were on the ground. One incapacitated, clutching his head. Randall was standing over another of them, kicking the man in the ribs. A third man was trying to grab his loose cricket bat as it skittered away on the sidewalk, and the fourth was bending over, spitting blood after Layne had just hit him.

Randall kicked the man leaning over for his cricket bat. Layne smacked the bleeding man again, sending him to the ground. Layne spun him over and removed his wallet. Stuck it in his back pocket. Might come in handy later.

When Layne looked past him, he could see more men with bats homing in on them. One man in the crew was holding a shotgun, loading shells as he marched. Randall's eyes drifted over there, too, and he flexed his jaw.

"Go!" Randall said.

Layne gripped the flashlight and ran. Feet pumping, chest burning. Randall hot on his heels. Layne set his sights on the car parked around the corner, but as soon as they made that turn onto the next street, two cop cars with screeching sirens appeared, a blur of flashing lights.

Layne grabbed Randall by the shirt collar and tugged him toward the nearest alley. The cop cars raced past, lights whirling. Yellow stripes with blue-and-white checkered sides.

"Damn it," Randall said. "Those cops will block us off from the warehouse."

"Forget that. We need to get to the car now before they seal off this block."

Layne leaned out of the alley as the cops raced toward the warehouse behind Luna Park. For a moment, the street was empty save for a few onlookers leaning out of shop and restaurant doors.

The car sat two hundred feet away, waiting. Their best bet to escape.

"Get your keys out," Layne said.

"Got it."

Layne pushed off from the alley wall and sprinted with everything in him toward the car. They made it in a couple of seconds and slid inside their respective seats. Both of them panting, breathless. Randall jabbed the keys in the ignition as a few of the incoming Union men changed direction toward their car.

Randall jerked it into drive and sped away. Slammed a fist into the steering wheel. "Shit! Shit, shit, shit."

"What the hell happened back there?"

"Looks like Union figured out where the Reds were keeping their gear before we did. That was a gang war."

"Maybe leaving is a mistake," Layne said, his head now clearing of the adrenaline. "We should go back and try to get the sniper rifles. Take them down to the water and dump them in the ocean."

Randall shook his head as he swerved at the next intersection and joined the street, car wobbling. "That ship has sailed, little brother. If the Union don't snatch them, the Reds will get them out of there before the cops descend on the place. We'll never find those weapons again."

22

————

AT HIS APARTMENT, LAYNE EXAMINED THE BRUISE ON his back in the bathroom mirror. The size and shape of a football, it ached anytime he stretched at the waist. He'd had much worse, but a cricket bat to the lower spine wasn't anything to scoff at.

He dug through the minifridge in the kitchen to retrieve another of his Victoria Bitter beers and eased onto the couch. Every movement made his back ache.

He picked up the remote control from the end table and flipped on the TV. The channel tuned to an in-progress game, which Layne learned was Australian Rules Football when a graphic informed him. A large field with giant goalposts on each end. At least thirty guys on the field. The announcers spoke in a rapid clip, and with their accents, Layne couldn't understand any of it.

After spending a few fruitless minutes trying, he gave up. He picked up the remote to change the channel. But his eyes were tired, and he had no desire to flip around a dozen channels to find something interesting to watch. So he turned off the TV and stared at the wall instead.

A second later, a knock came at his door. Layne slid his shirt on and crept across the living room. Picked up the steak knife from the nightstand next to the door and jerked it open.

Tilda stood in the doorway, glow from the porch light blanketing her like an angel. She glanced down at the knife. "Is this how you greet all your houseguests?"

"How the hell did you find me?"

"I work in intelligence, mate. There's not a lot you can do in Melbourne that I can't uncover. Good to see you again, by the way."

Layne dropped the knife on a small stand next to the door and waved her in. She waddled inside and held her hands behind her back as she took stock of everything in the living room.

"How do you like your serviced apartment?"

He shrugged. "It's fine."

"Exsie neighborhood."

"What?"

"It's posh."

"Is it?"

Tilda lowered herself onto the couch, grunting as she did so. Layne only now realized how much she'd aged. Had to be pushing fifty now or at least on the wrong side of forty-five. She still had that spry look about her, though. Cunning, smart, ruthless. He hadn't known her beyond operational friendliness, but they'd worked together in Montreal, Texas, and once in Peru. Each time, she'd invited him to come visit her in Melbourne, and he'd always smiled and said he would someday.

She flicked through magazines on an end table next to the couch. Layne hadn't yet looked through them. "I reckon you haven't had the time to explore the neighborhood, though."

"Not really."

"Some unsavory types turned St. Kilda into a dog's brekkie earlier today. Gang war between two organizations known as Reds and Union. Did you know anything about that?"

Layne slid into the chair across from her. "Why are you here, Tilda?"

She frowned, probably a little annoyed he hadn't answered the question. "Two things. One, I've got the equipment you asked for. Tomorrow morning, take the Alamein line to Auburn station. Walk a block over to Burwood Road. Come back east, and you'll find a guitar shop. Walk in the back and ask for Rohan. He'll make sure you're happy, but be careful with him. He's an odd one."

"Thank you."

"Wasn't easy to arrange all this on short notice. And I need to be clear: Rohan will *lend* you some gear, and he's expecting you to leave it in good nick."

"Nick?"

"Good condition. Don't bang it up or be wasteful."

"Understood. I can promise you I will put it all to good use."

She gave a subtle shake of the head at this. "I don't want you to take this as an insult, because you've always been one of the most capable operatives I've had the pleasure to work with. But you're in over your head at this stage."

"I appreciate your concern. What's the second thing?"

Tilda sighed and leaned forward on the couch. "Just want

to give you a word of warning, mate. You've been dropped into the middle of a situation that has a lot of bloody moving parts. The ASIO is involved in what's going on with Randall. And I'd like to offer a professional courtesy to you, from one spook to another: leave it alone. Get on a plane and go home before you land yourself in trouble."

"I hear what you're saying, Tilda, but I need to see this through. Until I find out the truth, I'm not going anywhere."

She nodded, chewed on her lip. "I figured you'd say as much." As she stood, she extended a hand. "Good luck to you then. And try not to get yourself killed, yeah?"

23

IN THE MORNING, LAYNE AWOKE IN A PANIC. REMNANTS of a dream about riding his motorcycle evaporated as his eyes adjusted to the window's light slicing across the room.

Tomorrow night, there might or might not be an assassination attempt on Governor Phelps's life. Randall might or might not be involved somehow, and Daphne might or might not be setting Layne up to fail for some unexplained reason. All the information he'd received from Tilda yesterday only muddied his thought processes.

So much bullshit going on, Layne felt like he was still jet-lagged. One of the people close to him was lying, but he didn't know which one, and he didn't know why. If he had the answer, he could blaze a clear path forward. Without it, he was wandering in the dark, taking shots at shadows.

He looked at his burner phone, hoping to find a missed call from Randall. Turned in bed and then remembered the bruise from the cricket bat. Groaned.

He dialed Randall, and it went straight to voice mail.

Sighing, he opted not to leave a message. Instead, he sent a quick text:

Nash Bridges needs to talk.

And then he left the phone on the counter to hop in the shower. Ten minutes later, when he returned, there was no text reply. Layne sighed at the phone and put on some clothes to meet the contact Tilda had set up for him.

But first, he needed to prepare himself. Tilda had described the weapons dealer as *odd*. Layne considered taking one of the knives in the kitchen, but he had no sheath or other good place to stash it. Possibly he could fashion a sheath from the shower curtain, but even then, carrying a knife seemed too bulky. Too likely it would be discovered. The idea occurred to him to engineer a clone of the clothes hanger fist-blade he'd made on the day he'd arrived, but a piece of wire wrapped around his wrist would be too obvious.

An idea struck. A modification of the clothes hanger knife. He dug through the clothes he'd bought upon arrival to find the one long-sleeve shirt in his possession. Then he removed the wire clothes hanger that had come with it and unwrapped the wire until it became one long piece of metal. From there, he bent and curved one end until the last couple of inches had been turned into a flat-ended circle, like a platform in the shape of a coil. Then he used a kitchen knife to sharpen the other end of the hanger.

He inserted the hanger up his sleeve until the flat, coiled base pressed against his armpit. It still stuck out of his sleeve a couple of inches. So he shoved the hanger in until the sharpened tip was fully hidden.

He stood before the bathroom mirror and practiced. When he pulled his arm back, the flat end pushed against his armpit, making the pointy end jut out from his sleeve. Not as slick as a retractable pistol, but it was the best he could do with his current materials. And a pointy clothes hanger wasn't as good as a knife, but it was much stealthier, and he could slash someone's throat if he had to.

———

SERENA SIPPED coffee as her eyes danced over the laptop screen. A surveillance camera feed looked down from the mantel over the fireplace into a living room populated by a couch, a recliner, an end table, and one small television.

But she didn't care about the furniture. Serena was concerned with the cat lying on a rug next to the couch, batting at a small furry toy mouse. He was on his back, kicking the mouse into the air with his rear paws and then batting it to the ground with his front paws. The kitty had been at this for five straight minutes. Serena envied his ability to remain entertained by mundane tasks.

As she watched, the cat kicked the mouse into the air and then missed it with his front paw swipe. It smacked him in the face and then tumbled onto the rug. The cat, startled, jumped to his feet, eyes searching the room as he meowed. Serena giggled. Wished she had sound to match the black-and-white surveillance feed. But it had been hard enough to install the camera in her neighbor's clock without damaging it and also without him finding out about it. Adding a microphone would've been much more complicated.

She glanced between the window blinds to see Layne strut along Davis Street toward the train station. Target on the move. He was wearing thick, black glasses and a shaggy-haired wig. He was either trying for porn star or college professor. She wasn't sure which one.

Serena whipped out her untraceable satellite phone and sent a text to Daphne:

Any word on whereabouts of Rattlesnake?

A moment later, the return text came through:

Negative. Stand by for instructions.

Serena sighed as Layne rounded the corner onto Toorak Street. She hated this. Sitting by, taking notes, barely encountering any action. What good was it for her to languish on the sidelines while the clock ticked down to zero?

The people out there causing all this havoc were enacting their plans. Taking action. Serena, meanwhile, was nothing but a glorified babysitter.

To hell with this.

She snatched her ankle holster and left the apartment.

24

LAYNE DUCKED INSIDE THE GUITAR PLACE ON Burwood to find himself in a seedy pawnshop with guitars hanging everywhere like stalactites of meat in a slaughter-house. Snaking coils of amplifier cords cut across the floor. Six-stringed instruments jutted from the walls and ceiling, poised to fall.

"G'day," said a burly man at the counter. Looked more like a bookie than a person knowledgeable about musical instruments. "You after something in particular, or are you happy to browse?"

Layne stepped up to the counter so he could keep his voice low. Made sure his clothes hanger blade wasn't poking out of his long-sleeve shirt. "I need to speak to Rohan."

"Rohan, eh?"

Layne nodded.

"Don't get a lot of requests to talk to our guitar tech. And what do you want with that bloke?"

Layne shrugged but didn't break eye contact with the man.

The other man paused a moment, then waved him toward a door behind the counter. The man cracked the door open and then stepped back, as if he were afraid of the evil spirits that might escape. Muted black metal music from tiny speakers leaked out through the door.

Layne pushed through the door and shut it behind him. The room was dark, lit only by a single desk lamp at what appeared to be a workstation-type table.

The lights in the room flicked on. Tools hung from the walls. Guitar parts splayed about everywhere. And in the corner, standing next to the light switch, a gangly man with a shaved head and glasses so thick they made his eyes bug out like a cartoon. He lifted a phone and tapped on it. The music ceased, leaving the room in utter quiet.

"I heard you asking after me out there," the man said in a deep voice. "How do you know my name?"

"Tilda sent me."

The man puffed out his cheeks like a horn player, then waved Layne forward. "Sorry for the cloak-and-dagger, mate. But if Tilda can vouch for you, then I suppose you're all right with me."

"I appreciate that."

The thin man stepped out from around the desk and sauntered toward Layne. Despite his gaunt appearance, he had Popeye-quality forearms, which he crossed over his chest. "You're here to pick up supplies?"

"That's right."

"And what will you be using these supplies for?"

"I'd rather not say."

"Not much for conversation, are you?"

Layne turned his palms up toward the ceiling and said

nothing. He breathed as the man across the room raised eyebrows at him. Still, he stayed silent.

"Let me get one thing clear, Tilda's friend: you cross me, and I'll paint the streets with your blood."

"Excuse me?"

Rohan slipped his hands into his pockets. "You heard me."

Layne hesitated. Rohan appeared ready for a fight, and Layne had no desire to engage in a scuffle inside a room probably well stocked with armaments. He didn't think he'd have much trouble with this guy, though. He could unleash his sleeve blade and make one good swipe across the man's face to get his attention. Funny how the tough would crumble as soon as they felt a little blood warming their skin.

Still, good chance Rohan was currently armed underneath his clothes. And Layne needed him.

"There's no need to be hostile."

The man narrowed his eyes. "You haven't seen hostile yet."

"Look, either you help me out, or you don't. If you want to stand here and be a tough guy, I'll be on my way. I don't care about this posturing and pissing-contest bullshit. I'm too old and have too little time."

The man paused, eyes still dim, scowl on his face. Layne felt the pressure of the sleeve blade trigger against his armpit. Readied himself to extend it but still held out hope he wouldn't have to.

Then Rohan's scowl turned into a smile. He tilted his head and let out a wispy cackle. "No dramas, mate. Let me show you what I've got for you."

When he turned his back, Layne let out a sigh. What a weird guy.

The weapons dealer opened a cabinet in the back and pulled out a series of items. Boxes of 9mm and .45 rounds. A Beretta, a Desert Eagle, and a Mossberg shotgun. Finally, ceramic body armor.

"This isn't made of magic fairy dust," Rohan said as he hoisted the vest onto the counter. "Don't think you can take on a firing squad."

"Not the first time I've worn body armor."

"No, I reckon not. But you'd do heaps wise to remember your mortality, regardless."

"What about explosives?" Layne said.

"Sorry. Tilda didn't give me all the time in the world. The Mossberg is my own private piece. I expect you to treat it as such."

"Understood."

Rohan reached back into the cabinet and pulled out one more item, a small felt bag.

"What's that?"

Rohan opened the bag and drew out an item about the size of a pair of toenail clippers, hiding inside a leather sheath. He removed it. It was a small blade, about two inches in length. "Concealable knife. Good for getting out of handcuffs. Can also pick easier locks or gut a man's throat if you're close enough to him. It's no match for a high-quality knife, but it'll do the job in a pinch."

"Thank you for this."

"Whatever you're getting into, with this much gear, I hope you have backup. If there's ten of them and one of you, it won't make a shit how many guns you have."

Layne made no response, and Rohan tilted his head as Layne loaded the items into a large duffel bag.

"You get caught with these," Rohan said, "you will not

utter my name. You will not utter the name of this shop where you found me. I don't care who you're mates with at the ASIO. If you mention me, I'll come after your family."

Layne considered reflecting Rohan's tough-guy words but decided against it. Let the man have his superiority. Instead, he looked the tall arms dealer in the eye and said, "I never get caught."

25

AS HE LEFT THE GUITAR SHOP WITH A DUFFEL BAG OVER HIS shoulder, Layne entered a street abuzz with activity. Four black Chevy Suburbans rolling down the road. Morning light bounced off the shiny midnight exteriors of the cars. A few other people had left their respective shops and breakfast diners to wander out to the street and check the commotion.

Layne caught the attention of a man watching the cars roll by. "What's going on?"

The man regarded him with a raised eyebrow. "Mayor and the governor are doing a presentation at Camberwell Station. Kicking off groundbreaking on new platforms."

"Camberwell? Where is that?"

Now the man looked at him as he would a confused child. "It's just up the road past the servo. Next station after Auburn."

Layne dashed down Burwood toward Auburn Station. Popped in a fresh piece of nicotine gum as he ran. He dipped into the alley that would lead him toward the platforms and then ditched the duffel underneath a dumpster before the station, along with his armpit clothes hanger knife. Took a quick look around to make sure no one had seen him.

He formulated a plan. Confront the governor about why he wasn't taking the threats against his life seriously. Look him in the eye and make sure he understood the gravity of the situation.

Given the security around him the other day, Layne would have to be a little more sneaky. He expected to encounter security teams for both men merging in one spot. And likely, the giant with the slicked-back hair would be running the show.

Layne followed the tracks toward the next station to the east, Camberwell. Feet crunching through rocks alongside the tracks, his chest burning from the dry air. The morning heat created streams of sweat running down his forehead. The long sleeves of his shirt weren't helping, so he rolled them up as he ran.

Halfway there, he slowed so he wouldn't attract attention to himself. He made it to the area in about ten minutes with an even jog.

The train station was elevated, with ramps leading up to the platforms and ticket office. Brick structures with large overhead panels to hide the station from the sun. Both of the ramps Layne could see were stuffed with people. Some held up signs for the governor, some for the mayor. Parents hoisting little kids onto their shoulders to glimpse these politicians.

And at the top of the ramps, Governor Phelps stood next to another man, who must have been the mayor of Melbourne.

Scattered throughout the people standing around to

witness the presentation were a few members of the security team. They were wearing plainclothes but were easy enough to spot. Layne did locate the giant with the slicked-back hair near the closest entrance.

Layne began to push his way through the people to reach the ramp. Was formulating what he would say when he got a chance. But he figured going straight up the ramp would be a bad move and would expose him to security in only a few seconds. Possibly, after his recent attempt to speak with the governor in Alexandra Gardens, everyone in the security detail would be on the lookout for him.

The man next to Phelps turned to the crowd and raised his hands. "We'll get started in a few minutes. Just working out some logistical problems with the audio equipment."

Layne shifted past the ramp and headed toward the rear of the train station. He crossed the tracks and slinked close to the actual platform next to the tracks. No one standing back here, and he had a straight shot to the mayor and governor from this angle.

But his sneaky back passage didn't last long.

As Layne raised himself onto the platform, several members of the security team ascended the ramp and gathered near the governor. They made a wall between Layne and his target.

He tried to slink away so he could circumnavigate to a different platform and approach that way, but it was too late. The giant turned his head toward Layne and grinned. Said something into the sleeve of his dress shirt. Some new guards appeared at the other end of the platform. Both exits were now sealed off.

The giant marched across the station on a path toward Layne.

Time was running out. Other security would converge on him soon. He strode along the platform, only a few feet from the governor. The men in their black suits approached cautiously, none of them running or drawing weapons yet.

"Governor Phelps," Layne said, keeping his voice low, "why did you ignore the warnings about your speech tomorrow?"

For a second, Layne's and the governor's eyes met. They held each other's gaze in silence for the brief moment it lasted.

Layne could see the confusion in his eyes. Had he not been warned?

"Him," said the giant, loud enough for those nearby to hear but lower than a shout. "Someone grab that bloke."

Layne skidded back toward the far end of the station platform as security converged on him. He pushed a guard out of his way. Tried to make a break for it. Two men had now appeared at the far edge of the platform—the one away from the governor—both of them in fancy suits, wearing mirrored aviator sunglasses. Arms wide, blocking his path to the ramp away from the station.

There wasn't anywhere for him to go, but he turned right, facing one of the inner platforms. The two security men reacted, making a move toward him. This opened a wedge between them.

Layne threw a shoulder into one and grabbed hold of the man's arms. Since he was already powering forward, he used the leverage of the man's weight to twist him out of the way, opening up the path to the train tracks. Back the way he'd come.

Layne let go, sending the man backpedaling, landing on his ass. The other man clapped a hand on Layne's shoulder, and Layne dropped to one knee and vaulted the man over him. Threw him flat on his back.

Layne leaped over the downed man, the edge of the platform in sight. The platform shook as an incoming train squealed and whooshed.

A hand landed on his ankle, and he kicked at it to free himself. Train incoming. As Layne ran, he saw the giant on his heels. Still not running. They probably didn't want to cause a panic.

Layne took off, leaping onto the tracks. The train horn sounded, blasting in his ears. He scrambled past the tracks and hoisted himself up a chain-link fence to a parking lot on the other side. The train roared behind him, an express that had no intention of stopping at the station.

Through the parking lot, he connected with Burwood Road and dashed across it. He slipped between two buildings. Doubled back to Burwood to get a glimpse of how many were behind him in pursuit. The giant, plus the two he'd thrown to the ground and one more.

Layne rushed across the street and through an alley. On a wall next to him was some sort of gum art thing. Hundreds of pieces of chewed gum stuck to the surface. So weird. But he didn't have time to judge the merits of gum art now.

At the end of the alleyway, he turned right and hopped a tall fence, using his feet to gain leverage. He dashed across someone's backyard and then vaulted another fence to reach the next yard. Once he was two more over, he stopped and knelt next to a small swimming pool. Listened. He heard the shuffling of footsteps on the other side of the wooden fence.

They ran right past him.

As soon as the footstep noise dissipated in the other direction, Layne hopped the fence and ran back toward

Camberwell Station. At a distance, he could see guards shuffling the mayor and the governor down the steps, pointing at a Suburban. Security protocols would demand they move any VIPs out of the area after a break like this.

No way was Layne going to speak to the governor again today.

But a new and unexpected development drew his attention. Out of the corner of his eye, along a row of shops, Layne spotted *Wharf Rat*, the restaurant Randall had suggested they eat at yesterday.

Layne meandered along the street, looking casual. And inside Wharf Rat, head down, talking on a phone, Randall was eating breakfast.

26

LAYNE PAUSED, EYING HIS BROTHER THROUGH THE restaurant window. Phone up to his ear, chatting with someone. His head was down, and he was forking little tomatoes into his mouth. He seemed unaffected by the chaos of the evacuating governor and mayor. There was no direct view of the train platform from here.

After a moment, he took out his wallet, dropped money on the table, and stood up. Never taking the phone away from his ear, he left the restaurant and hoofed it up the street in a direction opposite the train station.

Layne broke into a jog. He wasn't sure why, but the fact that he'd been unable to connect with Randall so far this morning bothered him. With only a day left until the alleged assassination of Governor Phelps, for Randall to have any amount of radio silence with him seemed unusual.

Layne weaved through the pedestrians to pass the restaurant. He approached the edge of the block carefully, then peered around it. Caught a glimpse of Randall disappearing into a back alley, still on the phone.

Layne took off after him. He slowed at the edge of a brick building as Randall spilled out of the alley and then diverted to a nearby street. Layne crept along and watched Randall enter a business district, a collection of clothing shops and coffeehouses. He opened the door to a coffee shop and approached the counter.

Layne spotted a fish-and-chips place on the other side of the street, and he kept his head down as he crossed the street and went inside.

He sat at the counter and took out his hand mirror, then pointed it at an angle so he could see the coffee shop on the other side of the street. No direct line of sight from here. Randall ended his phone call and ordered a coffee. Waited at the end of the counter for a minute, rocking back and forth on his heels with his hands in his pockets. Randall picked up his order and then sat and drank it uneventfully for a few minutes. If he knew he was being observed, he gave no indication.

Layne's brain spun with possibilities. Asking himself what he hoped to accomplish. Asking himself if, after the events of the last few days, he finally believed what Randall had been saying or if it was time to engage his mission and kill his brother.

Merely thinking of that as a viable option twisted Layne's stomach. For the first time since arriving in Melbourne, he considered the mechanics of how it would work. Actually ending his brother's life.

This was the perfect opportunity to do it. The nearby neighborhoods were jigsaw mazes of alleys and tree-shrouded backyards. Layne could follow Randall, incapacitate him, and dispose of him easily. Nothing he hadn't done dozens of times before.

But something still didn't add up. Layne couldn't let go of the feeling that Randall could be telling the truth about all this. If he was, that made Daphne a liar, which Layne didn't yet know how to reconcile.

Randall tapped on his phone and then lifted it to his ear. A moment later, he stood up. He navigated a path, not out the front door but to the back of the coffee shop.

Something wasn't right. Randall was swinging his arms around, gesticulating. Having an argument on the phone. Curiosity burned at Layne, and he had to get an ear close to the conversation.

This phone call could be a crucial clue.

Layne rushed out the front door. He crossed the street and walked in a wide arc until he could see the back of the coffee shop. There was Randall, talking on the phone. Facing away, one arm holding the phone and the other moving through the air, driving home whatever oral argument he was making.

Layne hovered near the front of the coffee shop and scrambled to think of how to creep within earshot. If he ventured into the alley behind Randall, his older brother would definitely hear the footsteps. If Layne went around the building to the other alley, he didn't know if that would get him close enough to eavesdrop.

Then it hit him. The coffee shop stood only one story tall, and there was a collection of milk crates lining the outside wall. He stacked six of them in a pyramid and then wrenched his arms up, barely grabbing on to the edge of the storm drain jutting from the side of the building. He took a breath and focused. If this thing gave way, it would screech, and he'd be exposed.

But it held. He pulled himself up to the roof and sneaked

across the gravelly surface, close to the rear. He stopped short of being able to see Randall. It didn't matter because he could now hear his brother talking below.

"What I care about," Randall said to someone on the other end of the phone, "is Abdul Abbad."

He stopped talking, and Layne resisted the urge to inch toward the edge of the rooftop. Randall would certainly spot him out of the corner of his eye. Instead, he closed his eyes and tried to still his breathing so he could focus.

Randall groaned. "No, Jerry, that's not what I'm saying. If someone puts a bullet in him or a drone locates and obliterates his camp before Phelps can get there, then this is all for nothing."

Layne slipped a pen out of his pocket and wrote *Jerry* on his palm.

"Right," Randall said. "You have no idea how hard I've worked to make this meeting happen. No, no, I know you have, too. I'm not saying . . ."

Another pause. Layne considered the possibility that this phone conversation was for his benefit. Randall hadn't been at the train platform, but he'd been near it, possibly checking up on the governor. Maybe he'd seen Layne's outburst and was putting on a play to convince him he was truly interested in getting the governor on that plane to Pakistan the day after tomorrow.

But Layne didn't think so. All this felt genuine to him. Besides, Randall wouldn't have had a clear view of the train station from the restaurant.

Randall said something at a low volume, and Layne leaned a little closer to the edge, turning his ear toward the ground. Bits and pieces of the conversation floated up to him, but not enough for Layne to put any context to the random words.

Something shifted. That sense of invasion of privacy, physical, like a sudden drop in airplane cabin pressure. The hair on the back of Layne's neck rose. He tilted his head to the left and the right, but he couldn't see anything.

Someone was watching him.

He didn't want to make it obvious he'd found her, but his shadow was definitely nearby, with an eye on his activities.

———

FROM HER PERCH atop the dry cleaners next to the fish-and-chips shop, Serena studied Randall through the crosshairs on her Walther PPK. He was talking with someone, as he had been for the last several minutes. An animated conversation, full of angry expressions and exaggerated hand movements. She wished again she had the parabolic mic handy, but it wasn't something she could have slipped into her purse.

Randall in the alley and Layne on the roof of the building.

She had a perfect shot, right here, right now. Would take one quick press of the trigger, then she could pivot her wrist a couple of inches and put a bullet in Layne, too. This street was barely occupied, so she wouldn't even have to run. Civilians hearing the suppressed shot would probably think it was an indiscernible bird call from the heavens.

The outburst at the train platform had been too much. Either Layne was working with his brother to prevent the Pakistan trip, or he was just an imbecile. Maybe he was too old; maybe his skills had softened.

That last possibility was a hard one for Serena to swallow. Although she'd never met Layne Parrish in person, she had known everything about him for years. Ever since taking his place as the star operative for an organization with no name within the US government. A team of highly trained specialists, dedicated and loyal and ruthless. Layne's exploits and adventures were the stuff of legend. He had no plaque or congressional medal commemorating his service, but those within her organization didn't need them. They kept the stories alive between them. Passed them down.

When Daphne had explained no one would ever know of Serena's service to the country, she'd been okay with that. The way they talked about Layne, she wouldn't ever be forgotten. If she could achieve half of what he had done, they would tell stories about her, too.

Layne Parrish used to be one of the best. Now, clouded by his brother, he'd lost it. Had become the sort of person others would distance themselves from for fear of that person's foolhardiness getting them killed in the field. Such a shame.

Serena wanted to put a bullet in him for that fact alone. A horse put out to pasture; a dog sent to live at a farm upstate. Field operatives weren't supposed to get old. They weren't supposed to retire. They were supposed to go out in a blaze of glory like someone in one of those dumb, nationalistic country songs.

Right here, right now. The perfect opportunity to remove both of them in a single second. She knew she wouldn't miss. Serena knew she could tag them both with barely any effort at all.

She slipped out her phone and sent a message to Daphne:

Have Rattlesnake and Boy Scout in my sights. Clean shot. Please advise

She stared at her phone as the little dots below danced to indicate an incoming reply. This went on for ten seconds, twenty seconds, starting and stopping. A couple of times, the dot dancing halted for several seconds. Each time, she looked up, expecting to see her targets dispersing. But they each stayed in place, Randall on the phone and Layne hovering above him.

Finally the reply came back.

Negative

She gritted her teeth and clenched her phone hard enough to feel the screen bow under the pressure. Serena had not so far been one to question orders, but all this uncertainty was driving her crazy. Making her wonder if she was being tested. A loyalty exam.

If that was true, she was failing miserably and wasn't sure if she cared anymore. This mission had ventured into crazy land from the first day.

And now, even with the perfect shot, she had no permission.

Randall Parrish was in the pocket of a mercenary group from India or Pakistan, engaged with terrorists, but Daphne still wouldn't let her take the damn shot.

She lowered her pistol. Heaved a breath and reminded herself of why she did all this. The ultimate goal. She had no choice but to trust Daphne and therefore trust the mission as Daphne wanted to orchestrate it.

After a few more breaths, she'd calmed down. Had

accepted the situation. She arched her back to stretch and slid her pistol back into its holster.

And then, a half second later, Layne turned in her direction. Their eyes met.

She winked at him.

27

WHEN LAYNE PUT A FACE TO HIS TAIL, HE SOLVED nothing, but knowing her would make things easier. This must have been the same person to attack the fleeing gang-banger on French Island. The eyes in the crowd observing him at Federation Square. The same eyes he'd felt on him since arriving in the country.

Someone sent by Daphne. For what purpose, he still didn't know.

The brown-skinned shadow disappeared from her rooftop, and Layne opted not to follow her. If she was as good as he figured her to be, he didn't think he could tail her. Not here. Not easily.

As Randall dispersed, Layne considered following him but wasn't sure what that would achieve. Randall had been speaking with someone named Jerry about ensuring Phelps's trip to Pakistan happened. He and this Jerry person had a vested interest in securing a meeting between Phelps and Abbad. What that interest was, Layne didn't yet know.

Maybe it was as Randall had said. He wanted Phelps to defuse Abbad and keep his group of followers at bay.

Or maybe there was something else going on. Something beyond what Layne could see.

He evacuated the rooftop and texted Daphne that he needed to speak with her. Told her to meet him at his apartment in South Yarra.

He reclaimed the duffel bag and hiked down the street, steering clear of the train station in Camberwell in case the governor's security team was still hunting him. After fifteen minutes, he reached Auburn and was able to sprint to catch a train only a few seconds before it left the station.

On the train ride home, his mind spun like a top. Who to trust? The more he learned, the more he became certain that Daphne was keeping something from him. She had some reason to withhold info and to give him false information. But the endgame still seemed too muddied, too vague.

At his apartment, he texted Daphne again and told her he was ready to see her. While he waited, he inventoried the gear Rohan had given him. Wasn't sure what to do with the tiny lockpick device. The blade was sharp enough he didn't want to put it in his pocket, even in a sheath. But it was too small to attach to a belt.

Then, when he sat, he knew what to do. He lifted his right foot up onto the opposite knee and shoved the blade into the side edge of his shoe sole. Jabbed it all the way in until only the tip of the tiny handle was sticking out. Someone searching him probably wouldn't find it unless they knew what to look for. Might be useful if he was disarmed and had to attack someone. One flick, and he could slash open any throat.

He checked his watch. Eleven minutes since he'd texted

Daphne. He knew she had to be nearby but couldn't imagine what was taking her so long. After another five minutes of staring out the window, he got up to open the door and check for her. And he found her waiting on his front doorstep.

"You couldn't invite yourself in?"

She shrugged. "I thought it would be rude."

"You drugged me and brought me to literally the other side of the planet. You're concerned about manners?"

Daphne pouted, hands on hips. "You're still mad about that?"

He ignored her as he stepped away from the door and she strutted inside, wiggling her hips as she went. She slid onto the couch. Raised her feet up onto the plain wooden coffee table and tossed him a sultry look. The same look that would have boiled his insides ten or fifteen years ago but had lately worn thin.

He flared red eyes at her. "What is the point of all this? If you wanted to kill my brother, you've had more than one chance to do it. I drew him out in the open for you, just like you wanted. But you're still sitting on the sidelines, watching."

"There are still too many unknowns."

"What's really going on in Pakistan?"

"I've already told you everything. Phelps is going to meet with Abdul Abbad to talk him out of whatever plan he has. To keep him from making moves toward extremist actions."

"That's the truth?"

She nodded. "As far as we know, it's accurate intel. And I've given it all to you now so you can do your job."

"You have proof that Randall is working for this insurgent group in India to kill Phelps and/or Abbad?"

Daphne let out a long sigh before answering. "Not conclusive. Your brother is the slipperiest bastard I've ever encountered. He's only gotten better at it since he disappeared in South Africa."

"So?"

"Well," she said, "proof is something we hoped you could provide."

A moment of silence hung in the air between them. Their eyes locked, and he searched for meaning. Layne now felt certain she was lying to him. But he couldn't figure out *why*.

He cleared his throat, ending the silence. "There are some who think this Phelps assassination is a smokescreen for something else. A ruse to keep all the authorities occupied."

"Who thinks that?"

"I have a local contact."

Daphne pursed her lips. "Even if there is a *chance* the assassination attempt will happen tomorrow night, we need to proceed as if it's a certainty. We can't drop the ball on this one. And that means you have one day left to get us something on Randall we can use. Or you kill him. Or if you can't do that, you put him in a situation where we can get to him once we've learned all we can. Those are the only options here. There's no shiny, happy solution where we all walk out of this holding hands."

"I think you've got the wrong guy. You should be looking into these two gangs. The Reds and the Union. They're at the heart of all this."

"You seem sure of yourself."

"I don't understand how they tie into Pakistan, but once we have that, we can put all the rest of these pieces together."

She gave a hard shake of the head. "Negative. Stay focused on the road ahead, not these detours. Get the proof about Pakistan and then take out Randall. If you can't get the proof before the governor's speech tomorrow night, take him out regardless."

Layne flexed his hands into fists. "No."

She smiled, chewing on her reply for a few seconds. "Your first training assignment in Seattle? Randall didn't think you'd be able to do it. And then, after, he was mad you didn't take out the dog in the downstairs bedroom."

"I know. I recall you being mad, too. But, in the field, it was my decision to make."

"I understood why you did it. But what I've always wanted to know is: What would you have done if the dog had woken up and raised its head? If you only had a fraction of a second to react before the dog started barking? Would you have pulled the trigger then?"

Layne breathed, stared at her, but made no response.

"You think I'm shortsighted?" she asked.

"I think you've got the wrong guy."

Daphne stood and ran her hands over her skirt to straighten it. "Fine, Layne. You've got one day left to prove it. One more day, and then I salt the earth."

28

SERENA CHECKED HERSELF IN THE BATHROOM mirror. She pulled down each of her eyelids and frowned at the redness marring the whites around her pupils. She didn't sleep well when traveling, which meant she didn't sleep well most of the time.

"You need a vacation," she said to the woman in the mirror. The woman in the mirror looked grim, tired, and in need of a multiday stay in the woods with only a set of hiking poles and a tent. Italy, New Zealand, or Canada. Somewhere outside of cell phone range.

But not yet. Maybe next week. Assuming this all turned out well and she didn't have to spend the next few weeks listening to Daphne rant and rave about how the mission went to shit as they performed a full autopsy on it in endless meetings.

With a sigh, she left the restaurant bathroom to return to Daphne. Her boss was seated at the table, a slice of cheesecake in front of her.

As Serena negotiated the crowd at the bar, a tall, well-built man holding a cluster of empty beer bottles in each hand entered her path. Blocking her from reaching Daphne's table.

"'Scuse me, miss?" he said.

Since he was directly in her way and the space between the bar and tables was too slim to evade him, she stopped. Glared at him. "Yes?"

"I'm here with my mates, and it's my shout. So since I was on my way to the bar anyway, I wondered if I could get you a drink."

"No, thank you."

"It's just that when I see a pretty lady at a place like this without a drink in her hand, it bothers me a bit."

He beamed, throwing every ounce of energy into charming her. She gritted her teeth.

"Why should I care if you're bothered?"

His devilish grin faltered a little, but he pressed on. "That's all right. I like my women a little feisty."

She leaned in close to his ear and whispered, "I have a Microtech Halo knife in my back pocket. It's five inches long, serrated, and it's very hungry. If you don't get out of my way, I'm going to give you a set of new and permanent dimples on your cheeks."

He laughed, nervous, and took a step back. His face twitched, an expression indicating he couldn't tell if she was being serious or not.

Serena didn't bother to explain herself any further. She pushed past him and marched toward Daphne's table. This time, he let her slide on by with no hesitation.

When she sat, Daphne flicked her eyes at the man standing at the bar with hands full of empty beer bottles. "Did you make a friend?"

Serena cleared her throat and placed her hands on the table. Said nothing.

Daphne popped a bite into her mouth and moaned. "Tim Tam cheesecake. You have to try this."

Serena leaned forward. "Are you sure this is a good place to talk, ma'am? There are at least a hundred people in here."

"You're so much like him," Daphne said with a grin. "It's uncanny."

Serena drummed her fingers on the table, awaiting a response.

"Don't worry so much. It's been vetted. We have a man at both the front and rear exits, as well as four on the roof. Plus, it's loud enough in here that I'm sure we'll be fine."

"I'd feel more comfortable talking outside."

Daphne slowly shook her head as she swallowed another bite of her food. "Okay, okay. Let's go." She lifted her hand to her face as if wiping a spot of dust from her cheek. Glancing around, she whispered into the sleeve of her blouse, "We're moving."

She gobbled one more spoonful of the cheesecake and then dropped a fifty-dollar bill on the table. Serena followed her outside, and Daphne twirled a finger in the air, a signal to her entourage.

They slipped into the alley behind the restaurant, and Daphne leaned against the brick wall. "Okay, you seem on edge this evening, so there's clearly something on your mind. Let's talk about it."

"Why won't you let me kill Rattlesnake? I had a clean shot this morning."

Daphne sighed. "Because I still have questions. Layne keeps pushing me toward the Reds, but all our evidence says there's nothing there aside from some well-organized thugs trying to get a bigger piece of the pie."

"I can look into them if that would help."

"No, I don't think that's necessary. We'd do better to stay on task. There's a good chance Randall is leading Layne down this gang sidepath to keep him away from Abdul Abbad and Pakistan."

Serena breathed, thinking the situation over. There was something about Daphne's actions that didn't sit right with her. But she brushed it aside. Without a clear notion of where to go, sticking to the plan was the best bet. "Understood."

Daphne opened her mouth to respond but paused as she slipped her phone out of her purse. "Ah, good. Our contact is here."

Serena crossed her arms. Contact?

Daphne thumbed the button to accept the call. "We're in the alley around back. It's secure."

A man standing at the head of the alley stepped aside as a figure shrouded in shadow entered. Wide, heavyset. A woman. A shock of red hair atop her head.

"Serena Rojas, this is Tilda MacMillan, from ASIO."

Serena extended a hand as the new woman joined them deep in the alley. "Nice to meet you."

"I'm heaps busy at the moment," Tilda said. "Don't mean to be rude, but if we could make this quick?"

Daphne nodded. "Of course. How is it going with Layne?"

"Been using a bit of reverse psychology on him. Telling him to stay away from Randall."

Serena folded her arms and watched the nonverbal communication between her boss and this new woman.

A moment later, the light dawned on her. The intel had said Layne knew someone at the ASIO but hadn't revealed the identity of that person. This Tilda woman must be it. That also might explain where Layne had gone yesterday when Serena lost sight of him for a few hours.

Why was Layne's friend feeding information to Daphne?

"Is your reverse psychology working?" Daphne asked.

"I think so. Layne's always been an unpredictable character, but he's also too much of a cowboy to leave his brother high and dry. He'll set him up, and we knock him down."

"If only it were that simple," Daphne said. "Plus, we're under a time crunch."

Tilda grunted. "You know this attempt on the governor's life is all a smokescreen, right? Something else is going on, but we don't yet know what that is."

Daphne took a napkin from her purse and wiped cheesecake remnants from between her fingers. "We're starting to come around to that thinking, yes. But it doesn't hurt to be prepared." She then pivoted and honed her eyes on Serena. "When we have our proof of Randall's ties to Pakistan, then Rattlesnake is open season. Twenty-four hours. And if Layne won't do it, then you're up. You good with that?"

Serena narrowed her eyes. "Yes, I'm good with that."

29

AFTER SUNSET, LAYNE LEFT THE APARTMENT ON SOUTH Yarra to accomplish a few things. Mainly to get food and take a walk to clear his head. Tomorrow night, the governor of Victoria would give a speech at Fed Square, and there was a good chance someone would try to kill him there. Or maybe not.

Maybe he would give his speech, go home and sleep for a few hours, and then board a plane for Pakistan, as planned. There he would meet up with his college roommate Abdul Abbad, and he would persuade his old friend to cease his attempt to acquire more advanced weaponry. And everyone would live happily ever after.

Probably, though, some of or all those things would not happen.

Layne headed up Davis Street toward Toorak. There was a fish-and-chips place to the west he'd seen and wanted to try. Of course, there were a dozen fish-and-chips restaurants on Toorak between Davis and Chapel, but this one looked clean and always seemed busy inside.

Half a block to Toorak Street. Every hundred feet, street-lamps flicked on to mark circles of light in the blossoming darkness.

And Layne knew he was being followed. The same young and attractive shadow from earlier today? This time, she wasn't content to watch him from afar, apparently. She was traveling with him, mirroring his movements. Maybe this time she would strike? She'd done nothing in Camberwell earlier.

Perhaps she wouldn't hesitate now.

Whatever her goal, Layne wanted another chance to steal a look at this shadow.

He checked the surroundings. There were trees on the street right next to the sidewalk on either side, bursting up through the pavement. None of them were wide enough to hide behind. Any odd movement, and his shadow would spot it. He could dart between a couple of the buildings on this side of the road, but that was the same problem. The shadow needed to stay oblivious.

Instead, he picked up the pace and headed toward Toorak. Wished he'd brought along his pocket mirror, but any reflected light from the streetlamps would give him away.

An apartment building butted up to the end of the next side street, and as soon as Layne reached it, he rounded it and looked up. Above his head, an awning jutted out from the building. Green cloth stretched over metal piping. Had to do quick math to decide if it would support his weight.

Layne pushed off from the side of the building and grabbed hold of a piece of that piping and then hoisted himself up. At the corner of the awning, he used the inter-section of the pipes to brace his hands, and he raised his legs and pressed his feet against the building. Now suspended, no part of his body was visible below the awning.

He braced his abs to hold himself in place. Supporting his weight in midair would become too hard in a few seconds. His elbows were already shaking.

But he didn't have to wait long. He hovered in space for three seconds before his shadow strolled nearby, pistol out and pointed at the ground. But it wasn't the woman from earlier today. This was a man. A large man, tall, with broad shoulders. A bodybuilder.

Layne waited for him to pass underneath, then he released his grip on the awning and plummeted downward. He landed on top of his pursuer, knocking them both to the ground.

Layne tried to snatch the gun, but the man was too quick. He'd already scurried out from underneath Layne and was rising to his feet. Layne bounced up, and they faced off, twelve inches from each other.

The man spun, and Layne flicked a punch out to knock the pistol from his hand. The gun went flying and clattered along the sidewalk, out into the street.

The guy inched toward the gun, and Layne matched his steps. They both paused, evaluating.

The man shot a fist straight at Layne's face. Layne pivoted, turning his shoulders and angling his neck to clear the blow. It mostly missed, except for one knuckle that grazed his chin.

The man's body swung away, and Layne knew he would run. Layne snatched him by the arm and pulled it back toward him, then delivered three quick punches to the man's midsection with his other hand. The guy's abs were as solid as punching a concrete wall.

He dragged the man deeper into the alley to keep away from prying eyes, then he flipped the man around and laced a hand underneath his jaw. "Who the hell are you? How did you find me?"

The man said nothing as he grunted and strained against Layne's grip. Layne felt the man's leg raise, and before he could react, a heel slammed down on Layne's foot. Startled, Layne loosened his grip.

The man darted forward through the alley. He planted his feet and raced left, back along Davis Street toward Layne's apartment.

Layne burst into action, chasing after him. The sun had set, but it wasn't yet completely dark. Anyone on this street who happened to look out their front window would see two madmen tearing down the sidewalk. Fortunately, there was no one out walking at this moment. The side streets were the only places in Melbourne you could steal a few moments of peace away from the crowds.

The man had blazing speed in him, and Layne struggled to keep up. Cardio hadn't been his forte for a while, and his chest heaved as he ordered his legs to pump harder.

Fifty feet separated them as the man dodged the trees shooting up through the pavement. Nearing the end of Davis, the road split at a Y intersection, and Layne guessed he would turn left. But he also knew once they were past Davis, he would have a harder time grabbing him. Layne didn't know these neighborhoods well enough to engage in an obstacle course.

Layne gritted his teeth and pushed ahead with everything he had. The man was about to pass the last tree on the block.

Layne pulled out ahead of him to the right. He placed one

hand on the tree and used his inertia to spin around it, placing him directly in front of the attacker.

Layne head-butted him, knocking the guy back a step. He snatched the larger man by the arm, spun his bulky torso to face the other way, and then Layne laced his arms underneath the man's armpits. With all his force, he dragged them both to the ground again, to make them less visible. He scooted back toward a wrought iron fence in front of someone's house.

Behind them, a small dog yipped. The fence clattered as they struggled against it.

"Tell me who sent you," Layne said, barely able to keep the man under control.

At first, the guy was using both hands to smack at Layne's tattooed forearms, then one hand slipped down to his waist.

Layne watched the glint of streetlamp light flash off the blade as the man drew the knife. He raised it and angled the tip so he could drive it into Layne's side.

The man's hand tensed around the blade. Biceps bulged, prepared to stab.

Layne reacted. He released his grip on the man and pawed at the blade to change the direction of his swipe. He latched on to the man's wrist and bent it a few inches outward. At the same time, he shifted his hips in the opposite direction, trying to squirm away from the oncoming blow.

The blade whiffed through the air.

At the last second, Layne applied pressure, pushing the knife a few inches forward, away from his body. The blade rammed into the man's chest. Layne helped guide it in, pushing until he could feel blood coating his hand.

The man gagged and sputtered. Heaved deep breaths.

Only then did Layne realize he'd stabbed his target in a place likely to kill him in a few seconds. A mortal wound. Even if Layne tried to apply pressure or dress it, the man's death was a certainty.

"Damn it," Layne said. He let go of the former attacker, who tried to crawl forward but fell on his face. The knife jutted out to the side, blood draining down the hilt.

Layne flipped him over. "Who sent you? Answer me."

The man said nothing, only stared up in surprise as the life drained out of him. His hands slipped down to the blade, but he lacked the strength to yank it out.

In a few more seconds, he stopped fighting. His lungs deflated, and his eyes became glassy and unfocused. Layne removed the knife and wiped blood on the man's shirt.

His safe house serviced apartment was blown. Useless. Layne was drenched in blood, sitting on the sidewalk next to a dead man. Not a bit closer to the truth.

INTERLUDE 3

LAYNE SHUDDERS AS THE COLD ENTERS HIS BONES. HE'S on one flank of the doorframe, Randall two feet away from him on the other. Both of them with combat shotguns and body armor. They've opted not to wear helmets because of the reduced field of vision. Daphne wasn't a fan of that decision.

Layne taps the device protruding from his ear. "Say again, Control?"

Over the tiny speaker, Layne can hear Daphne clearing her throat. "We're showing lots of heat signatures on the opposite end of the building. We think that's where they're keeping him."

Randall raises his eyebrows. "What did she say?"

"The intern is probably being held at the far end. A lot of them are together, so it's a boardroom or a kitchen or storage. A big room."

"Any word on the laptop?"

"Control: Laptop?"

"Negative," Daphne says. "It's a one-floor office building,

so it shouldn't take you long to search. But be careful. Some of the areas are too shielded for us to register heat signatures. Assume not all hostiles are in this back room."

"Understood. We'll be careful." Layne shakes his head at Randall. "Laptop location unclear. And we'll be blind in some spots in the building."

Randall purses his lips. "I don't like that."

"It is what it is."

"Okay," Randall says, his eyes searching upward. "Time to go knock on some doors, then. Ready?"

Layne grits his teeth and nods. Randall pauses to grin at his little brother. "You're getting good at this, you know. She told me you're almost ready to graduate."

It's been a long journey to here, from starting his training in Houston with Daphne to his first kill in Seattle. Stops in New York, Boston, Sacramento, Bolivia, Germany, Qatar, and more than a few others. Many he doesn't remember. He'll see the inside of an airplane, the inside of a hotel room, and then a few passing shots of desert or woods or a faceless city muddled with skyscrapers. Sometimes a landmark will stand out, like the Statue of Liberty or the glass pyramid in front of the Louvre, but otherwise, it's all a blur. He imagines it's what rock stars on tour must feel like.

Layne doesn't want to worry about that right now. All he wants to focus on is retrieving the laptop and finding the senator's intern, hopefully alive.

"Go," Layne says.

Randall picks the office building's door lock and swings it open. They're greeted by a small room with a desk built into the wall. Reception. Twin hallways mark either side of the desk, leading off into the unknown.

Layne points at his chest and at Randall, then at each of the hallways.

Randall shakes his head. Flicks his chin at the one on the left. He intends for them to stay together. Layne considers it, then agrees that it's a smarter plan.

They shuffle by the desk and enter one hallway. It's cramped, with closed doors on either side. Plates marked with names of various people Layne has never heard of. There are voices, far away, beyond the edge of the hallway. That's where they expect to find the intern, maybe even the laptop.

Six doors on each side between them and the closed door at the end of the hallway. Layne tilts his head to the right, then points at Randall and then along the left.

Randall nods and heads to the first door on the left. He presses an ear against it for a moment, then opens the door and levels his shotgun. Whisks it around to each corner of the room. He leans in for a moment and then withdraws and shuts the door.

Layne does the same at the first door on the right. He opens it into a small office with a desk and a bookshelf decorated with business books about productivity and some framed pictures of a family in bright winter gear, standing in front of a ski lift.

Layne closes the door and then shuffles to the next one on his side. Randall has already opened his next door. He lifts a hand in the air to gain Layne's attention and curls his fingers to ask Layne to join him. Raises a finger to his lips and then points at his own ear. Layne understands his brother is telling him not to inform Daphne about what he's found.

When Layne approaches the open door, Randall grins.

Points into the room. Inside, there's a table, a small LCD monitor, a minifridge, and no other furniture. On the table is a stack of porn DVDs, and a long, pink vibrator sits next to them.

"What the hell?" Layne whispers.

Randall shrugs, smirking.

"Say again, Boy Scout?" Daphne squawks in his ear.

"Disregard, Control," Layne whispers. "We're still searching."

None of the other doors in the hallway unearth rooms as interesting as the sex shop closet. They don't reveal any hints about the location of the intern or the laptop, either. The door at the far end of the room is blocked. The knob won't turn.

Randall removes a lockpicking device, but Layne stops him. Has a feeling this door is booby-trapped. Rigged with explosives or something similar. That the knob won't turn even a fraction of an inch stands out to him as strange.

He points to the doorknob, and Randall seems to understand. The older brother turns back down the hallway, and Layne nods. They return to reception and navigate back to the other hallway.

As soon as they venture inside, Layne can tell something is different. Ten feet into it, two men emerge from an open door. Both sporting M16s slung over their shoulders.

Randall raises his shotgun, but Layne already has his Beretta out. Two quick taps of the trigger. One bullet blasts a hole in the head of the man on the left, the other in the neck of the man on the right. Both of them stutter and fall to the ground. Dots of blood color the walls on either side of the hallway.

Layne regains focus after the spurt of adrenaline abates.

The noise-suppressed shots aren't deafening, but they're loud enough to attract anyone within earshot.

"Let's move," Randall says.

They break out into a run. At the end of the hallway, figures appear from an open door. The bullets fly before Layne can even make out their faces. A blast smacks him in the chest. His vest keeps the bullet from shredding him, but it still hits him hard enough to stop him in his tracks. Like running into a wall at full speed, chest first. He can't breathe. Staggering, his body wants to collapse from the shock.

An instant later, another bullet punches through his left forearm. An inch or two above his wrist. A white-hot pain sears up and down his arm. And then, he can feel warm blood rushing over his wrist. The blood flow is worse than the pain because it's the sensation of his life escaping in a flood of red. It's pure panic in liquid form.

Layne shudders and falls to his knees. Hears the rumble of Randall's shotgun above him. He wants to withdraw and clutch his arm to stop the bleeding, but he can't. They're in the middle of a firefight. He has to take aim and rid the area of any remaining hostiles.

Layne lifts his head. Points his shotgun at the collection of men at the end of the hallway. With his left hand incapacitated, he's unable to steady the barrel. Finger on the trigger, he wedges the shotgun stock into his armpit to help stabilize it. Blasts a couple of times. The spray nicks the wall as it spreads, exploding powdery bits of drywall into the air like a cloud.

Randall keeps shooting, and after a few seconds, the end of the hallway clears out. A pile of bodies littering the carpet.

"Go," Layne says, struggling to breathe. "Get the intern.

Come back for me once you have the laptop. I'm only going to slow you down until I can control this bleeding."

Randall drops to one knee and throws an arm around his little brother, snaking under his armpit. Hoists him to his feet. "Not a chance, Boy Scout. Put some duct tape on that wound and get your feet under you, because you're coming with me. We're doing this together."

And he drags Layne down the hallway. Weapons raised, droplets of blood flinging onto the carpet underfoot.

30

LAYNE STEPPED OFF THE TRAM AND DUCKED INTO A nearby coffee shop across the street from the house. He slid into a booth and opened the map, then compared that against the address on the ID from the wallet he'd lifted off the cricket bat-wielding man in St. Kilda yesterday. The name on the license was Kurt Lawton; the address connected to a house on the other side of the street from this coffee shop.

Today was the day. The last day.

Layne's back hurt from the shitty hotel bed he'd slept in last night. Not only that, but how hard he'd had to work to incapacitate the attacker near Davis Street. Any motion brought a twinge of pain and slowed his movements. Maybe he was getting old. His body beginning the slow descent into atrophy.

He couldn't take a punch like he used to, for sure.

And who had been sent to take him down? Most likely, it had been someone from the failed warehouse raid in St.

Kilda. Good chance one of them had seen him and Randall fleeing the scene.

No time to worry about that now.

"Sir?" said a voice behind him. Layne turned to see a man with a dreadlocked mullet frowning down at him. "We're not open yet."

"Sorry," Layne said and took his leave of the shop. He now noticed the closed sign on the front door. Little things like that bothered him—the small slips of reason. The Layne Parrish of ten years ago would never have risked attention by doing something stupid like walking into someplace he wasn't supposed to be in public.

Shirking the tiny details led to death more often than not.

He waited for a tram to power through the middle of the street, then he crossed after it. Paused on the sidewalk and casually strolled past the house. It was a one-story ranch home with blue siding and what appeared to be two bedrooms. Curvy palm trees out front shrouding the house. Nothing decorating the yard other than a propane grill that seemed untouched for quite some time.

Layne navigated the fence around the back and circled behind the house. By the backyard, he ducked into an alley next to the house and glanced at the windows into the kitchen. Saw nothing to indicate anyone was home. After another moment, the street thinned out, and he was able to slip over the fence unseen. He crouched, eyes on a patio door leading into the kitchen.

He crept across the yard, checking over the fence to make sure no one was watching. The house was still. Seemed in the clear. At the back porch, he paused again, focusing his ears for nonambient sounds. This early, he might find his target asleep inside.

Layne hovered near the back door. Shifted the Desert Eagle protruding from his waistband. He mentally practiced drawing it. Straightening his arm and closing one eye to aim.

A minute passed, and then two. Not a single peep of anything inside the house.

He made quick work of the window over the sink. Went up with no trouble. He could have just as easily picked the lock on the patio door, but the window seemed less likely to have an alarm.

He slipped in through the window and placed his hands on either side of the sink. Working his abs, he drew his torso inside and pivoted around to lower his feet to the ground. After the various squabbles of the last few days, his body screamed at him to take it easy.

The open kitchen was a straight shot into the living room. Decorated with posters, mostly black-and-white advertisements for the *Collingwood Football Club*. One large poster shouted about *Magpies Footy*. The bird on the poster and the logos matched the insignia on the clothes of the Union thugs at the warehouse in St. Kilda.

Layne crept into the living room, breathing slowly so his heartbeat wouldn't interrupt his hearing. As far as he could see, the house was completely empty. Maybe after getting his ass kicked in St. Kilda, Kurt had decided to take a small vacation. No evidence of a spouse or children anywhere.

Now Layne had to figure out how to turn this breaking and entering joyride into something useful.

Kurt, the owner of the wallet, had been one of the cricket bat swingers behind the warehouse. Thugs from the Union —or at least, that's what Randall had said. Made sense, since he and Randall were about to break into a building owned by the Reds when the attack happened.

So Layne figured he should look around for some evidence of what this gang was up to. How they fit into the plans of the Reds and how all it connected with Governor Phelps.

Low-rent organizations always left a paper trail somewhere.

And to be honest, Layne wanted proof his brother wasn't lying to him. Everyone wanted to poison Layne against Randall. To say he'd changed, but part of Layne refused to believe it. Randall had done nothing but help Layne since he'd arrived.

There had to be a way to clear his brother's name. Or find proof he was lying. Layne would settle for either one at this point.

He started in the living room, opening closets and drawers and flipping over couch cushions. Looking for guns, drugs . . . something.

The living room search bore no fruit, so he moved on to each bedroom in succession. He scoured them for information. Found a box full of pistol magazines under one bed, but nothing else incriminating. In the medicine cabinet, he found a few vials of what appeared to be either cocaine or high-quality meth.

After fifteen minutes of searching, Layne was ready to give up. Then he entered the garage, and everything changed.

The concrete and drywall space was primarily home to a motorcycle, covered with a bedsheet. Seeing those two wheels sticking out underneath made Layne miss his Harley.

But no, he'd left that behind on the day he realized one slip might leave his daughter without a father.

The irony of that decision occurred to Layne, now standing in a house where he could eat a bullet for trespassing.

Along the opposite wall sat a file cabinet. Unlike the rest of the room, there was little dust on it. Layne approached and then reached for his phone, but the nonsmart flip phone had no flashlight on it, so instead, he raised the blinds on the singular window in the room.

He knelt in front of the file cabinet. There were fingerprint smudges on the cabinet drawers. Layne started at the top. Inside, he found a treasure trove. Ledger books filled with records of gambling transactions, plus the sales of guns, drugs, and a few other line items recorded in such a way as to make them too vague to discern. Probably human trafficking or worse. Despite both Tilda and Daphne claiming Reds and Union were small-time, Layne seemed to keep finding evidence to the contrary. They had big aspirations, at least.

The second drawer revealed no new information. Same with the third. There was no fourth drawer, so Layne shoved them all closed, sighing.

He sat on the floor next to the bike, staring at the file cabinet. There had to be more than this.

"Okay, Kurt, what have I missed?"

Something caught his eye. Bits of dust and drywall powder were scattered across the floor, but next to the file cabinet, the dust there had streaked as if someone had attempted to clean it and only given it a single swipe with a broom. A ninety-degree arc of less-dusty floor. Subtle, but still noticeable.

Exactly the pattern you'd make if you moved the file cabinet a quarter turn.

He shoved the file cabinet to the side and found a cutout space in the wall behind it and a safe sitting inside that space. Short, about two feet tall and one foot wide. Digital keypad on the front.

Layne knew this model. A Paragon 760E, one of the most commonly sold safes throughout the Middle East and Europe. Not the most secure safe in the world, but not the easiest to crack, either.

He stared at the ten-number keypad on the front. The safe had a sixteen-digit factory override code, and that was all he needed to unlock the thing.

But he couldn't remember it. If he'd had his regular phone, he could log into his home server and retrieve the info, but sitting here, he couldn't remember the code.

Layne practiced a few memory exercises to recall the info. He thought about the last time he'd used that code. There had been a safe owned by a Colorado Springs man who'd changed his personal code one night when drunk and then couldn't remember it. He'd hired Layne to break into his safe. Layne had used the override to solve the man's problem.

Layne pictured himself in that man's bedroom, kneeling in front of the safe, tool belt dangling. There had been a furry cat weaving in and out between his legs as he'd worked on it. He visualized his fingers moving on the keypad.

A bolt of memory appeared. Layne typed in *624887*, then he paused. If the override code was entered incorrectly, even once, the safe locked for good. Only the actual factory that had manufactured it could unlock it at that point.

His hand hovered in the air. He flexed his hand and

blinked a few times. Visualized his fingers gliding over the keys.

Entered *0095647721.*

The red light on the front of the safe winked and then turned green. Layne grinned as he pulled the handle and the safe swung open. Inside, among rolls of cash, some jewelry, and a couple of pistols, he found something unexpected. A notebook detailing the comings and goings of Randall Parrish. Explicit timetables listing where he'd been, times he'd placed phone calls, flights he'd taken.

Layne scoured the flight records and found nothing indicating Randall had been traveling to the Middle East. He did see several flights back and forth between Melbourne and Berlin. Layne recalled his first conversation with Randall the other day, when he'd said he was acting on behalf of a certain European country.

Did Kurt Lawton or his Union buddies think Randall was employed by the Germans? Were they going to use that against him somehow?

Layne flipped the page to find a photo of Randall taped to the inside of the notebook. In the grainy photo, Randall was holding a cell phone to his ear. Below was listed the date and time of the phone call, only one week ago. And below the photo:

Contact: Gerald Ferguson
Berlin
Current: BND
Former CIA? NSA? Find out his angle.

Layne stared at the name. Gerald. In Camberwell, behind

the coffee shop, Randall had been on the phone with someone named *Jerry*.

Same guy? Seemed likely.

Realization dawned. Randall was working with American intelligence via Berlin. Daphne might not even know about it since the organizations often operated in silos. And for whatever reason, this contact in Berlin wanted to make sure Phelps got on that flight to see Abdul Abbad.

That would explain why Randall had given Layne only the bare essentials of intel. To protect whoever was running him from the United States. But none of this info answered the question of why Randall was in this operation to begin with. How Randall was tied to Australia.

Layne checked his watch. Twelve hours until the governor's speech. Time enough to reach the internet café and check out what Phelps was doing today. Layne decided to have one more go at preemptively saving the man's life.

31

ACCORDING TO GOVERNOR Phelps's Wikipedia page, he took a stroll through the Royal Botanic Gardens every morning after breakfast. The gardens were not far from the outdoor venue where Layne had tracked him at the festival the other day and were also adjacent to the mansion where the governor lived. Map searches revealed several pathways into the gardens and just as many exit points. A wide-open place to access the governor.

Which also meant increased security to offset the ease of access.

Sitting at the internet café, Layne checked his watch. He had no idea when "breakfast" was, but it was early enough that Layne thought he could intersect the man's garden jaunt. Maybe even get a few seconds of face time with the governor. A few seconds was all Layne needed.

The confusion on the governor's face yesterday still bothered him. Something about this whole situation wasn't right. Twelve hours away from the governor's speech, he had no concrete plan about what to do later today. No solid fail-safe to keep the governor alive.

Even though he didn't have the time to spare, Layne made another video chat call to Inessa. The video window remained black for several seconds while the call tried to connect. Eventually, after almost a full minute, it morphed into a bright sunny day at the edges, and Inessa's beautiful-yet-stern face filled the middle of the window.

Layne opened his mouth to say hello, but Inessa sighed and handed the phone to Cameron, who was sitting at the top of a playground slide. Red nose and foggy breath pushing out from her tiny mouth.

Layne recognized the plastic playground as the one in the park near Inessa's house.

"Daddy!" Cameron said, her eyes bubbling over with excitement. "Me and Mommy are at the park!"

His daughter's smile erased all the pain in his world. She made everything feel like cartoons and popsicles. Being here, on a job, it was too easy to forget the feelings he had when in close proximity to her.

Layne didn't want to interrupt park time, and he didn't want to hear more snide comments from Inessa, so he kept the conversation brief. Told his daughter a million times he loved her. Promised to call in a couple of hours to read her a story at bedtime.

When the conversation ended, Layne experienced a pang of loneliness like a bullet hole in his chest. With stinging at the corners of his eyes, he cleaned up his activity at the café and headed back toward the South Yarra railway station.

On the train toward downtown, Layne texted his brother, and the message came back:

Randall: *I'm working on recovering the crate we've been having so much trouble with. Have an opening. Want to come with? I could use the backup.*

Layne: *I've got another path. Can you go it alone?*

Randall: *Yeah I'll be okay. What you working on?*

Layne: *A more direct route. Might help or might backfire*

Randall: *That sounds exactly like something you would do.*

Layne: *This shouldn't take long. We can reconnect in a couple hours*

Randall: *My thing might take all day. Will probably turn my phone off or put it on vibrate. Will check in as soon as able, but may not be able to respond immediately.*

Layne: *Okay*

Randall: *If nothing else, I will meet you at the square*

Layne: *North end. I have a good idea where the action will be coming from.*

Randall: *Sounds good. I'm signing off for now.*

Layne slipped his phone back into his pocket and stared out the train window. Trees and houses whipped by in a blur. The train shimmied back and forth as it raised up over a bridge, chugging and grunting to gain elevation. Large billboards pushed up against yellowing buildings. One bright billboard proclaimed: *Buy Your Kids a Future. Buy Australian-Made.*

He didn't like being unable to contact Randall for hours, but he wasn't surprised. Randall had always been the lone wolf type. The impulsive type. He would show up at Fed Square with only seconds to spare, his hair mussed and a mischievous grin on his face. He would claim, in hindsight, that he always knew things would work out and saving the day was easy. Drove Layne crazy how his older brother could live by the seat of his pants for his entire life and somehow get away with it.

Layne exited at Richmond Station and crossed the street to cut through a park toward the botanic gardens. The midmorning heat already leaving him drained and heavy. Sweat slicked his back and thighs.

He raced over a bridge to cross the Yarra River and found himself at the edge of the park. A lush green environment smacked him in the face. Trees and plants Layne had never seen before, like the cover of an Isaac Asimov book set on a faraway planet. Strange bird sounds echoed through the air.

But what worried Layne wasn't the alien flora and fauna. He noted a few security guards stationed in an arc. That meant the governor was here, out for his morning walk, somewhere nearby.

Layne considered his options. After the incident at the Camberwell station yesterday, if any of these guards saw him, they wouldn't hesitate to slam him to the ground, Taser him, or maybe even put a bullet in his brain. He'd considered donning the body armor, but it was much too warm out to conceal it under a jacket. Approaching the governor wearing a lot of clothing was a surefire way to end up dead as a suspicious character. He hadn't even brought a gun because of how bad it would look to be caught with one.

And Layne anticipated a 90 percent chance of being caught today. That was an acceptable risk for what he was about to do. What mattered was how much alone time he could gain with the governor before the inevitable descent of the security team.

He hung back under a tree with spidery limbs jutting out like a curtain. Knelt, waiting for a chance to spot the governor. Did the presence of these guards mean he was nearby, or were they spaced out along the property? How long until they were on the move, scouting in a wider-area sweep?

Maybe waiting here was a mistake.

He slid left out from under the tree and inspected the nearby grounds. A small pond shrouded by trees stood off to the north. Behind him, the south opened out to Richmond Station. To the west and east sat hillsides that descended into fields of flowers. None of it seemed like a good place to hide and grab the governor as he strolled by.

Layne continued to slink left, keeping an eye on the one bodyguard within range. The man had his back to Layne, staring out over the pond. As Layne crept along, he spied the far edge of the pond, where a bridge connected two sides of a slim point over the water.

That was the optimal place. Under the bridge, he could wait unseen. The problem was getting there. Security and lots of open space between here and the destination.

He crept, low to the ground, to the edge of the trees on his left. There was a break in the coverage for about sixty feet until he could enter the shade of the additional trees at the periphery. To maintain overhead tree-shadow coverage, he'd have to keep a wide arc. Swing far away from that bridge and then double back. But he'd be safely hidden in the shadows the whole way. The main problem was what to do if the governor made an appearance before Layne could move into position.

He studied the open space between the trees where he was aiming. A single security guard hovered near that far cluster of trees. He stood opposite the other security guard back at the edge of the pond.

Layne kept him in visual contact in case anything about his position changed.

After a brief silence, the guard by the trees lifted a hand to the coiled earpiece jutting out like a pig's tail. Nodding. He was getting a message. Then he raised a walkie-talkie and spoke into it, and made a hand signal toward the other man.

Layne's pulse raced. Governor Phelps was en route to this area. Had to be. Still enough time to make it to the bridge?

The man near the trees turned inward, away from Layne.

He took his shot. Abandoned the trees and raced across the field of flowers, his sights set on the bridge at the far end of the lake. He met the trees nearby and came to a full stop when Governor Phelps and that same slicked-back hair giant from before emerged on the other side of the bridge.

The governor looked puzzled. The security guard's mouth dropped open. Only the sound of chirping birds filled the air.

Layne had maybe three or four seconds. "Governor Phelps, has anyone warned you about the assassination attempt on your life tonight?"

The governor's head cocked. His forehead wrinkled.

"Grab him!" said the security guard. In a flash, three more guards came out of the trees.

"Skip your speech tonight," Layne said as arms snatched him. He resisted the urge to pull free or throw any punches.

Eyes on the governor, trying to reinforce his last message. He opened his mouth to say more, but a fist cracked him across the jaw.

32

TILDA MACMILLAN SWUNG OPEN THE DOOR TO THE Richmond police station and strutted inside. She slipped a tissue from her purse and dabbed the perspiration on her brow. This heat would be the death of her, for sure.

Two officers stood behind a glassed-in booth at the other end of the room. One of them caught her eye.

"Evening, miss. Can I help you?"

Tilda approached the desk and opened her ASIO badge. She set it on the booth's counter and tapped the top of it with one finger. "You have a man in custody named Layne Parrish. I'd like to see him."

The two cops shared a look, hesitating.

"Is there a problem?"

"Not at all, ma'am," said one of them. "It's just that this bloke attempted to assault Governor Phelps. We've been waiting all day for the chief to get here since this suspect is lacking a passport or any ID at all. We're not supposed to do anything with him until the chief arrives."

Tilda, still holding her badge open, pushed it across the

counter, closer to their faces. "And I'm telling you that I'm here to collect him. I don't give two shits what your chief does or doesn't do, and I don't want to hear any more about it. Now, on you go. Let me inside."

One of the cops jumped to his feet. "Of course, ma'am. Please, follow me."

The cop pressed a buzzer to open a nearby door, exited the booth, and then he opened the door for her. Led her down a hallway, past an open room buzzing with activity. Uniformed police, detectives, and other personnel going about their jobs. The cop turned at the end of the room and escorted her to the holding area. A cluster of six cells in a line.

Layne was sitting alone in a holding cell, knees to his chest. Aside from the cot, he had a combo dunny/sink and a Bible. Staring down at his forearms, holding them together. She noted two matching tattoos, both fat little cherubs. One seemed devilish, tinted with red, and the other tinted with blue, more angelic. He was studying them.

He looked up at her, a giant purple bruise on his cheek. Lip split, dried blood on his chin. His expression didn't change at the sight of her.

"Did you have to rough him up?" Tilda said.

"No, ma'am. That wasn't us. Governor Phelps's security team delivered him to us like that. We offered him medical attention, but he's been noncooperative."

"I see. You can leave us now. And unlock his cell, please."

The cop hurried off to a panel and pressed a button. Layne's cell door slid open, but he made no motion to stand or move.

Tilda swept into the cell and lowered herself to a knee to be on his same level. "Hello."

He nodded, and she could hear the creak of his bruised jaw as he opened his mouth. "Hi."

"You caused a bit of a shitstorm, old friend."

"I didn't think they'd arrest me. I was only anticipating a beating."

"You anticipated wrong."

He cleared his throat. "What time is it?"

"Just before five."

He scowled. "I definitely missed the bedtime window."

"The what?"

"It doesn't matter now. We're running out of time. Something is wrong here, Tilda. The governor has no idea there's going to be an attempt on his life tonight."

She reached out and patted his knee. "I told you, mate. There will be no attempt on the governor's life. It's all smoke and mirrors, set up by your brother."

"Why would he do that?"

Tilda shrugged. "I have no idea, but we're working on it. All you'll do by galloping into this situation is put yourself in harm's way, for no good reason."

"You know I'm bad at sitting on the sidelines."

She stood. "True enough. Come on, follow me."

He groaned as he stood, placing a hand on his lower back, and winced as he limped out of the cell.

"They really did a number on you," she said.

"The governor's men take his personal space very seriously."

She put a hand on his shoulder as she guided him through the hallway and out into the lobby. Layne had to sign a couple of documents for a prisoner transfer. Tilda didn't care; whatever they had to tell their chief was fine with her.

Out onto Flinders Street, Layne and Tilda watched the sun fading into the lower sky. Trams and trains and buses and cars nearby filled the street with the energetic sound of motion. But Layne seemed still, a statue against all the activity.

"When you were in Uluru with your family," Layne said, "did you eat crocodile? I saw that on a TV show once."

She laughed. "No, but I had it when I was younger. It's like rubber. Something you would only eat if you were desperate."

"I see." He paused, chest heaving. "Is Governor Phelps a good man?"

Tilda shrugged. "I reckon so. He's not one of those career-politician types, or at least, he wasn't always. Phelps was a tradie who saved money and got a loan to open his first business. He played that well and made some more money, then college in America, then went into politics. As far as I can see, he's done good things. He's worse than some and better than others. You know how that goes."

Across the street, a young mother corralled a toddler with one hand while she held an infant in a sling across her chest. The toddler danced along the sidewalk, resisting all attempts by her mother to hold her hand. Layne smiled at her, a wistful look in his eyes.

"I hear you don't have a passport," Tilda said.

Layne nodded.

"I can help you. You know Daphne Kurek is using you, right?"

He nodded again.

"If you want, I can get you out of the country. Boat to Tasmania, then on a cargo plane to Los Angeles by morning."

His eyes dropped to his shoes, and he said nothing as his shoulders rose and fell.

"You could be back with your daughter by tomorrow night. Well, actually, through the magic of the international date line, you'd be back with your daughter in a few hours."

She could see the wheels turning in his mind. Still, all he said was, "I don't know."

She handed him a slip of paper. "Have a think on it. Call this number if you change your mind, yeah? The boat leaves at nine tonight, so don't dally."

33

TILDA OPENED THE DOOR TO THE LITTLE INDIA restaurant and navigated through the tables as the glorious scent of curry washed over her. Stomach rumbling. Little India had the best ratio of Indian patrons to white patrons, and that's how you know it's a quality ethnic restaurant. After this meeting, Tilda planned to get a korma to go. Maybe some naan if they had it fresh.

She scoured the restaurant and located the lanky brunette at the back, drumming her fingers on a glass carafe of water. Tilda sat down across from her. "The vindaloo is excellent."

Serena shook her head. "Not hungry."

"If I might say, dear, you would enjoy Melbourne a lot more if you weren't so sullen all the time. Amazing coffee, unique art galleries. Can't be beat."

"I'm not sullen. I'm focused."

Tilda shrugged. "If you say so."

"Where is Boy Scout?"

"I just sprang him from jail. He's not in good shape. Phelps's people roughed him up quite a bit."

"What's his next move? Any hint?"

"No idea. I offered him a chance to get out of the country on a boat to Tassie and then a plane home. One quick phone call, and she'll be apples."

Serena's eyes widened. "You did what?"

Tilda resisted the urge to tell this young operative that she wished Layne would accept. Wished he would get the hell away from here and not involve himself in any of it. But to keep up appearances, she said, "Oh, don't fret. He won't take me up on my offer. He won't be able to resist chasing after his brother."

Serena pursed her lips. "You seem sure of that."

"I've known him for a long time. We worked together in Singapore on a job, long before either of us had any wrinkles or made noises when we sat down or stood up. He can't resist plucking the damsel from the train tracks."

Serena frowned at this. Perhaps she thought herself a "liberated" woman, and the *train tracks* comment triggered her social justice buttons. Tilda cared not if Serena was offended, however.

"You and Daphne work well together?" Tilda asked.

"She's excellent at what she does."

"But you're so young, what do you have to compare it to?"

Now Serena looked quite angry. "I'm not as young as I look. Maybe I haven't been doing this as long as you, but this isn't my first time out of the gate."

Tilda lifted her hands in surrender. Figured she'd better back off before the young lass decided to flip the table over and cause a scene. She lowered her head and filled a glass with water from the carafe.

Neither of them said anything for a moment, and Tilda studied Serena's face. "What's on your mind?"

The younger woman hesitated, then leaned forward. "It's not my place to say."

"But you have doubts, yeah?"

"I don't understand why we need proof about Randall Parrish. Why we can't just take him out and be done with it. Why would we let a threat walk around unchecked, with *carte blanche* to do whatever he pleases?"

Tilda considered her answer before speaking. "It's not so simple. You spend months planning an op, and it's over in a day or three. Then you might spend years defending your actions, wishing you'd done it differently, endlessly hashing it out in meetings behind closed doors. Measure twice and cut once. That's what my grandad used to say."

Serena's jaw tensed, which made Tilda grin.

"You're passionate," Tilda said, substituting *passionate* for the word she wanted to say, which was *inexperienced*. "And you're not used to second-guessing your decisions. It's all part of that lovely, red bureaucratic tape we all have to bind ourselves with in this business."

Serena poured water from the carafe into her glass, then she ran fingers up and down the side for a few moments. Red nail polish. Fingers clicking as they danced along the surface of the glass. "Maybe so. But there are too many things about this that don't make sense."

"And that's the way it is, dear. Those of us who are good at this don't always know the way to go, but we get good at pretending that the outcome was the thing we intended all along."

34

LAYNE WANDERED DOWN FLINDERS WITH THE PIECE of paper in his hand. On it, a phone number to call Tilda's contact so he could escape. Leave the country for good. A boat, then a plane, then another plane, and then home. Then he could swoop up his daughter and plant a million kisses on her face. Nestle next to her in bed and listen to the thumping of her miniature heart.

He didn't know if he'd ever wanted something so badly in his life.

As he powered on his phone, a slew of text messages from Randall filled the feature phone's little screen. All of them begging Layne to reach out. He'd been stuck in that jail cell for several hours, with no lifeline to the outside world. He didn't even know how Tilda had found out about it.

Layne dialed the number.

"Where the hell have you been?" Randall whispered, breathless, as soon as he picked up.

"Jail."

"Oh. That sounds about right. Anything I need to know?"

"Not really. All that matters is my operation from earlier today failed in a big way."

"Roger that. There are still a few cards we can play. How quickly can you get to St. Kilda?"

"I'm not sure," Layne said. "How far is that from downtown?"

"It's about a half hour by train from the CBD." Randall paused, sucking on his teeth. "It's too far. Never mind, little brother; I'm about to handle this by myself. No sniper rifles, no sniper."

"What are you going to do?"

"I'm following a truck I think is carrying their payload."

"You have any backup at all?"

"Nope. Don't need it. Proceed with your plan at Fed Square; but you'll only need to be a last-resort fail-safe. I'm going to end this now. Expect a text message from me as soon as it's done, then you can buy the drinks when we celebrate."

The call ended with a click, and Layne stared at the phone. He became aware of the people moving around him on the sidewalk, cars rushing by, the water in the river below. Somewhere, a busker played didgeridoo.

He strolled a few feet forward, eyes on the phone. Mind swimming.

Next to a nearby bridge, a street vendor pulled down canvases from easels. Pictures of the river and of the Melbourne skyline. The vendor, a gray-headed and shriveled man with paint on his clothes and face, lifted a hand to Layne. "You after a painting, mate?"

"No thanks."

"It's closing time. Dirt cheap."

"Sorry, but I don't have any place to put it."

The man shrugged. "Such is life, eh?"

He turned back to his activities, folding the easels and packing them into a large rubber storage bin. Layne waited another moment, watching. Then he descended a ramp next to the water and strolled along the Yarra for a block or two. He came to another bridge and found a bench, so he sat. His whole body felt like a single, throbbing ache.

The light breeze off the river misted a cool dampness across his face. He sighed, letting the sounds of birds gliding across the water soothe him. Two young ladies jogged by, having a breathless conversation as their arms and legs pumped. They paused their conversation for a moment to smile at him, and Layne lifted a hand in reply.

He could go home. Today. Just a phone call.

But if he did that, he was possibly leaving the governor to die. Possibly abandoning Randall, who may or may not have something to do with the governor's possible assassination.

No. Layne no longer followed that narrative. Whether Daphne was manipulating him or had simply received bad intel, he didn't know. And it didn't matter.

At least one life, and maybe several others, were at stake.

Layne lifted the paper and read over the phone number scrawled across it in black ink. Ten digits for a way out of here. He gripped the phone in his other hand.

35

SERENA CAUGHT UP TO LAYNE AS HE MOPED DOWN Flinders Street. Tilda had been right; the governor's people had beat the shit out of him. She wondered if he'd even put up a fight.

She also didn't know whether she would have stopped him from approaching the governor if she hadn't lost him in South Yarra earlier today.

This man, the one she'd heard so much about over the last couple of years, didn't seem in full control of his faculties. Didn't seem like one of the government's top operatives over the last fifteen years. Seemed to be a mess, actually. Sometimes he was clever and ruthless. Sometimes he was befuddled and slow.

If the best and brightest eventually lost their skills, what would happen to her when *she* turned forty? Would they send her off with a cake and a watch and a house by Lake Tahoe? Get a job working as a security consultant for a Fortune 500 company?

Daphne and others in the organization talked little about

what happened to the older operatives when they were no longer useful. Likely, that was by design.

Her phone dinged, so she slipped back across the street and answered it. Daphne's number on the caller ID.

"Yes, ma'am?"

"Are you in position?"

"I'm following him right now. He was released from holding a few minutes ago."

"I'm sending a team to the assumed location. You should be there when they arrive, regardless of what he does."

Serena paused, considering. "I would advise against it."

"Why is that?"

"I think we're going to spook the snipers. Maybe even spook Boy Scout. If this assassination attempt does happen, I think you should leave it to me. I can do this. I can handle this."

Their phone conversation went silent as Serena watched Layne ramble down a walkway, having a chat with a street artist as he broke down his mobile shop. The man tried fruitlessly to sell Layne a painting.

"Fine," Daphne said. "I will let you have autonomy on the ground. But if this goes south, I'm holding you responsible."

Serena hitched a breath. She had not expected Daphne to cave like this. The mission protocol wouldn't allow her to engage solo, not with so much on the line.

What kind of game was Control playing?

Daphne cleared her throat. "But you *will* stay on Layne, you *will* find out what role he intends to play, and you *will* keep the governor safe. You have twenty minutes to find a solution. Am I making myself clear?"

"Clear. I have to sign off. Boy Scout is on the move."

Serena ended the call as Daphne was beginning to say

something else. She wouldn't be happy about that, but Serena didn't care. She couldn't lose Layne now.

The end of the conversation had rattled her. There had to be a good reason for Daphne to act that way, but what could it be?

Layne descended a ramp and spent a few minutes sitting by the water, staring out over it. Then he lurched to his feet and continued walking. A block later, he entered the National Gallery of Victoria, an art museum at the north end of Fed Square.

She hustled along after him. Waited a full minute before cracking the door to find a dark lobby inside. The clock on the wall promised the gallery would close in about fifteen minutes. She checked the gun in the concealed holster, making sure the safety was off and wouldn't catch on her shirt if she had to draw. She visualized whipping her hand back to snatch it. Nothing she hadn't done hundreds or thousands of times before, but it never hurt to be prepared.

There was no ticket taker at the lobby and no other people present. The silence of the room bothered her. No Layne. She ventured a few tentative steps toward a black curtain, which she assumed led into the gallery proper.

At the curtain, she reached out one hand and swept it back. On the other side, dimly lit paintings covered the walls, little wall plaques next to each one. But no people.

A hand grabbed her from behind. Jerked her back, so she was now off-balance. Another hand quickly slid under her shirt and stole her pistol.

She tried to latch on to anything nearby as she was dragged to her left, through a door. Her hands couldn't find purchase to stop her assailant's momentum. She ground her feet into the floor to regain her footing, but she had no leverage.

Strong hands jammed her up against a door, bumping her head. She blinked a few times before she could see the shape in front of her.

Layne Parrish, holding her pistol.

He ejected the chambered round and then popped out the mag. He shoved it into his back pocket and held out the pistol to her, butt-first.

"I can't have you shooting me," he said, "but I have no intention of stealing your sidearm. If you have a spare magazine on you, please do not make a move for it. I'll be forced to break your jaw."

He didn't seem befuddled or slow now. He had a cold calculation in his eyes, despite the bumps and bruises on his face.

She accepted the gun and slid it back into the holster concealed beneath her shirt. Gave him a blank stare.

"You've been following me all week," he said. "I've been calling you Shadow. What's your name?"

She paused, considering. Then decided it didn't matter. "Serena."

"Good, Serena. I know why you've been following me, and you should know I don't blame you for doing your job. But I would like to know why you didn't take the shot yesterday when we were in Camberwell."

"I didn't have permission."

"If you'd had permission, would you have done it?"

She bit her lip. "Yes. I would have taken out your brother. Probably not you."

"And why is that?"

"You don't know this, Layne Parrish, but I've known all

about you for years. I studied you. All of your assignments. Your successes, your failures. I know all of it."

"But you did have the authority to take me out if you'd wanted to? As an acceptable mission parameter?"

She nodded.

"Do you know an agent named Gerald Ferguson, or Jerry Ferguson, based in Germany?"

"Never heard of him. He CIA? NSA? FBI?"

"I don't know. I think my brother has been feeding him intel about Abbad. I'm not sure why he's doing it, though."

"Ask Control."

Layne shook his head. "I don't want to ask her. Do you understand why?"

Slowly she nodded. "I do."

"I'm not sure if this Jerry Ferguson figures into things, but it could be another piece of this puzzle."

She shrugged. "Yeah, could be. I've only been around for a few years, so I don't know everyone."

Something in his face changed. "You took my job when I retired."

"That's right."

"Then you must be smart enough to know something isn't right here. This whole thing feels off."

Serena averted her eyes but only for a moment. "You're right. Daphne hasn't been straight with me, and it's driving me crazy."

"That's pretty much par for the course when it comes to Daphne."

A pause floated in the air, neither of them speaking.

"What do you want to do?" she said.

He checked his watch. "In about fifteen minutes, Governor Phelps is due to give a speech across the street at

Fed Square. I think this Reds gang might put a sniper up on the roof. I know a good way to access the atrium roof so we can have the best vantage point. Want to come with me?"

She let the question hang in the air for a few beats and then crossed her arms. "Can I have my pistol magazine back, please?"

36

LAYNE AND SERENA TRAVELED EAST ON FLINDERS, PAST Fed Square, a block down to Russell Street. A snaking maze of train tracks exiting the station to worm out into the rest of the city. After the bridge over the tracks, Layne waved her on as he hopped over the barrier to the ground below.

Serena looked at him funny, but Layne didn't bother to explain. He lowered himself down the side of the barrier and to the ground. Snatched the duffel bag. Plenty of pedestrians traversed the sidewalks, but he figured they wouldn't see him down here, fifteen feet below them.

Serena climbed down after him and put her hands on her hips. "When did you stash that?"

"Late last night," he said. When she frowned, he added, "You're a good shadow, but you're not perfect. I assumed I'd get in some trouble after visiting the governor. Always have a backup plan."

He withdrew the body armor, the two pistols, and extra magazines. Considered taking the shotgun, but he had no way to conceal it. The body armor made his polo shirt bulge, but no use in worrying about that. Would have to hope no one paid too much attention to him.

He offered the body armor to her, but she shook her head. "It'll only slow me down."

"Suit yourself."

Layne's phone dinged, and he raised it to see Randall's number. "Yes?"

Out of breath, his brother said, "It didn't work. I couldn't stop them. The truck lost me on a side street."

"I understand."

"I'll get there as fast as I can, but I'm at least a half hour out. You'll have to take care of this until I can get there. So sorry, little brother."

Layne looked at his phone as the call ended.

"What was that?" Serena said. "Problem?"

"It's happening. We have to move now and tag our shooters."

"What are you thinking for when we get there?" she asked.

"I think we're going to walk out onto that atrium and find two shooters lying prone near the edge that faces the stage. Maybe three. If we don't find anyone there, we'll be able to spot wherever they are hiding from that position. How are you with a pistol at medium-to-long range?"

"Very good."

He checked his watch. Ten minutes until the speech. "Let's get to the atrium."

They rushed back along the tracks to the rear of Fed Square. Scores of people were converging on that location, filing through the opening to the west, under the atrium. With Serena on his heels, Layne dashed back into the NGV, at the northern end of the atrium area.

The gallery was now closed, but the front door had remained open. An emergency exit sign covered the door to the right. Layne squinted to examine it. Alarmed, connected to the building's main power.

After a moment, he knew what to do.

"You don't happen to have superglue or epoxy, do you?"

She patted her pockets. "No, but I have tape. A few inches of electrical tape."

"That should be good enough," he said as he took it from her open palm. At the top of the emergency exit door, he identified two magnetic sensors. One on the actual door and a matching one on the doorframe above it. The alarm would trigger when they separated from each other as the door opened, so Layne had to make sure they stayed together. He reached up and tugged on one to detach it from the door, then he taped it to the one positioned on the doorjamb.

His hands pressed easily and opened the door. The strips stayed together, so the alarm did not sound.

"Clever," Serena said.

"We got lucky. This is a very outdated way of alarming a door."

They both drew handguns as they entered the dark stairwell. Only a smattering of running lights near their feet provided any illumination. With his Beretta pointed low, Layne climbed the first flight of stairs. Based on the building's height, he figured they had four more flights to go.

First floor, he could still hear the PA system outside and the low roar of the crowd. A woman was speaking over the sound system.

At the second floor, Layne could only hear the rumble of the building's air conditioner. Same at the third and the fourth.

Then they reached a door marked *External Access*. The roof.

"You ready?" he asked.

"Want me to go first?"

He tapped a thumb on his vest.

"That won't help you much if they shoot you between the eyes," she said.

"I'll take my chances."

Serena nodded, so Layne raised his pistol and kicked open the door. Jumped outside.

The roof of the NGV was a maze of air conditioners and banks of solar panels, angled like rows of corn. A hundred feet to their left, the arch of the glass curved over the atrium. Up at this height, a vortex of hot wind swirled, pilfering the moisture from his skin.

Serena pulled even with him. She tilted her head at the far side of the atrium, then flicked her chin toward him and to the other end. He nodded, and they set off in their separate ways.

Layne snaked through two air conditioners out into the rows of solar panels. The purplish-red sky above sent a little glare off the panels, and he squinted to maintain his developing night vision.

He raised the pistol when he had the atrium in sight. A curve of glass, connecting this building to the one next to it. He moved deliberately, checking left and right each time he came to a break in the solar panels. If Layne and Serena had done their job and masked their approach, there would be no ambush. But aside from the expected one or two snipers, no telling how many others they might find up here.

Layne reached the end of the solar panel rows without spotting a single combatant. He stepped out onto the glass atrium. The lights from below shone up through it as the sun plummeted behind the skyscrapers to the west.

In another fifty feet, he reached the highest point of the atrium curve and gained an elevated view of the ACMI building on the other side. More solar panels, air-conditioner units, and some vent piping.

There was no sniper on that building or anywhere on the atrium. He chewed on his lip and let his eyes scour over every inch of the rooftop again. Maybe he'd missed something.

Serena appeared on the far side, and he waved a hand to catch her attention. He pointed past the atrium to the ACMI building on the other side. She nodded and headed in that direction. Still needed to check it. Maybe the sniper had crouched behind one of those angular solar panels.

They both began the descent over the atrium curve's apex to the other side. Layne looked down through the glass below at the dense crowd meandering, taking tables at restaurants, or passing through to grab a seat to hear the speech.

On the other side of the atrium, Layne and Serena met. He flicked his pistol at the banks of solar panels. She frowned, and he could tell what she was thinking. But there *had* to be something here. Had to be some sign of the Reds' plan.

They stuck together this time, moving as one through the rows of solar panels. Down one, then back, until they'd made their way along four separate paths. No sniper.

The only thing left was a small door in a standing structure, the size of an outhouse, jutting out of the building beyond the solar panel farm. Roof access for the ACMI building.

Serena pointed at the door. Layne raised his pistol at it, and they crept forward. He felt his chest constricting. This had to be the place.

Near the door, Layne jumped to the other side. Beretta up, finger on the trigger.

No one there.

"What the hell?" he said.

They rushed toward the edge of the ACMI building. Layne squinted at the rooftops of the surrounding buildings, but he saw nothing at all out of the ordinary. Not even a single person or object that seemed like it didn't belong.

They gazed down at the square to find hundreds of people in folding chairs, sitting opposite a stage. On that stage was a podium and a microphone, but no Governor Phelps standing behind it.

Layne checked his watch as the sun finally reached ground level in the west. The time ticked to 7:04 p.m. The speech should have started already.

"What's happening?" Serena said. "Where's our shooter? Where's the governor?"

Layne shook his head. Had he been wrong? Was it not a sniper? His eyes trailed over the crowd. What if the Reds were going to use a bomb instead? There were enough people gathered here to cause some serious carnage.

But where was the governor?

"I don't know where he is," Layne said.

A woman in a business suit strutted across the stage toward the center. A few people clapped as she cleared her throat into the microphone. "Ladies and gentlemen, I'm very sorry, but the speech has been canceled for this evening. Please go about your normal business. Again, I apologize."

Her words sank in as Layne felt a lump form in his throat

and a headache pulse at the back of his head. There was only one possible explanation. Everything came together like a bolt of thunder. He understood.

Randall.

Randall had done this. He'd orchestrated everything and pulled all the strings.

"There is no speech because this is a decoy. It was always a decoy."

The weight of his failure hit him like a sledgehammer to the face. His body felt heavy. Knees weak. He sat on the atrium as the air conditioners whirred around him. Heard the distant rabble of people talking and walking. His head throbbed, the ache worming down into his neck and shoulders.

A memory stood up inside Layne's head. Insistent. Layne was ten years old, his brother fifteen. Both of them playing *Monopoly* with their parents. Layne barely old enough to grasp the game but knowing he wanted to win. And then, going bankrupt two hours into it, the first one in the family to lose. The way Randall had smirked at him as Layne's last dollar disappeared after he landed on Randall's Baltic Avenue. And Layne knowing, somehow, that his brother had been cheating at the game. Knowing it but being unable to prove it.

"What do you want to do?" Serena said, frowning down at Layne.

He wanted to tell her to do nothing because there was nothing to do. They were beaten. He'd made the poor decision to trust his brother, despite knowing better from the start.

Heat from the glass atrium warmed his legs. The light from below highlighted the tats on his arms. Years and years of tattoo parlor torture to decorate his skin a little at a time. His eyes rested on the cherub with the light blue tint.

When Layne looked up at Serena, something happened. An idea formed in the back of his mind. A possible answer and a way to regain the upper hand.

It was a long shot, yes, but there was a chance. He slipped out his phone and struggled to remember the number. Since he had no idea what time it was on the east coast of America right now, he had no choice but to roll the dice and hope Harry was awake.

PART III

THIEVES AND PALADINS

37

HAROLD BOUKADAKIS COULDN'T SLEEP. AND NOT only last night. For the last several nights, he'd awoken multiple times, had stared at the ceiling, turned over and over. Restless and irritable. Stressed about not being able to sleep, which in itself kept him from falling back asleep.

So tonight, after the fifth time he'd woken up and tapped his phone to check the time, he'd given up. Had quietly slinked out of the bed so he wouldn't wake either his wife or the snoring border collie who shared the bed with them. He took his phone and closed the door behind him as he crossed the living room and settled into his home office.

He knew what the problem was. Worry. A general, pulsing anxiety that he couldn't shake. It had been with him for a week so far and would remain with him for another week until his three partners came back into town. Only then could they finish what they'd started.

Even so, there seemed to be no way out of this alive.

Harry sat down at his desk and stared at the piece of paper. A stats sheet for a level fifteen cleric in tabletop

Dungeons and Dragons. The constitution, dexterity, and charisma stats were all excellent, but his strength and wisdom attributes were lacking. The real problem, though, was the current level of hit points.

Before Jeremy, Ethan, and Danny had left town for their conference, they had been in the middle of a campaign. In the depths of the hill giant's castle, Harry's cleric had opened a locked door that had been booby-trapped. A crossbow triggered by a string attached to the door had impaled Harry and left his cleric with almost no hit points. Right after that, his three partners had paused the game so they could go home and get ready for their trip.

One roll of the dice, and the cleric stood on the precipice of death, frozen in paper limbo.

And now Harry had been stewing over it for a week. Should have made Ethan's thief or Danny's paladin open the door. Harry wasn't supposed to be frontline! He was a cleric, damn it. Clerics were supposed to hang back and cast spells to protect and heal the rest of the party. Not charge ahead and open risky doors to take crossbow bolts to the chest.

Harry sighed and tapped the piece of paper. This was a problem.

His phone lit up and then skittered across the desk. He snatched it with a tired grip and held it up to his face. The brightness of the screen made him wince, and he needed a couple of seconds to regain focus. When he could see, the Caller ID showed *unavailable* as the origin.

Normally Harry did not answer phone calls if he didn't recognize the number. So many damn robocalls and solicitors these days. Harry's circle of friends and family was very small, and the majority of the people in the world he talked to on a regular basis lived in this house with him.

Still, he pressed the button to accept the call.

"Hold on," he whispered as he crept back out into the living room. The window in front faced east, a meager Virginia sunrise beginning to lighten the sky from black to purple.

He tiptoed over to the door across the room and slid it open. Inside, his son was still sleeping, a comic book resting on his chest as it rose and fell. Harry shut the door and lifted the phone to his ear.

"Who is this?" he said as he strolled into the living room. "Do you have any idea what time it is?"

The voice on the other end was scratchy but understandable. "Harry? It's me."

Took him a full second for the *me* comment to register. When it did, Harry drew in a breath. "Layne Parrish? Is that seriously you?"

"Hey, man. Long time no see."

"Holy crap, Layne. Why the hell are you calling me so early?"

Layne sighed. "I'm sorry, but this is an emergency. I need you to do something for me, and it's kinda, sorta what you might call not exactly ethical."

Harry glanced first at the room where his son was sleeping and then back at the door to his bedroom, to where his wife and dog were still dormant. "Hang on," he said and then held the phone against his chest as he crossed the living room back into his home office. Once that door had shut, he held the phone to his ear again. "What's going on?"

"I'm going to text you a phone number. I need you to trace it and give me a real-time location that can be updated on the fly. Can you do that?"

"Theoretically, sure, I can do that."

"I'm in Australia. Does that make a difference?"

Harry resisted the urge to ask why retired Layne was in Australia. He knew better than to ask too many questions when it came to Layne Parrish. "It does make a difference, yeah. When do you need this?"

"Right now. Like right this second."

"Well, I can start to work on it now, but it'll probably take me a couple of hours. Maybe more. My VPN has been acting up lately, so I'll probably have to go into the office."

"No, don't do that. No one can know about this."

Harry raised his free arm in exasperation. "You're not giving me a lot to work with here."

"I know. And I'm really sorry. This is important, man. I wouldn't bug you if it wasn't."

Harry sighed as he sat down at his desk and thumbed the power button on his desktop tower. "Okay, fine. Send me the number."

38

LAYNE, HEART PUMPING SO FAST HE FELT A LITTLE dizzy, ended the call and immediately texted the phone number to Harry in Virginia. Then he took two pieces of nicotine gum from their packages and chewed them both at once. Made his throat tingle.

Serena met his eyes. "Randall?"

He nodded.

"Are you sure?"

"No," he said. "But it makes the most sense. He's spent this entire week pointing toward this gang, the Reds, that they would conduct an assassination attempt on Phelps here tonight. To push me and everyone who might be interested into gathering at Fed Square. A friend of mine tried to convince me there was no assassination attempt, but I didn't listen."

"Meanwhile, they snatch him and take him somewhere else when no one is looking."

"Seems that way. Looks like you should have taken that shot yesterday."

Serena frowned. "This whole thing has been one big soup of sloppy intel. That's not your fault."

He slipped the phone back into his pocket. "I'm not sure about that. I shouldn't have trusted him. That's on me."

"None of that matters anymore. What do we do right now?"

"My contact is going to track Randall's phone. It might take him thirty minutes or more to establish the connection. Until then, I know a place we can investigate. It's not a guarantee, but it's the best option on the table."

They extracted themselves from the rooftop of the building and scrambled down the stairs back into the NGV. The front door was now locked, so they opted to leave by the service entrance on the side.

They joined a stream of people wandering out of Fed Square. Confused about the lack of a speech. Shrugging, going back to their bars and restaurants, filtering out to Flinders Street to board trains. Not a general panic because this whole thing had been designed to keep the public in the dark.

But why? Why the hell would Randall Parrish want to kidnap the governor of Victoria? Could Randall actually care about disrupting the governor's plans to meet with Abdul Abbad in Pakistan? And if not, what else could it be?

They had no leads and no compass.

Layne and Serena returned to his duffel bag. This time, Layne would definitely take the shotgun. He removed black jeans, a long-sleeve black shirt, and a tin of shoe polish.

"Do you have dark clothes with you?" he asked her.

She put her hands on her hips. "I do."

He swabbed black shoe polish on his face and handed the tin to Serena. "You come by train, or do you have a car?"

She pointed at a Toyota Camry parked across the street.

"You want to drive, I assume?" she said.

He nodded, and she tossed him the keys.

As soon as his seat belt was on, they headed toward the Reds' building on Bourke Street. He drove in the wrong lane for a few seconds at first. The steering wheel living on the other side made him reevaluate everything he thought he knew about street lane perspective. But like riding a bike, it came back to him in short order. Serena bracing a hand against the window and gasping helped pull him back to reality.

"You going to tell me where we're going?" she asked.

"Possible hideout." He glanced at her out of the corner of his eye. "Why are you helping me? Why did you agree to throw away your mission?"

"I didn't throw anything away. My mission was to keep an eye on you and Randall and to take him out if you weren't willing or able to do it."

"And take me out, too?"

She pursed her lips but nodded. "If I knew for certain you were compromised. Sorry about that."

He waved a dismissive hand. "I understand."

"Regardless, the mission parameters have changed somewhat, but I'm still within the core mandate."

"Daphne won't be happy with you."

"That's par for the course. Don't think I've had an op yet that didn't end with me being dressed down in her office." She let her eyes drift out the window as a tram chugged along the center of the street. "Plus, all that watching was boring as hell."

Layne grinned, despite the tension in his neck. He remembered feeling the exact same way when he'd been her age. The stakeouts so lengthy, he wished someone would start shooting, so he'd have a reason to cop an adrenaline buzz. "We're going to the Reds' hideout on Bourke Street. I have a feeling we'll find the governor there."

"How certain are you?"

He shrugged. "Not very."

She nodded and spent the rest of the car ride loading various weapons, ejecting magazines, testing the springiness of the loaded bullets. Layne observed out of the corner of his eye. For someone so young, she seemed to know exactly what she was doing.

When she reached into the back seat for new clothes and changed in the passenger seat, he did try to avert his eyes. Stripping down to her underwear in front of him didn't seem to bother her at all.

Once they were at Bourke Street, across from the McDonalds, Layne eased into a curbside parking spot. He eyed the street, and there was a handful of pedestrians about but not many. A nearby streetlamp flickered and then died, so he figured they could chart a path underneath that one and avoid any prying eyes.

"What's the play?" she asked.

"There's a roll-up bay door across the street, behind the building. We enter through there and work our way up. If the governor is here, that's how we find him."

"I get the feeling you don't think he's on-site."

Layne was about to respond when he glanced at the building. The sun had set, but not a single light was on in any of the windows facing the street. Odd. She was right. He didn't think they'd find what they were looking for inside.

"One way or the other," he said, "we're about to find out."

They rounded the back of the car and inventoried their

gear. Layne eyed a few pedestrians as he donned his body armor. Some of them tossed looks at the two people in dark clothes with black shoe polish on their faces. But no one lingered long enough to cause a problem.

He opted for the shotgun this time. Loaded in the shells and stuffed his pockets with more. Serena chose pistols. As she jammed a magazine into the first, she paused to check her phone. Frowned.

"What's up?" Layne said.

"Daphne wants to know where I am." She made eye contact with Layne for a second, then stowed her phone. "I'll text her when we're done."

They crossed the street and slipped around the back. Layne raised the door leading into the garage, a little at a time. Made almost no noise at all. The room was dark, only vague shapes visible. But Layne recalled the layout from last time.

He crept across the room with Serena close behind him. A tense hand grabbed the handle of the door as he sucked in a deep breath. Swung the door open and raised his shotgun.

On the other side stood a bald man in a dirty wifebeater, leaning over, about to insert his key into a nearby apartment door. Layne watched the guy's hand strike out in slow motion, the other keys on the keychain dangling in space.

The man gasped and reached a hand toward the back of his pants. Layne reacted. Jabbed him in the chest with the butt of his shotgun, knocking him back a step. The man had barely placed a finger on his pistol when it flew from his grip and tumbled onto the stained carpet. Serena kicked it away.

Layne jabbed him again, this time in the jaw. The man

staggered and sank to the ground. Hands on his face as blood leaked out from between his fingers.

Serena raised her pistol, but Layne held out a hand. Even with her noise suppressor, it would be too loud. She lowered the gun, and Layne smacked the man in the jaw one more time with the butt of the Mossberg.

"Stop," the man said, spitting blood. Scowl on his face. Bulky shoulders heaving up and down.

Layne leaned in. "Where is the governor?"

"I don't know what you're talking about."

Serena raised the pistol again, and the man shied away from it. Still, he held his face high. Fire in his eyes.

"We don't have time for this," Layne said. He dropped to one knee, eye to eye with the man. "Tell me what I want to know, or I let her put a bullet in your eye."

The man grinned. "You don't know nothing. You're just a baby in nappies, screaming at the edge of his crib for Mummy."

Layne sighed and punched him in the jaw. His head smacked against the wall, and he sank to the floor, fading fast. His eyes closed, and his head lolled to the side.

Serena pointed at him. "You're just going to leave him here? Like this?"

"It's okay," Layne said. "I don't think we're going to be here long."

They encountered no one else on the first floor. Same with the second floor. And every floor after that. Each time they turned another corner or passed another open door and found nothing, Layne's chest constricted another few inches.

The Bourke Street apartment building was a ghost town.

On the fourth floor, in the last apartment they checked,

they stood at the window, overlooking the lights of the city. As Layne watched the cars and trams blink down the streets, all the little lights in the buildings, he felt empty. The brief hope of finding something useful on Bourke Street had faded and left him lower than he had felt on top of the atrium.

"I can call Daphne," Serena said. "She might have some ideas."

Far off in the distance, a light blinked. An explosion. "See that?"

"There's one over there, too," Serena said, pointing in the opposite direction.

Columns of smoke rose from where the two points of light had been. Someone was causing havoc in the streets of Melbourne tonight.

And then Layne's pocket buzzed. He retrieved his phone to find Harry's number on his caller ID.

39

LAYNE AND SERENA RACED ON THE HIGHWAY TOWARD some town out east named Lysterfield. Randall's phone had been tracked there, used within the last hour. As they escaped the city and the nearby suburbs, the landscape changed from tall buildings and highways to two-lane roads and grassy pastures filled with cows, sheep, and the occasional hopping kangaroo.

Layne drove as Serena navigated, using the GPS on her sat phone. Out this far, there were few streetlamps. Mostly dark space, occasionally broken by oncoming headlights or lights from houses set back from the road.

"You inform Control?" Layne said.

Serena nodded. "Right around the time of the speech, there was a series of attacks across the city. That's what those lights were we saw from the building on Bourke Street."

"Diversion."

"Exactly. A highly coordinated one. All the operatives are scattered, and she's trying to get everything under control."

Layne sighed and stared at the white line on the road and the bushes whipping by on either side. For a full minute, they stared ahead in silence. Layne could almost hear the thump of his heart in his throat.

"I miss my cat," she said out of nowhere.

"Say what?"

"First thing I do when I get back is I'm going to buy him an expensive toy. One of those automated things that spins in a circle so they can chase it. You know what I'm talking about?"

"No clue. I'm a dog person."

"Well," she said, "I hope that works out for you."

Layne swallowed and said nothing.

In another couple of minutes, she pointed him toward Wellington Road and then had him slow to a stop at Brae Road, a dirt path snaking up into the hills to the south. Layne pulled the car into the brown grass next to the road. When he killed the engine, silence boomed in the car.

"What's the deal?" he said.

She tilted her head toward the road while staring at the GPS map. "It's a quarter mile or so up. I have no idea if we'll find an outpost or stragglers or what on the way between here and there. How about we gear-up here and walk the rest?"

"Sounds good to me."

Serena paused, staring at him. A hint of a crooked smile curling the edge of her lip.

"What?" he said.

"I'm glad I didn't shoot you when I had the chance, Boy Scout."

"Me too. And you should know: I despise that code name. I always have."

Her smile dissipated. "Understood. Let's get on with it."

They rounded the car, and Layne snatched the Mossberg and then filled his pockets with ammunition and pistols. Really regretted not being able to procure any explosives from Tilda's gear guy. No better way to make an entrance than to blow a door off its hinges, particularly if you set it to detonate and then sneak around to the back door while everyone is freaking out and pointing their guns at the new hole in the room.

Properly armed, they stared at each other for a moment at the back of the car. Some animal howled in the distance. Without streetlights, Layne could only see Serena under the glow of the moon above. She had a ruthless beauty to her he found uncommon and intriguing.

In a way, she reminded him of someone he knew a long time ago. Someone he tried not to think about and had become more successful not thinking about as time went on. Layne hadn't realized the resemblance until that exact moment.

But he was less concerned with her looks right now than he was with her ability to avoid taking a bullet during this operation.

"Best case?" she said. "Governor Phelps is still alive and being held in a room in a house up this road."

"We should assume exterior and interior guards. We follow them to where they're thickest, and we'll find him there."

"Agreed. Go in with force or quietly?"

He paused, thinking it over. "Quietly. If their goal is to kill him, they'll put a bullet in his head the second we show our faces."

With that, they set out on the dirt road up the hill. The

brown strip cut a line between two dense forests on either side. The usual night sounds Layne had come to know over the last few days provided a soundtrack as feet shuffled through dry dirt. Weapons up, senses on full alert.

Something small and furry darted across the road up ahead, and Layne hesitated.

"Wombat," she said. "Like a hairy pig. Nothing to worry about."

"I wasn't worried," he said, and she grinned in response.

At the top of the hill, Layne spied a two-story mansion set off to the side, obscured by a dense line of trees. Lights gleaming through the dark. He checked Serena; she glanced at the sat phone and nodded. They both ducked and continued a little closer until Layne could see the whole house through the forest. Seemed like a plantation-type home, a large rectangle, maybe eight or ten thousand square feet. Two smaller buildings flanked either side—one likely a garage, the other a toolshed. Surrounding the property, science-fiction-looking trees with giant limbs. The two independent buildings were dark and quiet, so Layne figured they could bypass them.

"How many bedrooms you think?" she whispered.

"I'd guess four or maybe five. Enough that we'll have to do some navigation on the inside."

Layne paused under a tree and let his eyes adjust to the difference in light near the house. The second floor sported a front-facing balcony, and Layne spied two armed men hanging out on opposite ends. In the wide open space in front of the house, several cars were parked in the grass. One man was sitting on the hood of a car, a phone screen lighting up his face. A shotgun cradled in his lap.

"I count three," he whispered.

She leaned in and rested a hand on his shoulder as she pointed to the side of the house. Her hair was tied up and pinned against the nape of her neck, but he could smell her shampoo. Strawberries.

"Missed one out there in the woods," she said. "Nestled up in the tree. See him?"

Layne squinted and did see a figure positioned in a tree at the back of the property. Sitting in the crook of two branches, fifteen feet off the ground. Not moving at all, barely more than a shadow.

"Good eye," he said. "Let's take care of him first, then make our way around the back. See what we're dealing with there." He hesitated as he noticed something around the man's neck. After a moment of squinting, he had a good idea of what it was. "Wait. See that thing he's wearing?"

Her brow creased as she bit her lip. He pointed to the goggles sitting on the man's collarbone.

"Night vision," she said.

"Be careful. I'll take out our monkey."

She tilted her head left, away from the man in the tree. He nodded, and they set off in separate directions. Layne's focus stayed on the man up above, checking the whites of his eyes to spot where he was looking. He continued to delve deeper into the forest, away from the house, to avoid the man's line of sight.

Once he was far enough out to pull even with the tree guard, Layne worked his way back, now behind him. He crept within a few feet of the tree. Remained mindful of crunching stray twigs, each step carefully settling onto the ground before applying full weight. He focused on his breathing and keeping a reasonable heart rate. In, out, silent and measured.

He slipped the knife from its sheath on his back belt loop. Now he had to make a decision about how to bring the target out of the tree. The spotter was too far up for Layne to climb the tree and snatch him without alerting him or others. Too high for Layne to jump without making noise. Gunshots would be way too loud. And if Layne did something like shake the tree, the spotter might call out. Layne could wait for him to come down on his own—maybe at a shift change—but that might take several minutes or even hours. Minutes and hours Layne did not have to spare.

He didn't like any of his options.

As far as he could see, there was only one choice left. He turned the knife around so he was holding it by the tip, then he hefted it a few times to measure its weight.

Layne had zero room for error if he wanted to pull it off. An inch too high or an inch too low, and this would all be over. Not since his twenties had he felt good about his knife-throwing accuracy.

He raised the knife, hoisted it over his shoulder, and took a few deep breaths. Focused his eyes on the slim spot of flesh below the man's chin and above the night-vision goggles.

Attempting this was nutty. The odds of success were slimmer than he could imagine.

Layne let the knife fly.

It tumbled through the air, spiraling up toward the tree. And it hit. Sank right into the man's neck. His hands flew to the spot of the incision, and that made him lean in his tree branch nook.

Layne almost laughed. A thousand-to-one shot, and he'd nailed it.

A second later, the spotter tumbled, and Layne tried to catch him. He was a weighty man, though, and the impact caused them both to tumble to the ground. Made way too much noise. As the man gurgled and flailed and flung blood all over, Layne wrapped his arms and legs around the dying man to keep him contained. Hand over his mouth. When the squirming slowed, Layne scooted out from underneath him and crawled a few feet south to get a look at the guards in the front of the house. Saw nothing had changed.

He returned to the dying guard and withdrew the knife from his neck. The man's hands were around it, drenched in blood. Layne pulled it free and then wiped both sides on the man's shirt. Sheathed his knife, wiped spots of blood from his own face, and then resumed his route around the house.

The back of the house opened to a large field, ending at a line of trees marking the surrounding forest. There was a strange basketball court, but the hoops had no nets and no backboards. Some Australian version of the game.

The back of the house looked just like the front, except without a grand porch for entry. Limited lighting, only illuminating a few small circles around the perimeter. There was a second-floor balcony with two guards, but no additional guards stationed in the back. Layne spied Serena across the way. She pointed up toward the balcony, and he nodded across the distance to her.

He pointed at the side of the house, meaning they could approach that way and stay out of both the guards' vision and the circles of exterior lighting. She moved closer to the corner of the house, and he did, too.

When Layne reached the side, he dropped to a crawl so anyone looking out of the windows wouldn't see him. Serena did the same. A glass-walled sunroom jutted from the back, with a single door leading into it. Layne and Serena slinked toward it, just like recruits shimmying through the mud beneath barbed wire.

And then he heard footsteps. The rustle of equipment. For a moment, panic overcame him when he realized how disadvantaged he was, here on his stomach, on the ground. A trigger-happy guard could put a dozen bullets in his spine in the time it would take Layne to get his weapon out.

Layne spun onto his back to find Randall standing over him. An M4 carbine rifle pointed down at him. The elder Parrish shook his head slowly.

"I had a feeling you would find me," Randall said. Brotherly look of disappointment on his face.

Two more heavily armed men emerged into view on either side.

The sound of footsteps across the way. Layne pivoted his head to see Serena racing off into the woods. Randall and his two accomplices spit a few shots into the dark, but the shots were not accompanied by a scream or the sound of a body hitting the ground. Layne squinted into the darkness and couldn't see any signs of her.

Randall knelt. "No worries. If she's here or out in the woods, we'll get her sooner or later. Come on, little brother, on your feet. We have a lot to talk about."

40

LAYNE OPTED NOT TO FIGHT, MORE OUT OF CURIOSITY than anything else. He had to know what could make his older brother do all this. What the India/Pakistani mercenary group could offer that would make him kidnap and want to kill the governor of Victoria.

Randall and his two accomplices, dressed in black-and-white *Magpies* clothes, hoisted Layne to his feet. They wrenched his hands behind his back, threw zip-tie cuffs on him, and then relieved him of all his weapons. Layne didn't know why, but they left the body armor on him for now.

They said nothing as they dragged him inside the house and escorted him through the kitchen, then a living room, and up a set of grand stairs. Opulent decorations everywhere. A giant chandelier like a thousand glass daggers hanging above their heads. Layne counted the number of guards he saw as they moved from room to room. At least eight, but there were likely more.

At the top of the stairs, they turned left, and Layne noted a still-wet streak of blood on the banister.

"Is Governor Phelps alive?" he said. His captors gave no reply. Pushed him down the hall to the third room on the left. Randall opened the door into a bedroom with a large bed, a dresser, and a desk. Layne's eyes flicked to the window leading outside.

Randall must have noticed the window, too, because he pulled Layne back out of the room. "Actually," Randall said, "let's put him in the big closet on the first floor. Hurry up now."

Back down the stairs they went. Turned left, crossed the room into a hallway. Layne spotted four doors along the way. Only one open, leading into a bathroom. In his head, he built a floor plan based on everything he was seeing.

The big closet they pushed him into was more like a dry storage room, with shelves stacked with canned food and flour and other kitchen paraphernalia.

Randall waited until one of the men had stood Layne in front of a chair, and then he used a knife to cut the zip tie. Both of Randall's henchmen trained assault rifles on him. For a brief moment, Layne was unrestrained, and Randall grinned at him. Probably waiting to see what he would do. But Layne wasn't about to try an escape attempt now with armed men staring him down. And obviously, Randall knew that.

The older brother pointed at the body armor and then flicked a finger toward the ceiling. Layne lifted the vest over his head and dropped it on the floor. Randall patted down his shirt and pants and then motioned to the chair. Layne sat.

Randall lifted his shirtsleeve to scratch his shoulder. Inked there a black tattoo of a bird, with the word *Collingwood* written underneath it.

"Open your mouth," Randall said.

Layne obliged, and Randall peeked inside, moving his head around to check every angle.

One of the men handed Randall a roll of duct tape, which he unrolled over both of Layne's wrists and ankles, securing him to the chair.

"Is the governor still alive?" Layne said.

Randall nodded.

"*Why* is he still alive?"

Now Randall chuckled. "We need him to make a video. So far, he's not been as cooperative as we'd like."

"Why are you doing this?"

Randall angled his head toward the two henchmen, then he waved them away. He tested the duct tape securing Layne by tugging on the bound limbs, checking the tension. Layne had almost no give. Then Randall picked up a corkscrew on a nearby shelf and tossed it across the room, far away from Layne.

Once the two had collected Layne's things and left, with the door shut behind them, Randall knelt to meet Layne's eyes. "I never wanted you to come here, little brother. I didn't want you to be a part of this."

"A part of what? How much are they paying you?"

Randall's eyes twinkled. "Paying me? I thought you would have figured it out by now."

"Enlighten me."

"Daphne tried to sell you on this whole myth about Pakistan. About some mercenary group and Abdul Abbad and all that."

"No, *you* tried to sell me on Abdul Abbad."

"True, I may have misled you about the connection. But

the truth is: I don't give a shit about Abbad. I don't give a shit about Pakistan. This is all about Governor Phelps."

Layne took in a breath as the realization settled over him. "Reds and Union. There is no contact named Gerald Ferguson in Germany, is there? Your phone call behind the coffee shop in Camberwell yesterday morning."

Randall pursed his lips. "Now you're starting to get it. Also, I saw your little wallet theft after that warehouse mess."

Layne scowled. "You planted the notebook in the wall."

"I did."

"Putting it in a locked safe was a nice touch."

"I thought it added a hint of authenticity, plus I knew you would figure out how to break into it. You have to believe me, though. I wanted to keep you out of this. I thought if I could placate you, keep you busy, you might stay out of my way long enough for me to do my job."

"And what is that?" Layne asked.

"Everything I told you about the Reds was true. They were going to send snipers to Fed Square to take out the governor as retaliation for the shitty deal he brokered for them. But we got him first."

"Who is we?"

"Union, little brother."

"You're part of an Australian gang?"

"We're not a gang. We're a family."

Layne gritted his teeth. "No, man, I'm your family. These are just some thugs who've brainwashed you."

"You're not my family. I had no idea about you and your wife splitting up or even getting married. You didn't tell me about the birth of your *child*. What kind of brother does that?"

"I assumed you were dead, you know, when a decade goes by and I don't hear from you."

"Did you even look for me?"

Layne felt himself getting flustered, so he took a breath. "I was told not to. That rushing off to South Africa would endanger our other operations there. You could have reached out, too, you know. What the hell have you been doing for the last ten years?"

Randall stood to his full height, flexing his fists. "I've been here and other places, fighting the good fight."

"'Fighting the good fight.' I can't believe this propaganda bullshit you're spewing. I think I would have rather you become a foreign agent. At least that would make sense."

"Believe it or don't," Randall said, "but there's more going on here than you realize."

"Such as?"

Randall strolled around the room, his hands in his pockets. He settled by leaning against the door. Arms crossed, staring at Layne. "Do you remember our first op together, in Seattle?"

Layne nodded.

"I remember how nervous you were," Randall said, smiling. "Shaking while you were trying to eat that meatball sub."

"So?"

"That man you killed in the house across the street, Omar Naseer? Was he a bad man, or was he someone who believed the things he was doing were just?"

Layne cleared his throat. "I know what you're doing, Randall. You're not going to win me over with a *shades-of-gray* argument here."

"Fine. Then all you need to know is I'm doing what I believe is just."

"And you ended up a gang member."

"Like I said, the Union is not a gang. We're a family. We're trying to do good things for the world."

"By killing a politician. And you refuse to see how twisted that is."

"If killing him serves the greater purpose, then I'm all for it. He's just a man. Ideas are bigger than a man."

Layne gritted his teeth. "You can't even be objective about the words coming out of your own mouth."

"I know you never liked the code name Boy Scout, but it fits you. Sometimes you have to get your hands dirty. That's the way the world works."

"Fine, Randall. What is your greater purpose?"

"The governor will record a statement, denouncing the Reds and encouraging the ASIO to investigate them. So far, they've completely flown under the radar. When they're out of the way, we can do good things in Australia. Put good people in power. People who can negotiate with other countries and ease tensions between the east and the west."

"Easing tensions?"

"The west is blind to the threat from China and Southeast Asia. From here, we can make a real seat of power to keep them from gaining too much influence. We can make a difference. Maybe it doesn't look like it from where you're sitting, but I care more about America and her future than any of those idiots in Washington."

The door opened, and the two guards leaned in. Randall held up a hand, and the men stood there in the doorway, clutching their guns. Awaiting orders.

"If the governor doesn't do what you want, are you going to kill him?"

Randall paused, then nodded. "Would you shoot a wolf to keep him from entering your henhouse?"

"It's not the same thing. I don't care what your end goal is. Your methods are sick."

"That's fine. I don't expect you to understand right away. But I do need to go check on our friend upstairs, so I will give you a few minutes to think about it."

"Want us to wait in the room, sir?" one of the henchmen said.

Randall swished his lips around, considering it. He neared Layne, and he tugged on Layne's wrists and ankles again, checking the strength of the duct tape. "That won't be necessary. You can wait outside so Boy Scout here can have time to reflect. If I leave you in here, he'll find a way to convince one of you to shoot the other one."

Randall dropped to a knee. "These men are two of my best, in case you get any ideas about breaking out. When I come back, I'm going to give you a chance to walk out of here alive tonight. We'll see if you've thought it over and had a change of heart."

"And if I don't, you'll kill me?"

"I meant it when I said I didn't want this for you. But you're here now, and we can't put that toothpaste back in the tube."

"So you *will* kill me."

Randall frowned. "No, little brother, of course not. I'll have one of my men do it."

41

SERENA SPENT A FEW MINUTES IN THE THICK OF THE woods, hiding behind trees and keeping low to the ground. They sent only two guards into the woods after her, and it wasn't too challenging to elude them. They'd proceeded in a straight line from where she'd entered the forest. All she had to do was skirt a couple of hundred feet to the left and find a large tree stump. She positioned herself on the far side of it and then waited. One of them came close enough she could hear his feet shuffling through the underbrush. Then his walkie-talkie squawked, and he said something unintelligible in response. A few seconds after, he hustled back toward the house.

After another minute or two, she worked her way back, mindful of anyone lingering in the trees. Texted Daphne and then waited, watching. Still two guards on the balcony and one out in front of the house, among the vehicles.

Judging by the number of cars out front, she expected about a dozen people inside. Possibly more.

She knelt in the grass when the guard slid off the hood of

the car. He wormed through the parked cars, weapon up. The two men on the balcony remained, but two more joined the group, standing on the front porch. All of them with walkies, chatting. Organizing a search party.

Within a minute or two, they would launch a more thorough search through the woods for her. Maybe with high-powered flashlights or dogs. Maybe they would burn the forest to the ground.

The phone in her pocket buzzed. She whipped it out to find a text message from Daphne.

Fastest ETA 90 minutes to mobilize and arrive at your location. Best we can do. Tilda MacMillan is en route with ASIO strike team. ETA 60.

Serena grimaced. An hour was too long to wait. Whatever plan Randall and his people had for Governor Phelps would escalate now that their location had been compromised.

She wrote back:

Understood, Control. I can't wait 60 mins. Will have to improvise. Will advise of sit rep soon.

She held down the button to power off her phone and arched her back to stretch. Ran through a quick inventory of her gear. Certainly not enough to take on a house full of armed foot soldiers.

The man weaving through the cars emptied out of the makeshift parking lot and turned toward her direction. His eyes were still wide, still searching. Hadn't spotted her and hadn't thought to don his NVGs.

Serena's heart raced. She eyed the tree near her. Good leaf cover, a nice and sturdy system of branches. She holstered her pistols and scampered up the tree, twenty feet to the first intersection of branches large enough to support her. If his eyes drifted upward, she would be spotted, even with the dark clothing and black shoe polish.

The guard continued to skulk in her direction.

She had to decide. Killing this guard might be too loud. Might bring lots of unwanted attention. But every second that elapsed meant more uncertainty for both Layne and Governor Phelps. At some point, she had to take a risk and infiltrate that house.

The guard neared the tree and waited there. Leaned up against it. He hoisted his M4A1 rifle up onto his shoulder.

Serena readied her knife. How much longer would he stand there, right underneath her and perfectly still?

Screw the noise. If this man looked up, it was all over anyway.

With the knife edge pointed down, she let herself slip from the branches. Air whistled. The guard looked up at the last second just before she drove the tip of her blade into his chest. She wrapped her free hand around him to pull him to the ground and then quickly slapped it over his mouth. Twisted the knife, rocking it back and forth to widen the hole. He squirmed and whimpered, but his muffled bellows were lost in her palm. Blood rushed over her hand and down her wrist.

After a few seconds, she released her grip on him and pushed his limp body to the side. Heart pounding, a little dizzy from the contact. She sat up. Heaved a few deep breaths to center herself and shed some of the adrenaline rush.

And then something on the side of the house caught her eye.

Breaker box.

Keeping low and avoiding a view of the front, she crept across the yard and flipped open the panel to reveal a series of switches on the inside. Knife out, she held it against the main power cable protruding from the bottom of the box but then stopped herself.

The guards roaming outside had all been sporting night-vision goggles.

Instead of cutting the power cable, she sheathed her knife and flipped off all the switches with three quick flicks of her wrist.

The light from a window above her head went dark.

"Okay, Layne," she whispered. "You got four minutes. It's your turn now."

42

THE DUCT TAPE AROUND HIS ANKLES DIDN'T GIVE HIM much room to work with, but Layne started working his knees together and apart horizontally. The ceiling creaked above his head with footsteps shuffling back and forth.

After a minute, he'd loosened the duct tape enough to create some breathing room. A quarter of an inch, but it was enough to allow him to wriggle his ankles. Once he'd done that, he worked his right knee vertically to create more space. He took harsh, rapid inhalations to ratchet up his heart rate. Moved as quickly as possible to work up a sweat. In the confines of this little room with no air-conditioning, it wasn't too hard. Soon he felt slickness working against the duct tape, diluting the adhesive and helping his legs to progress more and more with each thrust.

After another minute, he'd worked his right ankle free. He lifted that foot until he'd wedged the heel of his shoe inside it, and then he pushed against the duct tape. It tore, making a *scritch* sound as it gave way. His whole foot was free.

He paused, stared at the door. The guards outside were still there. Didn't come in to check on him.

With a grunt, he hoisted his right foot onto his left knee. The problem was getting it close to his left hand since the duct tape allowed no motion at all for his arms. Randall had been more forgiving with the tape around his ankles, but he'd gone over his wrists dozens of times. No way could Layne wriggle out of that.

But he wouldn't have to. All he had to do was maneuver his right shoe closer to his left hand. Close enough for him to secure two fingers around the barely noticeable slit in the sole.

After gritting his teeth until sweat dripped down his forehead, he managed to push his foot close enough to get his two fingers on it. The little blade was buried deep, but he pried open the slit with his thumb and used his forefinger's nail to flick at the edge to draw it closer. He moved it out slowly. Back and forth, a little at a time, sliding up the hole in his shoe until it surfaced.

Had to be mindful of the clock. No telling when Randall would open that door again.

Thirty more seconds of working the blade out. Layne finally got two fingers around it, and then he yanked it free. He turned it around and inserted it back into the slit, sharp end out. He had to push even harder to move his foot toward the duct tape. His hip and quad muscles scolded him, but he gritted his teeth and ignored it.

Blade against the duct tape, he worked his shoe back and forth. The outer layer of the duct tape tore, then he went to work on the inner layers. After a few more swipes, he was able to wrestle his hand free. He plucked the blade from his shoe and slashed the duct tape on his other hand, then his other foot.

He stood, back aching. Heart still pounding against his rib cage, he had to take a breath to steady himself.

And then the lights went out. Total dark in this room.

Serena. Had to be her.

Did she know about the four-minute drill? Had that been her plan?

Instantly he heard shouts and footsteps shaking the ceiling above him. Then voices outside the door, bleeding through the walls. Layne grinned at the sound of chaos all around him.

Priority one had to be finding where they were keeping his weapons and body armor. Then the governor.

Like a light bulb blinking on above his head, he remembered the night-vision goggles the men outside had been wearing. Would they bother to keep them around inside? He would have to acquire some, or he'd be dead at the first unfriendly encounter.

Checked his watch. Three minutes and thirty seconds.

He opened the door to the storage room and burst into the hallway. There was one man there, not wearing goggles. Short guy, spiky black hair. Layne could make out only a hint of the man's silhouette as his opponent spun toward the sound of the commotion, M4 carbine raised.

Layne drove an elbow into the man's face. A gush of blood from the man's nose coated Layne's elbow instantly. Layne could barely see him, but he felt the man stumble back a step.

Layne grabbed the stock of the rifle, but the man was wearing a shoulder strap. So Layne tugged on it to wrench the man off-balance, then he hooked his ankle behind the man's calf and drove his free hand into the guy's shoulder to knock him back in the other direction. The man dropped to the ground with a thud. His head smacked on the cold floor. Layne punched him in the face two times, three times. Put his hips into it. Everything he had. Felt nose cartilage crumbling under his knuckles.

Layne snatched at the shoulder strap and jerked the rifle away. Eyes now adjusting, he could see the man's head lolled to the side, still breathing.

Layne hoisted the rifle and drove the stock into the man's head one more time for good measure. He paused there for another second to make sure the guy stayed on the ground.

Then he set out to his right. Thought about the layout of the house, at least from what he had seen when they'd dragged him in here. If there were nooks and crannies or secret passageways, Layne had no idea. Had to be extra careful.

He opened the first door on his left. A small office. He took one step inside, his eyes squinting through the dark to find grenades or tear gas. Anything to tip the scales in his favor since he seemed woefully outnumbered and running on fumes, too. But nothing except pens and pencils and spiral notebooks on a desk populated the room. Layne didn't have time for this. Clock was ticking. Under three minutes remaining.

Feet still trundled across the second floor above his head. Layne kept his eyes on the foyer of the house, at the end of this current hallway. He edged into the open room with the double-tall ceiling and massive chandelier. Layne kept back, shielded from view by the stairs.

He could see well enough in the dark now, but not as well as anyone would wearing night-vision goggles. There were still voices and feet moving everywhere. He couldn't make an informed decision about where the next attacker would come from.

Rifle up, he pushed along. Two men thundered down the stairs and embarked on a path straight for him, oblivious as to what they were about to encounter. Layne squeezed the M4A1's trigger and cut them both down. A short burst spliced them both across the chest. Been a long time since Layne had fired an M4 carbine, and he'd forgotten about the thirsty trigger. Press it for about a second and a half, and you find yourself with an empty magazine. He flexed his finger, mentally practicing quick taps for controlled bursts of fire.

These two he'd killed had been wearing night-vision. As he stepped over their bodies, he reached down and lifted a pair of goggles from one, as well as pocketing a few spare mags. He slid the goggles on and fumbled for the button on the side. With a whine from the electronics, the world turned an eerie, glowing green.

Checked his watch. About two and a half minutes left.

He pressed on through the foyer and turned toward the stairs. A man appeared at the top, and Layne spit shots at him without thinking. The blast from the M4 lit up his vision, and he shut his eyes against the blindness. Had been so long since Layne'd worn goggles, he'd forgotten about that, too.

Lucky for Layne, he tagged the man in the thigh on the first attempt. He tumbled down the stairs, stopping halfway, with limbs splayed out in all directions. Gasping, grunting, trying to grab the rifle that had fallen on the stairs next to him. Layne aimed for his head and gently stroked the trigger. One bullet into the man's skull.

Layne eased up the stairs. He could go left or right. Chose

right, in the direction of the bloodstain on the banister he'd seen earlier. Several doors on either side along this hallway. First door on the left was an empty bedroom.

Gunshots whiffed through the air. Layne shut his eyes and threw himself behind the open door. He inched inside, using the doorframe to shield himself. He guessed it would be the thickest object nearby for shelter.

"How did you get out, little brother?" Randall shouted from down the hall.

Before Layne could answer, more gunshots assaulted the hallway. The barrage lasted a quarter of a second, raining thirty or forty bullets in his direction. The doorframe above Layne's head splintered, raining wood chips on his head. Holes peppered the door. Shafts of green light poured through them.

He checked his watch. Ninety seconds left.

Layne leaned right and squeezed the trigger while he rotated the stock to widen the spray. The *ratatat* of the rifle fire drilled his ears.

Randall spit back another round of fire, and Layne held his position. Listened as carefully as he could between the shots to gauge if Randall was on the move.

This was not a battle he could win, firing from cover to cover. Any of them could circle around him, and Layne couldn't defend forward and flank at the same time.

And then the sound stopped. Layne opened his eyes and peered down the hallway. Randall was gone. No more shouting, at least from that direction.

Layne stood and proceeded to the next room. Opened the door and saw his body armor, shotgun, and pistols sitting on top of a bed. Arranged neatly, as if they'd been expecting him to return and claim them.

He set the M4 against the wall and hustled across the room. Raised his goggles and dropped them on the floor. He held up the ceramic body armor, about to put it on—

"Stop."

Layne turned to see the dim figures of two men in the doorway, assault rifles pointed at him. Night-vision goggles on their faces. He angled his wrist to glance at his watch again. About fifty seconds remaining.

"Drop the vest and put your hands above your head."

43

SERENA WATCHED THE TIMER TICK. SHE WAS crouched underneath the breaker box, one pistol pointed to the back of the house, one toward the front. Her head swiveled back and forth like someone in the stands at a tennis match.

She'd set the timer on her phone for four minutes. Hopefully that would give Layne enough time to escape wherever they were keeping him and make his way out. If four minutes came and he wasn't bursting outside, she would execute the plan.

Layne had to know about the four-minute drill, didn't he? It was something she learned about in her first year on the job. He would have to remember. Have to.

But the drill wouldn't matter if someone shot her before she could finish what she'd started. And her job was to stand here and guard the breaker box for two hundred and forty seconds. To watch the timer and wait.

Her head switched back and forth, front and rear, back and forth. Checking the shadows against the moonlight.

But no one had come so far. Ninety seconds remaining, and she could hear gunshots from inside. Shouts. Most everyone seemed to have run *inside* the house, not out. Maybe these Australian thugs didn't know about electrical wiring. Had no idea to check the breaker box when the power went out.

Footsteps came from the rear of the house. A walkie-talkie chirping. She angled one ear toward the back and closed her eyes to focus on the sound.

The footsteps grew a little louder. She turned and pointed both pistols toward the back. Silent, arms extended, fingers on the triggers. Blinked a few times to keep her eyes from becoming unfocused.

But this didn't feel right. The footsteps were too blatant. Too obvious. The walkie chirped again, louder this time.

Her eyes drifted up. The breaker box was at eye level, about five feet off the ground. Three feet above the breaker box sat a window with shutters on either side. She holstered the pistols, climbed to the top of the breaker box, and then hoisted herself to the window. A tiny lip of a ledge outside the window allowed barely enough space for the tips of her shoes.

The shutters were on hinges, so she grabbed hold of one and swung it perpendicular to the house. Scrambled up higher so she could sit on top of it. Fifteen feet in the air, sitting on an inch-wide piece of wood, held up by two metal hinges. It creaked a little but held her weight.

She pointed one gun at the back and one at the front. And waited.

An armed guard appeared from the back of the house. And then, as she'd expected, came the ambush. A second, silent guard with no blatant warning clues of loud footsteps and deliberate walkie chirps from around the front.

They started walking toward each other. Looking around for her, confusion on their faces. She aimed toward the front and then the back. Squinting, she lowered her rear-facing arm to compensate for the path of approaching steps.

Pulled both triggers.

She hit one in the head, the other in the chest. The one she'd hit in the chest had been wearing body armor, and he fell to the ground. Gasping, wincing, but not dead.

She scrambled to the ground just as the timer on her phone blared. Four minutes had passed. She lifted her pistol and shot the still-breathing guard in the temple.

At the breaker box, she flipped the power back on.

Then she rushed into the house via the front porch.

Inside, her attention first landed on a dead man on the stairs. That was good. Layne was still alive and had made a stop here on his way up the stairs.

A man emerged from the hallway on the second floor, and he skidded to a halt as his eyes landed on her. Serena raised a pistol and spit one shot. It nicked off the banister in front of the stairs and lodged into a wall.

The man raised his assault rifle and squeezed off a barrage of bullets. Serena felt a pinch in her side, like a bee sting. The world blasted white for a second, then she raised both pistols and filled the man full of holes.

She heaved a breath as she holstered one gun and checked her side. The bullet had nicked her, in and out. Blasted a chunk out of her right hip, but it didn't feel serious. She tested her weight on the right leg and found she could move without too much pain. Probably wouldn't bleed to death anytime soon.

She slid next to the wall and reached into her back pocket for the emergency Israeli bandage she carried on all ops. Ripped it from the package and lifted her shirt, then she wrapped it across her waist and around her hips, centering the gauze pad over the entry wound. Wrapped it around a couple of times, grimacing. Then she clipped it off and heaved a few deep breaths. There was duct tape back at the car, if need be.

With the bleeding under control, she lunged up the stairs two at a time. From the second floor, she could hear the chaos of shouts and the trampling of boots on the carpet.

She broached the top, weapons up. Looked left, looked right, not sure which way to go. Then to her right, a figure dashed down the hall. Silent, like a flash of shadow.

Randall.

He hopped over a dead body and disappeared into a bedroom, gripping a shotgun in his hands.

44

INSTEAD OF DROPPING THE VEST, LAYNE TURNED toward the two men standing in the doorway of the bedroom. They were dressed head to toe in black, with night-vision goggles protruding from their heads like cyborg attachments. Little dots shining on the sides of their heads.

The goggles Layne had been wearing were now sitting on the floor. While holding his vest, Layne couldn't see his watch to check the time. But he had to figure less than thirty seconds were remaining in the four-minute drill.

Unless Serena had been shot outside. If she had, Layne could see no way out of this room alive.

They raised their rifles but didn't fire. Layne was three feet away from the table where all his weapons sat, waiting for him. Maybe the M4 he'd set against the wall was a little closer, but he preferred the shotgun if he had to take on two at once.

"Put it down," said the guard on the left.

"Let's talk about this," Layne said, and then he took a

backward step toward the table. "I'm not who you think I am."

Both of them gripped their rifles, tensing. "This is Randall's brother?" the one on the right muttered to the other one. The left guard said nothing, only kept his rifle high, one eye squinted down the sight. Layne kept his attention on their trigger fingers, waiting for any hint of motion. He could barely see them in the dark.

And then, with a click, all the lights came back on. The two men screamed and dropped their guns as their hands rushed to their faces.

Layne leaped toward the table and snatched the shotgun. With two quick pumps, he created holes in both of the men. Shotgun cracking like a bolt of lightning. Sent them to their knees, and then they toppled to the floor.

Layne slid on the body armor and then snatched a box of shells and refilled the Mossberg. Had to blink a few times to adjust to the sudden brightness after four minutes in total darkness. He grabbed the pistols and slid them into his pants pockets. Hands shaking, heart racing, his vision streaked with stars. He couldn't remember the last time he'd been so high from adrenaline.

Something thudded behind him. Then the cocking of a shotgun. Layne paused, listening.

"That's it, Boy Scout," Randall said. "It's over."

Layne spun, and Randall's shotgun went off. He'd shot high, and the blast blew out a chunk of the wall over Layne's right shoulder. Little bits settled in his hair and on the back of his neck.

They stood, ten feet apart, shotguns pointed at each other like growling dogs. Each of them looking down the sights, fingers on their triggers. Two dead bodies on the floor between them.

"Who was the woman on the bed?" Layne said.

Randall cocked his head. "Huh?"

"The woman we rescued."

"Oh, that nice piece of ass we found tied up at Bourke Street? She did bookkeeping for us here and there. I was worried for a second she might recognize me that day, but I'm fairly certain we only met once."

"Is she alive or dead right now?"

Randall shook his head. "We wouldn't do that to one of our own. She's fine, as far as I know."

Layne said nothing and held tight to his shotgun.

"You won't pull the trigger," Randall said. "You know what we're doing here is the right thing to do."

Layne focused on his breathing. Reassured his grip on the weapon in his hands.

"I don't want to do it, Layne, but I will shoot you if I have to."

"I'm wearing level 4 ceramic- and fiberglass-reinforced plates. Your shotgun will barely bruise me."

Randall lowered the barrel of the shotgun, now pointed at Layne's legs. "I don't have to kill you, little brother. I just have to incapacitate you while I get the hell out of here. You've turned my whole operation into a cesspool of chaos, and it's time to tuck my tail and run."

"Where is the governor?"

"On the floor in the master bedroom, with a bullet in his head. He wouldn't record that little video, so he didn't leave me any choice. I figured you already called in the cavalry, so I don't have much time."

Layne said nothing. Out of the corner of his eye, he saw Serena slip behind Randall. Without making a sound, she raised a pistol and pointed it at his head.

"What happened to you?" Layne said.

"I woke up to the real threat, little brother. Now I'm trying to do something about it, since no one else seems to understand."

Layne bit his lower lip.

Randall grinned. With a flicker of his eyes, his finger closed around the trigger.

Behind them, Serena pivoted when a nearby door opened. She spit two shots from her pistols. Randall's head jerked to the side.

Layne kicked his legs out to fall to the ground, and as he sank, he pressed the Mossberg's trigger. The shotgun kicked back against his shoulder.

The blast hit Randall square in the chest.

A blur of flesh and blood sprayed outward, and his arms flapped as he staggered, tripping over one of the bodies on the floor.

Layne watched his brother twist and then fall flat on his back, his midsection torn open. Blood squirting and pooling instantly underneath him. His eyes open wide, his mouth sputtering.

Layne lumbered to his feet and staggered across the room. Shotgun up, pointed at Randall. His older brother, the one who teased him endlessly about the nickname *Nash Bridges*, was dying on the floor. As he tried to speak, blood bubbled and dribbled from the corners of his mouth.

A specific memory appeared in Layne's mind. A family trip to the Grand Canyon. Layne was eleven and Randall sixteen, back when the difference in their ages seemed as wide as the canyon itself. Their parents and the two boys stood against a railing looking out over the canyon. The wonder Layne felt at seeing the giant chasm in person. Mouth agape, eyes wide. And then, when he looked up at his older brother to check if he was experiencing the same sense of awe, Randall frowned at him. Rolled his eyes. An unaffected teenager, too cool to think anything during a forced family vacation was worth his precious attention.

With so much adrenaline pumping through his veins, it took Layne a second to realize Serena was talking to him. He looked up at her, then his eyes fell to the dark spot on the side of her shirt.

"Are you okay?"

She nodded, then whirled around and blasted her pistols down the hallway. She alternated, firing each gun like a Wild West sheriff strolling down a dusty street. Layne could barely hear the bodies hitting the floor as his ears whined from all the gunshots.

"Where's the governor?" she asked.

"Master bedroom. He might be dead."

Layne wanted to avoid viewing his brother's limp body on the way out of the room, but he was too shaky. Couldn't trust his feet. He had to look down as he navigated through the trio of corpses on the floor. His brother's expression demonstrated the last thing he experienced before dying. Surprise. Disbelief. Eyes stuck wide open. Pupils pointed straight up at the ceiling. Mouth pulled down into a horrified frown.

"Master bedroom?" she said.

"I think so."

She pointed down the hall. "I think it's back this way."

He joined her in the hall, and they crept along the carpet

until they reached a door at the top of the stairs. There were voices somewhere, but they were fading, not growing louder. The surviving gang members were fleeing the scene.

Layne flung the door open to find the governor sitting on the bed, a gag over his mouth. His hands tied with zip ties. Shaking, eyes full of panic.

But not dead.

Serena cut the zip ties and helped the governor to his feet. He seemed dazed, maybe in shock. Head lolling like his neck didn't work quite right.

Governor Phelps knitted his brow at Layne. "You?"

"Governor, my name is Layne Parrish. This is my colleague Serena. We're here to get you out of this building, but there may be more of these men coming. When is your flight to Pakistan?"

"They wanted me to record . . . something. A video for some reason. I didn't understand. I kept telling them—"

Layne set his shotgun against the side of the bed and put a hand on Phelps's shoulder. Gave it a solid squeeze. "Sir? This is important. I need you to listen to what I'm asking you."

The governor's eyes were vacant, like a wax figure. "I'm listening."

"When is your flight?"

"It's . . . it's not until morning. What time is it now?"

Layne checked his watch. "Midnight, sir. Do you have access to a private airplane? Can you charter something?"

Phelps nodded, his expression blank. "I do. I can call someone. There's an airfield in Cranbourne, and I think I can get a flight from there."

Serena nodded. "That's about forty-five minutes from here."

"Can you walk?" Layne said to the governor.

He blinked, absentminded. "I think so."

"We're going to get you to a car and escort you to Cranbourne. You should make that call right now, Governor. If we do this correctly, we might live through the night."

45

LAYNE STARED AT HIS HANDS AS THE CAR SPED ALONG A dirt road. Serena was driving, eyes focused, hands gripping the wheel. Grimacing. She'd swapped out her Israeli bandage and slapped a few inches of duct tape over the wound in her side.

In the back seat, Governor Phelps was on the phone, chatting with his pilot. After a brief conversation, Phelps pulled the phone away from his ear. His hands shook, and he needed a few tries to tap the *end* button.

"All good?" Serena said.

The governor nodded. "He already had a plane fueled for something else, and he said he can be ready by the time we get there."

Flashes of memory kept appearing in front of Layne's eyes. Specifically, the night his daughter had been born. Hovering over then-wife Inessa, holding her hand and encouraging her to push. Across from her hospital bed, the TV was on, muted. Some nature program showing a cheetah slinking through tall grass, hunting prey. Looking down at

Inessa's sweaty face as she heaved deep breaths and grunted. Knowing he didn't love her anymore. Knowing the baby she was about to deliver was not his, and the astounding confusion he felt over that fact.

But above all those heightened emotions, he kept thinking about Randall. Years before, how Layne's big brother acted when mutual friends of theirs had become parents. The light in Randall's eyes when they'd gone over for dinner and met the little one, cooing as it practiced tummy time on the floor. And as Cameron entered the world that night in the hospital, how Layne regretted the fact Randall would never know his niece because he'd been lost and presumed dead in South Africa.

He glanced down at his forearms, at the pair of cherub tattoos there. He held them together, their faces pointed at each other.

"You okay?" Serena said.

Took Layne a second to realize the question had been directed at him. When he turned his head, the world followed a fraction of a second too slow. Like being on painkillers. Nights like this used to be common for Layne Parrish back when he lived a different kind of life. Now he'd forgotten how to swallow all the adrenaline. It wanted to overwhelm him.

"What?"

"Are you okay?"

"I think so. I don't know. I shot my brother."

From the back seat, Phelps made a little whimper of a nervous sigh.

"This is all my fault," the governor said. "No one took this squabble between the Reds and Union seriously enough.

That person should have been me. I'm so very sorry, Mr. Parrish."

Layne didn't know what to say to Phelps, so he opted to keep quiet. He commanded his mind to shed itself of the extra junk. Had to focus on getting this man on that plane so he could safely travel to Pakistan. To do something good with all this mess.

"He used me," Layne said. "He tricked me into pointing all this attention at the Reds so he could swoop in and push his own agenda. Randall used me; Daphne used me." He glanced out the window at the trees rushing by. The headlights cutting a path along the green. "This bullshit is why I retired in the first place. You can't trust anyone, no matter how well you think you know them."

"I'm sorry, Layne," Serena said.

He glanced at her side. "You in pain?"

"I don't think it's bleeding anymore. I can manage." The phone in her lap vibrated, jiggling along her thigh. "Hang on one second." She answered the call, holding the phone between her ear and shoulder so she could keep both hands on the wheel. "Yes. Yes. We got him. Taking him to Cranbourne to board a small aircraft there. We'll get to Brisbane or Adelaide or somewhere within a few hours. Catch a flight from there. Right. Right. No, I understand. I'll advise again once we're on-site."

She ended the call and tossed Layne a frown. "Daphne can't mobilize anyone right away to meet us at the airport in Cranbourne. We're on our own for at least sixty minutes."

"We can't wait that long," Layne said. He took out the crappy feature phone and dialed Tilda.

After a brief conversation, he hung up and stared at the phone for a few seconds. So many pieces in play, he didn't know how they would all fit together. Too much was left up to chance and luck.

Serena gave him the eye. "You have an alternate backup plan?"

"I know someone in the ASIO. She's nearby. She can have a team meet us at the airfield to make sure the governor gets off smoothly."

"Tilda MacMillan?" she asked.

Layne pivoted in his seat. "How do you know that name?"

"Daphne introduced us a few days ago. She didn't mention it?"

Layne scowled. "No, she didn't. Tilda is sometimes mysterious and cryptic, and she tends to hand out information on a need-to-know basis only. It doesn't surprise me, though, that she knew why I was here and what I've been doing."

Serena shook her head. "What a mess."

"It doesn't matter. We could use the backup."

Phelps leaned forward. "Did you say ASIO?"

"Yes," Layne said.

Phelps slumped back into his seat and let out a whooshing sigh. "Oh, thank God. Don't get me wrong; I'm heaps grateful you sprung me from those awful people, but it's good to have someone from the home team. No offense."

"None taken," Layne said.

The fields and trees and slim roads became suburbs and late-night traffic. The roaring of trains along tracks. Layne used Serena's phone to navigate the little dot along the grid toward the small airfield.

Soon they were in Cranbourne. From the back seat, Phelps directed them where to go, past the train station to a small lot outside of a densely populated area.

Four semicircular hangars marked four quadrants of the airfield. Three long runways made up the middle section between the buildings. One hangar was lit and open, a plane sitting at the edge, with a couple of men attending to it. And a car parked not too far from that hangar, idling and dark.

Layne's phone buzzed as he eyed that single car. He read this message from Tilda:

We're over here. Will meet you at the plane.

"Is that her?" Serena said, pointing at the car.

"Yes, it's her. But wait. Stop."

Serena hit the brakes. "What's wrong?"

Layne checked the other three hangars. They appeared dark, but the shadows seemed off. That sense of foreboding, the same one he felt when he first realized Serena was following him, came to him now.

"This isn't right. Something is wrong about all this."

"What?"

"I don't think we're alone out here."

He reached down below his knees and retrieved his pistols.

ACROSS THE BAR, GLASSES CLINK. CONVERSATIONS warble in tones where certain words stick out, but the rest is gibberish. In this town, much of what people say is gibberish, but Layne Parrish is okay with that. He knows better than to become too enamored or too disillusioned with any particular person or ideology. Sometimes in the trenches, it's not about whatever reason the suits would have the public believe. It's about the guy next to you—making sure he gets out alive so he can have a future.

Layne stares at the whiskey and Coke in front of him. He's not much of a drinker. He did his fair share in college, but he soured on that recklessness once he entered grad school. There's only so much medicine you can consume without becoming numb to its painkilling effects.

Across from him sits Randall Parrish, older, wiser. He's worked in this organization for a few years. He's been around the world forty times in as many months. When Layne started this journey in Houston with Daphne, he wanted the same thing. He wanted adventure and passion and the satisfaction of knowing justice in the world would be on the rise because of his actions.

Now he's not so sure.

"And no one will ever know what we've done?" Layne says.

"You seeking fame, little brother?"

"No, it's not like that. It's just . . . does that mean there's no accountability?"

Randall sighs and sips at his glass of Yuengling. "Do you remember last year, in Toronto? The senator's laptop and the kidnapped intern?"

"Of course," Layne says, pointing at the scar on his arm. "You don't forget getting shot."

"Right. If you were FBI or ATF, you would have spent the next three months in committee meetings, testifying before Congress, fending off reporters. But you and I both know decisions in the field have to be made in fractions of seconds. We don't have that luxury of hindsight."

"And so that makes us above the law?"

"In a way. But we self-police." Randall leans forward a little. "And no matter what, we always look out for each other."

Layne thinks about Toronto. Randall insisted Layne get to his feet to push on through the hallway after he'd been shot. If Randall had done what Layne commanded and left him there, Layne would be dead now. Ten seconds after they cleared the area, a string of grenades obliterated that hall-way. Layne is only alive now because his brother forced him to complete the mission.

Layne sips at his drink. It tastes too sweet on his tongue. But he does like the burn when it slides down his throat. The irritation always returns him to awareness.

"You talk to Mom or Dad lately?" Randall says.

Layne shakes his head. "Not in a few weeks."

"What do they think you're doing with your time?"

"Working to get my LPC in Texas. Then I'll open a little private practice, maybe in Austin."

"That might be a hard cover to manage."

Layne shrugs. "Control says there's room in the budget to rent an office in Austin or Dallas, and I can fly there within the hour if they ever decide to visit me at 'work' sometime."

Randall tents his fingers for a few seconds. "You won't be in this line of work forever. Someday you can get that LPC for real if you want to."

"Maybe so."

"Start saving your money now."

A silence falls between them. More glasses clink, more blurry conversations move around them.

"Daphne," Layne says, leaving Randall to interpret his meaning.

And it seems that Randall understands the intent. "Yeah, I get it. She's intense and manipulative and sometimes hard to trust. If you slip up, she will be the absolute first person to toss you under the bus. But there is one thing you can count on from her."

"What's that?"

"She gets done what needs to be done, regardless of how she has to do it. And she loves this country. She will always put it first."

"The end justifies the means?" Layne asks.

"Sometimes it does. You have to respect her dedication at least. Right, Boy Scout?"

Layne rolls his eyes.

Randall chuckles. "I know you hate it, but your new name has stuck. It's not going anywhere."

A server approaches their table, a pretty and young white girl with blonde hair and blue eyes. She eases up to the table, making sure they both see her. Working at the bar, so close to the capital, Layne assumes she knows better than to surprise people by barging in on their conversations.

Randall points at his glass, but Layne waves her off. With a meek smile, she nods and disappears back toward the bar.

"I get what you're saying about Daphne," Layne says.

Randall dips his head and catches Layne's eye. "Are you still sleeping with her?"

"Off and on."

"I have to admit I was surprised about that."

"Why?"

Randall shrugs. "Doesn't that make Daphne your first since . . ."

"Since she died, yes."

Layne doesn't want to talk about *her*. Doesn't want to dredge up those memories, now several years in the past. Yes, in Houston two years ago with Daphne was the first sex he'd had in a long time. And while sleeping with Daphne did break the cycle of him seeing his deceased girlfriend's face on every woman he encountered in public, it still felt a little like cheating. And he hasn't ever stopped wondering if it was a bad idea.

"Sorry to bring up old shit," Randall says.

"It's okay. I'm fine."

The server returns with Randall's new beer and swaps it out for his empty glass. Like a ghost, she's gone in two seconds.

Randall leans forward and consumes half his drink in

one gulp. "You will be good at this. You're smart, cunning, and above all, you have a conscience. I can't say that about all the shadows on the team."

"I'll do the best I can." He points at the whiskey on the table. "I don't want this anymore. I'm done."

Randall pats the table and gulps the remainder of his drink. "Good. So you ready to go give them an answer and officially join your team?"

Layne places two fingers on the rim of his drink glass and rotates it on the table a few times. The condensation on the outside sends beads of moisture dripping like raindrops on a windshield.

"Okay, yeah. I'm ready to accept."

46

___

LAYNE MOTIONED SERENA FORWARD AS TILDA'S CAR parked near the hangar containing the airplane, in the final stages of preflight prep. Serena inched forward, not taking the car out of first gear.

"Talk to me, Layne. What are you thinking? Sharpshooters on top of the hangars?"

Layne checked the tops of the other three hangars. Squinted but couldn't see anything. Not enough light surrounding this private airfield. "No, I don't think that's it. But be ready for more cars to arrive, and it could be from any angle."

"It's so dark out here," Serena said. "Too many shadows."

"What's going on?" the governor said. He leaned forward from the back seat, his hands gripping the headrests behind Layne and Serena.

"We don't know yet," Layne said. "There may be some trouble. We want to get you as close as possible to the plane and let my contact provide security as you board. She's got backup in her car."

"Thank God," he said. "I'm ready for this nightmare to be over. I can't thank you enough for getting me out of that house in the bush."

Tilda's car parked right outside the open hangar, fifty feet from the plane. She stepped out from the passenger seat. The two doors in the back opened, and men in full body armor stepped out. Holding submachine guns across their chests. Stoic, motionless, like good soldiers. The driver remained inside the car, idling.

Serena parked on the opposite side of the hangar, a hundred feet from the plane. Tilda was standing in front of her car with her two cops, lips pursed.

Layne opened the car door and got out. The feeling of being watched intensified. Out here, he was exposed. But he couldn't figure out which angle the threat would come from.

"Had a bit of excitement tonight, did you?" she said as Layne got out of the car, on the opposite side of the hangar.

Layne didn't want to riposte Tilda's comment with sarcasm because he didn't feel up to it. Didn't want to discuss his brother's death. "You could say that."

Layne was about to remove his body armor and drop it on the passenger seat, but he still couldn't shake the feeling that something was wrong. That there were armed gang members nearby, ready to invade as soon as they saw the governor's face.

No one was in the hangar. He could see nothing out of the ordinary on the runways or in the other hangars. No lights of oncoming cars. But something wasn't right here. Had to be.

He opted to leave the body armor on.

In the back seat, the governor leaned toward the door handle, and Layne snapped his fingers and blocked the door.

"Wait, sir." Then he leaned back inside the car and spoke to Serena. "Can you park over there? Nose to nose with Tilda's car, as close to her team as possible? I don't want to take any chances."

Serena nodded, and Layne backed away from the car. He'd kept his two pistols, which clanked against his hips as he strutted across the tarmac.

He approached Tilda, and she held out a hand to shake. "You all right?"

"I'm fine."

"Randall?"

Layne shook his head.

Tilda frowned, letting a long, slow sigh escape her mouth. "I'm sorry, Layne. But I did try to warn you about him."

"You told me he was involved with a Pakistani militant group."

She pursed her lips and turned up her palms to the sky. "I did. I've spoken to Daphne, and it seems we had bad intel, about that and about the Union's plans. We can't win them all. And it seems like you made it out okay."

"That's a matter of perspective."

"Sorry, mate. I know this has been a rough week for you."

From the open door of the small airplane, a man in a suit leaned out. "Who has the governor?"

Layne raised his hand.

"Please let him know we're ready to leave as soon as is convenient."

Serena opened the rear door of the car, and the governor slipped out. He was still shaky, barely able to stay on two feet. Layne could now clearly see a purple bruise on Phelps's temple.

"Change of plan," Tilda said. "Governor Phelps, we'd like you to come with us."

"Wait. What?" Layne said. "Why would he need to do that?"

Layne's eyes fell on the driver in Tilda's idling car. He couldn't quite make out the man's face through the tinted windows. But there was something odd about him anyway.

Something familiar.

Layne's mouth dropped open.

"You know," Tilda said, "I should thank you for taking out Randall for us."

The driver's door opened, and the man exited the vehicle. Slicked-back hair. Wide, burly frame. This was Governor Phelps's head bodyguard.

"Carl?" Governor Phelps said, his head cocked in confusion.

With the speed of a bullet, everything made sense to Layne. Tilda was in league with the Reds. Her people were going to kill the governor at Fed Square, but Randall and his Union crew kidnapped him first.

Layne raised his pistols and shot each of the bodyguards on either side of Tilda. Two quick presses of the trigger, aimed a little high to compensate for the body armor. He tagged one in the forehead, the other in his left eye. Both of them immediately dropped, submachine guns clattering to the ground.

Slicked-Back Hair—a.k.a. Carl—whipped out a handgun the size of a small country and popped off a few shots. One hit Serena's car, and the others whiffed into the air. Serena grabbed the governor by the neck and dragged him to the rear of the car. Forced him to the ground, placing her body on top of his.

Tilda raced to the back of her car. Carl joined her. Layne squeezed his triggers a couple of more times as he backpedaled to meet Serena by the trunk. With their cars so close, they were only thirty or forty feet apart.

Bullets whizzed through the air, cracking metal, pinging off the concrete runways.

Then Layne remembered he'd stashed the extra magazines for the pistols inside the car. He had maybe eight rounds remaining in each.

He knelt on the other side of the governor, further shielding him. Serena popped up onto her feet, leaning around Layne, guns out. She rested her elbows on the trunk and blasted a few times. Layne's ears pounded from the proximity of the gun blasts.

They were pinned back here, with nowhere to go. A short distance to their left, an airplane to transport the governor to safety. A shorter distance in front, a firing squad.

47

"IT'S NOTHING PERSONAL," Tilda shouted from behind her car. "I tried to get you out of the country. Gave you a solid chance to flee from your Union brother and board a plane back home. It's not my fault you chose to stay."

Layne lowered his body to the ground to take a shot at them from under the car. But the tires were in his way. He couldn't see any viable targets from here. Couldn't move too far to the side, or he'd expose parts of his body.

"Why don't you send the governor on over here?" Tilda said. "It's time for his reckoning. He was supposed to die during his speech, but now we're going to have to improvise. You, Layne, can still walk away from this. The Reds have no beef with you, mate."

Layne leaned as far to the right as he could. Spotted the bottom half of a shoe sticking out from the other side of a tire.

"Get ready," he whispered to Serena.

Layne aimed, and Serena pulled the governor into a

crouch. She whispered into his ear, and he nodded vigor-ously, a look of utter panic on his face.

Layne closed one eye and centered the stray foot along the sight of his pistol. Took in a deep breath and then exhaled. When his lungs had expelled all the air, he took the shot. Hit Carl's foot. A spray of blood, a scream from the other side of the car.

Serena yanked the governor to his feet. The plane jutted out of the hangar a hundred feet away. A movable set of metal stairs with wheels leading up into the plane connected to the open cabin door.

Layne hesitated a second, tempted to open the rear door of the car and grab the spare magazines. But there was no time. He would be exposed for too long.

All three of them ran. As they hustled, Layne sidestepped, with his torso pivoted back toward Tilda's car. Squeezed off a few more shots. He counted down the bullets with each pull of the trigger.

Thirty feet from the plane. Twenty feet.

Tilda and Carl jumped up and started shooting, leaning over the trunk of their car. Their bullets pinged off the plane on either side of the open cabin door. The message was clear: try to board that plane, and we will pick you off before you can get inside.

Layne guided Serena and Phelps to the other side of the stairs, where the steel plates would shield them from bullets.

"These idiots are going to blow up the plane," Phelps said.

Serena leaned toward the edge of the stairs. "Suggestions?"

Layne pulled back to check the surroundings. The hangar had enormous ceilings and little cover. A few scattered tool benches here and there. The nearest enclosed space was an office at the back of the hangar. Too far away. If they tried to leave the cover of these stairs, they would find almost nowhere to go. Plain concrete, with just a few widely scattered mobile tool benches. Not much else.

Fortunately, he could say the same for Tilda and Carl. If they stepped out from behind their vehicle, they would have nowhere to hide, either.

They could sit here and take potshots at each other forever. Tilda and Carl were safe and secure in their spot. If Layne thought he could hit the car's gas tank from here, that might be something. But no, they were too far away. Gas tank would be a million-to-one shot.

But if the firefight lasted too long, they might actually hit something vital on the plane.

Plus, no doubt more Reds or Union or both were incoming. They had to get the governor out of here. Now. No time to wait for Daphne's strike team to arrive.

There had to be another way.

Layne noticed one of those mobile workstation tool benches was only about fifteen feet away. An idea formed. A stupid one, but it could work.

"I think I know what to do," he said.

Serena lifted her pistol over the stairs and fired a couple of shots. One bullet punctured a tire on Tilda's car. Air wheezed out like a balloon deflating. "What?"

"I'm going to rush them."

"Are you crazy?"

He studied the tool bench. "Not really. I need you to cover me, but only for a few seconds."

"This is not a good idea."

Layne pointed to the body armor covering his chest.

"That won't help if they blow off your kneecaps."

"True. I only need a couple of seconds of cover. Can you do that?"

Serena gritted her teeth but nodded anyway.

Then without warning, the shooting from the car stopped. Layne leaned over to check, but a rapid barrage of bullets pelting the stairs sent him right back into hiding. They'd switched from pistols to automatic weapons.

He had to go now. Any second, they would destroy that plane. Or maybe with assault rifles, they wouldn't feel squeamish about advancing.

No time left to debate the merits of the plan. Time to go.

"It's now," Layne said, and he leaped out of the hiding spot. Instantly bullets bounced off the concrete in front of him. He took huge strides toward the mobile bench and somersaulted behind it. It was a metal box on wheels, about four feet tall and three feet deep, with drawers jutting from the side. A metal bar attached to one end to maneuver the bench.

Bullets pinged off the workbench as Layne got his feet underneath him and latched his hands on to the metal bar. He pushed. The thing was heavy. Hard to get going. He had to dig his feet into the floor to make it roll along the concrete. Hammers and screwdrivers clanged from the top onto the floor around him.

Layne braced his abs and strained his legs to build momentum, and the workbench rolled ahead. Slowly at first. Dozens of shots pinged against the other side of it as he rolled it faster and faster. Momentum building. He could see shots ricochet off and punch little holes in the concrete floor.

Fifty feet of terrain to cover between him and the car.

Behind him, Serena blasted, again and again, keeping Tilda and Carl pinned to their hiding spot.

Layne pushed. The cart rolled. He came within thirty feet. Legs churning, bullets slicing the air all around him.

Twenty-five feet.

In another second or two, he'd be close enough for Tilda or Carl to shoot him from the side.

Layne gave the cart one last shove.

He stood to his full height and raised his pistols. How many bullets were left?

He squeezed both triggers right as a slug hit him square in the chest. Layne watched the gunpowder misting from Tilda's wrist, a venomous smile on her face.

He wobbled but didn't fall. Squinting, he aimed and shot her in the stomach. Next to her, Carl lifted an AK-47 to get a clean shot at Layne.

Layne ducked and pulled the trigger again as bullets whizzed over his head. Hit Carl in the arm, which sent the big guy spinning. Layne aimed again and shot him in the back. Serena added a few more bullets to Carl's body, which finally sent him to the ground.

And then, the pain of the shot to his vest appeared. Like a whack from a baseball bat, all the air rushed out of his lungs. He staggered, heaving, trying to catch his breath. The world dotted with stars.

He stumbled forward as Serena raced across the hangar and to the two bodies on the ground. Pistol up, she kicked away Tilda's handgun and Carl's AK. She circled around them, her mouth moving, but Layne couldn't hear a thing. The residual gunshots throbbed in his ears. Serena was barking orders, her face full of fury.

Layne, feeling like his chest had been crushed, rose to his

feet and lumbered across the floor to meet Serena. He staggered, and she laced her arm underneath his armpit to support him.

"They're gone," Serena said, practically yelling. "It's over."

Layne nodded. Had to lick his lips to form words. "Let's get the governor on that plane."

48

BY THE TIME LAYNE BOARDED THE CARGO PLANE THE NEXT day, his chest injury had abated to a dull throb. He still had a bruise like a purple dinner plate, but he was used to that.

He slid into his seat, grimacing. The cargo plane was an open space, with rows of seating on either side of the main area. Not exactly traveling in style, but the weariness in Layne's head and limbs told him he would be asleep in a few minutes, whether prone or upright.

A moment later, Daphne took a seat across from him, ten feet away.

She grinned. "Been a rough week, right?"

He inhaled until his lungs were full, to calm himself. "There are lots of seats back here. Please choose one not across from me."

"Oh, come on, Layne. You're not going to be mad at me forever, are you?"

"I shot my brother yesterday. I had to step over his corpse on my way out of that mansion. After that, I shot a woman

I've known for over a decade. Someone I counted among my most trusted friends."

The playful glint in Daphne's eyes soured, and she dipped her head a bit. "I'm sorry. I know that was awful for you. As far as operations go, this was one of the messiest and most unpredictable I've ever seen."

"Messy," he said, musing on the word.

"I'm sorry we weren't able to mobilize the team in time. Everything in the city was chaos right after the explosions."

Layne studied her face. "The thing is, I've spent the last twenty-four hours trying to piece it all together. Randall was Union; Tilda was with the Reds. Those parts of the puzzle are obvious. Now, I mean. Serena was only doing her job. But you," he lifted a finger and jabbed it in her direction, "your motivations were a lot more suspect."

"And you think you've figured it out?"

He nodded. "I've been thinking about the first time I mentioned Abdul Abbad to you, after I met with Randall. There was something in your expression, and it didn't register at first."

"Okay, so?"

"Abbad was always the target, wasn't he? And it had nothing to do with the governor. You didn't care about Reds or Union or Governor Phelps. Whether he lived or died or got on that plane or didn't . . . none of that mattered. It was always about drawing Abbad out of hiding."

"Abdul Abbad is a very bad man. A dangerous man."

Layne flexed his jaw to keep it from locking and continued to explain his theory. "If Phelps goes to Pakistan, then you nab Abbad when he surfaces. If Phelps dies in Melbourne, then Abbad comes out of hiding because his friend has died. Either way, you smoke him out of his hole."

She nodded. "That's right."

"Did you get him?"

"Phelps met Abbad outside of Lahore. We tailed the governor and picked up Abbad about an hour ago."

Layne gritted his teeth and stared at his feet as the plane's cabin door shut. "Good for you. And my trust in you was something you were willing to shred to make it happen, apparently."

"I understand the way you feel about all this. But I hope you will someday appreciate how there were bigger things at play. If you knew the truth, Randall wouldn't have trusted you. When we started, we weren't sure how he fit into every-thing, so we couldn't run the risk of him disappearing. We thought he was linked to Abbad, but that obviously turned out not to be true. We had to be careful while we pieced the puzzle together."

Layne wiped clammy palms on his pants. "I do under-stand, Daphne. And I forgive you. If removing Abbad prevents bad things from happening, then I can understand all of this."

"Thank you."

He leaned forward against the seat belt. "But let me be clear: even though I forgive you, I will never fucking trust you again."

"That's fair."

Even as she said it, one corner of her mouth still curled in a shadow of a smile. He knew she didn't believe him. And that was fine. She could make future plans in her head until she collapsed in orgasmic delight at the thought of all the empires they would unwind together. As long as Layne got to return home to his cabin and his daughter and his quiet life in a tiny mountain town, Daphne Kurek could think whatever she wanted.

"How is Serena?" he asked.

"She's recovering from her gunshot nicely. Already talking about the next op."

"She's not going to be punished for breaking her mission protocol?"

Daphne pushed out her lower lip and shrugged. "That's not your concern. But just between friends, I have no problem with it. She made a decision in the field, and it worked out. You know how it goes out there. You don't have time to draw up a *pro and con* board."

Layne considered the number of dead bodies left in the wake of all the recent decisions. He resisted the urge to lash out about how it all "worked out" and instead pursed his lips, opting to stay silent.

"You know, you two work well together. If you were to consider coming back full-time, I could pair you up. She's young and impulsive. You're this wise elder statesman who can turn her into something special."

"No," he said.

"You're too good at the spy game to leave this life behind."

"You always did know how to butter me up, Daphne."

"Plus, she could use a mentor."

"I agree on that last point. But whoever fills that role, it won't be me."

"Don't you want to be her Obi-Wan?"

"I'm not coming back. Not after this time. All I want to do is get home and see my daughter and never, ever leave her side again."

Daphne sat back and closed her eyes as the plane's engines spun up. "We'll see."

SEQUEL

Want to hear about the sequel? Join the reader group at www.jimheskett.com/free to learn more.

AFTERWORD

Dear Reader,

Unlike Micah Reed and Tucker Candle, the heroes of my other two thriller series, Layne Parrish began his life as a side character. He was not intentionally designed to be the main attraction.

I was writing the third book in the Micah Reed series, *Blood Thief*, and I wanted Micah to make a friend. Someone who was like him in some ways but very different from him in other ways. I invented Layne Parrish to fill that need. A man with a mysterious past who does not lack for self-confidence. A man who doesn't take any shit from anyone. Someone who could be a kick-ass action hero but also had a lot of humanity to him.

As Layne kept appearing in various Micah Reed novels, I saw the potential for Layne's story to unfold on its own. He had his own past demons to wrestle. His own future to plan.

And now, in your hands, you're holding the first installment of that journey.

The idea came from a scribble I wrote on a piece of paper one day. The idea was: An American man walks out his front door to find a kangaroo hopping through the neighborhood. How in the world did the kangaroo get there?

That became the genesis for this novel you've read. I'm an American, but I spent some time living in Melbourne and have wanted to write a story set there for a while now. A spy thriller with political intrigue and fistfights and explosions and guns and drama seemed like just the right kind of tale to set against that backdrop.

I hope I've done the Australian people justice. The slang is tricky to get right, and I'm probably a few years behind the times with how people speak there. But it was a lot of fun to write with terms like *heaps* and *bogan*.

I hope you enjoyed Layne's story and are eager for more. This journey has been a fun one for me, for sure. Thanks for coming along with me.

Do you want a free Layne Parrish novella? Join the reader group at www.jimheskett.com/free.

A NOTE TO READERS

Want to know when the next book is coming out? Join my reader group to get updates and free stuff!

If you enjoy Layne Parrish's adventures, you will also like my Micah Reed series. Layne himself appears in several of the books. You can get book 0 in the series absolutely free, and it's not available for sale ANYWHERE. Get it at www.jimheskett.com

Do you want a free Layne Parrish novella? Join the reader group at www.jimheskett.com/free

With that out of the way, thank you for reading my book!

Please consider leaving reviews on Goodreads and Amazon.

I know it's a pain, but you have no idea how much it will help the success of this book and my ability to write future books. That, sharing it on social media, and telling other people to read it.

Are you interested in joining a Facebook community of Jim Heskett fiction fans? Discuss the books with other people, including the author! Join for free at www.jimheskett.com/bookophile

I have a website where you can learn more about me and my other projects. Check me out at www.jimheskett.com and sign up for my reader group so you can stay informed on the latest news. You'll even get some freebies for signing up. You like free stuff, right?

For Eric and Brian

eBook published by Kindle Press
Paperback published by Royal Arch Books

Handmade with love in Denver, Colorado

Www.RoyalArchBooks.com

ABOUT THE AUTHOR

Jim Heskett was born in the wilds of Oklahoma and raised by a pack of wolves with a station wagon and a membership card to the local public swimming pool. Just like the man in the John Denver song, he moved to Colorado in the summer of his twenty-seventh year and never looked back. Aside from an extended break traveling the world, he hasn't let the Flatirons out of his sight.

He fell in love with writing at the age of fourteen with a copy of Stephen King's *The Shining*. Poetry became his first outlet for teen angst, then later some terrible screenplays, and eventually short and long fiction. In between, he worked a few careers that never quite tickled his creative toes, and he never forgot about Stephen King. You can find him currently huddled over a laptop in an undisclosed location in Colorado, dreaming up ways to kill beloved characters.

He believes the huckleberry is the king of berries and refuses to be persuaded in any other direction. If you'd like to ask a question or just to say hi, stop by www.jimheskett.com/about and fill out the contact form.

www.jimheskett.com

facebook.com/authorjimheskett

twitter.com/jimheskett

goodreads.com/jimheskett

youtube.com/authorjimheskett

Made in the USA
San Bernardino, CA
28 May 2019